STRATEGIES
FOR SUCCESS

STRATEGIES FOR SUCCESS

A NOVEL

BY

STONA FITCH

G. P. PUTNAM'S SONS
New York

This is a work of fiction.
The events described are imaginary,
and the characters are fictitious and not intended
to represent specific living persons.

G. P. Putnam's Sons
Publishers Since 1838
200 Madison Avenue
New York, NY 10016

Library of Congress Cataloging-in-Publication Data
Fitch, Stona.
Strategies for success : a novel / Stona Fitch.
p.   cm.
ISBN 0-399-13735-1 (alk. paper)
I. Title.
PS3556.I816S7   1992   91-31868 CIP
813'.54—dc20

The text of this book is set in Baskerville.
Printed in the United States of America
2   3   4   5   6   7   8   9   10

This book is printed on acid-free paper.

ACKNOWLEDGMENTS

Special thanks to Dan Harvey, editor and friend. Thanks also to Rob White, Dick Preston, Ginger Barber, Mitchell Loss, Gary Provost, James Ryan, Philip Johnson and Company, and my parents and family.

For Ann
J.A.T.H.

A SECRET

THERE ARE PLACES in the world a boy shouldn't go. Inevitably, he will seek them out when left alone.

I dodged along the overgrown fences between the watermelon fields and stayed behind tall weeds so my grandfather wouldn't see me. He had said the ruins of the First House hid nests of snakes, that there was a well where I could fall and never be found. But I kept walking until the fields gave way to woods, branches intertwined in a rustling canopy that reminded me of jungles from the news. I watched for Vietcong hiding behind tangled veils of chokeweed but saw only an occasional quail.

On foot, our land seemed endless, holding generations of Strides, cattle pastures, and a branch of the Ouachita River with banks dark as coffee grounds. Near the river was the fishing shack my father had remodeled into our home, and dozens of relatives lived along the road to Pine Bluff. My grandfather watched over us all from the widow's walk of the Second House.

When the First House burned in 1867, it left behind a cleared patch on the crest of a low hill, a foundation overgrown with vines, and an uncertain history. Rumor had it that Union soldiers burned the house because my great-great-grandfather Catlett

Franklin Stride was a Confederate hero. Another story had the fire starting from a hurricane lamp. Most of the family thought that Catlett had set the fire himself.

No matter which story was true, the house burned and Catlett Stride burned with it. For as long as I could remember, my grandfather had told me to stay away from the First House. And for just as long I found myself drawn to the quiet clearing, sheltered in a grove of pecan trees, protected by blackberry brambles.

My canteen was filled with warm vinegar, water, and sugar, since I had read in a paperback western that Kit Carson drank this mixture on frontier expeditions. Twelve years old, my bony arms barely thicker than broomsticks, I hoped this potion would give me strength, but I spat most of it out on the ground.

I stretched my T-shirt up to wipe the sweat and vinegar from my chin. August was so hot that summer that the cattle grazed at night and stayed in the shade all day, black shadows crouched in the crackling grass. Sparks from passing trains started brushfires until the state sent a chain gang from Little Rock to clear off the weeds next to the tracks. In the early morning, steam rose from the low hills around the river, and by noon the world rippled with a dizzying heat.

I reached the clearing, where broken stones jutted from the grass like ribs, cool even in the afternoon sun. That spring, my mother and I had waded along the river shallows, turning over stones like these to find black salamanders and scuttling crayfish that my fingers were never fast enough to catch. We would eat lunch on the railroad trestle and drop our orange peels into the muddy current. Against my grandfather's rules, we had explored what was left of the First House, and my mother taught me the names of the plants that grew here. Orange-tipped prairie paintbrush. Lilies of the valley. Pokeweed with its inky purple berries. She told me that Catlett Stride's wife, a full-blooded Cherokee named Kate Hands, had planted these flowers in her garden. A hundred years later they still grew wild among the stones, home now to jackrabbits and black, leathery snakes.

I learned secrets from my mother, family history that I hadn't heard at my grandfather's table. She had told me that after the fire, Kate Hands had come back to the smoldering ruins and built a boxy cabin the size of a dollhouse so that her husband's soul would have a place to live—a Cherokee custom. In spring, when cattle ranchers scavenged the ruins for wood, they took apart the house where his soul lived and used it to mend fences.

My mother had been sick, *tuberculosis*, the doctors said, a word that sounded more like another plant than a disease to me. Her hair was light brown, cut unfashionably short, and above her pale freckled cheeks her green eyes were shiny and tired. As spring gave way to the unnatural heat of summer, she couldn't go on walks anymore. She said she had a case of the wobbles, and I would find her leaning against the kitchen counter, her eyes squeezed shut. But she had seemed happy even as her strength slowly faded and the wobbles settled in to stay. I found out years later that most of this happiness had been chemical; she ate codeine tablets like peppermints.

I tried another sip of the rank Kit Carson brew, then put the canteen back in the knapsack my father had given me before I left for camp. It had been his idea to send me to Camp Iron Range, a boy's camp in northern Minnesota that he had read about in an outdoors magazine. I needed to see more of the world than Arkansas, he said. The northern part of Minnesota was a wilderness, and a summer of camping and canoeing would do me good. But we both knew this wasn't why I was leaving. When I boarded the Greyhound in June, my mother hadn't been out of bed for weeks and new doctors had come from Tulsa. My father quit his construction job and stayed home, leaving his dented pickup full of tools parked in the backyard. He read the newspaper and smoked cigarettes in the kitchen all day, made my mother's meals as best he could.

A month later, I stood on a basketball court in khaki shorts and a green T-shirt, yelling at my teammates, a tangle of tanned arms and crew cuts grappling for the ball. After a few awkward tries on the court, I knew the best place for me was on the sidelines, but I made up for my lack of talent with sheer volume. The camp director, a bronze-skinned man named Charlie, walked up the path from the mess hall. He stood at center court, took the silver whistle from around his neck, and sent out a shriek that stopped the game. In the quiet that followed I hoped he hadn't come to make us do road work, the camp's most feared punishment. Camp Iron Range was strict about its rules and we in Cabin 3 had failed our morning inspection thanks to evidence of the foot-powder fight the night before. Charlie walked toward me, his rubber sandals slapping on the court, and I was sure that he had found the stash of gum my mother had sent me, a few contraband sticks smuggled in with each letter.

"Larkin. Come on down to the infirmary for a minute."

The other boys watched me go, then started the game again. Charlie and I walked through red pines and birches along the rutted path that led to the dock and the nurse's cabin. I had written home on birchbark and said that I was having fun although I'd rather have been back in Pine Bluff, where the woods weren't quite so dark or the mosquitoes so large.

The camp nurse stood at the cabin door cracking her knuckles. Curly hair and a pointed nose made her look like a nervous white bird in her uniform. She was the only woman anywhere near Camp Iron Range, and older campers claimed they had seen her swim naked in Fall Lake late at night. I thought about her pale skin flashing as she dove down into dark water, then looked at the ground as I walked closer. Her thin ankles were covered with dark hairs and she had scratched her bug bites into scabs. Charlie nodded toward a comfortable cot reserved for the sick, the overheated, the queasy. Then he sat down and talked to the window in front of him.

"When I was in town, I picked up a message from your dad," he said. The camp was deep in the woods, miles from the nearest phone, and Charlie was our only link to the outside. He ran his fingers through his longish hair as he paced across the small cabin. Charlie was a jazz pianist who played with a band in Chicago. During the summer, he pounded the untuned upright in the mess hall, accompanied by the clatter of metal forks on plastic plates and the piercing chorus of a hundred boys eating and talking at once.

"I wish I didn't have to be the one to say this, but I'm just going to tell it to you straight." Charlie put on the black-framed glasses that hung on a shoelace around his neck. "I've been running Camp Iron Range for fifteen summers, and something like this only happened one other time." He turned to me and paused. "Your mother died yesterday in the hospital." The nurse walked quickly to the screen door and looked out at the lake. "I'm sorry."

Everything stopped. The nurse stood at the door. Charlie held his whistle in one hand. I sat on the cot, paralyzed, unable to breathe. We froze like mannequins for what seemed like hours; then I heard Charlie talking and saw his face come closer, out of focus.

"Hey. You okay?" His voice sounded too loud and I jumped a little.

I pulled in some air and said the first thing I could. "It's all right." I meant that it wasn't his fault, that I had known all along that this was going to happen, just as my father did when he sent me here. But then I started to cry and Charlie sat down next to me on the cot. The nurse crossed the room and perched on a chair, putting her pale hand on my scuffed knee. My stomach felt tied up in a fisherman's tangle, the kind of knot you had to give up on and cut out. I thought about my mother's letters, brief and printed on notecards like recipes. If she knew she was dying, she hadn't given me any clues, just reminders to take my salt tablets if I was out in the sun all day.

In a little while, I had cried all that I could.

"I'm hungry," I said. Charlie looked at me strangely.

"It's a normal reaction when there's been a traumatic shock," the nurse said to him, as if I were invisible. Charlie tapped my shoulder and we walked out of the nurse's office and past the mess hall to a small clearing where the camp station wagon sat covered with canvas to catch falling sap. He pulled off the tarp and we drove down the rocky camp road past a soccer field cleared from a grove of cathedral pines. Soccer players stopped to watch us pass, and I knew that I was no longer one of them, that I was different now, singled out.

We went to the A&W drive-in on the outskirts of Ely, the nearest town, and Charlie let me order whatever I wanted by yelling at an aluminum speaker mounted next to a menu. I asked for a hamburger, a large order of onion rings, and a root beer float. When the food tray came, the first taste of hamburger made me dizzy as I devoured it, smearing catsup around my mouth. I washed the food down with root beer, then spooned the ice cream quickly into my mouth. The onion rings sent out sweet steam as I bit into the golden crust. For whatever reason— a traumatic shock or the camp's steady menu of macaroni and cheese—food had never tasted this good. I hunted down every last crispy piece of crust lost in the folds of the wrapper.

"We better get going," Charlie said as he watched me finish. "We have to call your dad and tell him what time your bus gets in. It'll be a long trip but you'll be okay. You're a tough kid."

I started to cry again, deep sobs that hurt my stomach.

"You can come back next summer. We'll save a spot for you."

I wanted to stay in Cabin 3, and brush my teeth in the lake every morning, and skip rocks out across the water in the evening. Later in the summer there would be canoe trips, paddle decoration contests, a final soccer tournament. I thought if I stayed at Camp Iron Range forever, my mother might still write and send gum, would be waiting for me at home. But the time had come to leave, and as Charlie started the station wagon, I knew I wouldn't be coming back.

14

* * *

I spent the rest of the summer at home being sad, angry, or a sulky combination of the two. I plotted small crimes in my room late at night. Quart jars of brandied peaches and watermelon rind smashed to the brick floor of the Second House cellar. My father's best tools kept turning up rusted in the yard. Coins disappeared from my grandfather's collection and found their way to the railroad tracks, flattened into shiny disks. And I went to the ruins of the First House every day now that the long, hot summer was coming to an end.

I knelt at the hole in the crumbled foundation where I had been digging for the past week, and stabbed at the dirt with a sharpened stick, sifting through the soil with my fingers. I had collected pieces of blue bottle glass. Square-headed nails. Copper pennies the size of quarters. A tiny ceramic salt cellar with an even smaller rusted spoon. A brown bottle embossed with "Tinct. of Iodine." When school started in a couple of weeks, I would use these trading goods for playground swaps.

Everything I uncovered that afternoon seemed squeezed by a strong hand. Bottles were flattened, pieces of metal melted. An ivory domino folded in two shattered when I tried to bend it back. My great-aunt Opal, our family historian, had told me that the fire had spread quickly but all four children escaped by climbing down knotted sheets. There was nothing they could do to stop it, so they stood with their mother and watched as the fire blazed out of control and the bricks exploded, knowing that the flames that raced at the moon carried away their father.

I dug deeper into the ground and uncovered a rusty fork and a lead ball the size of a marble, which I stashed in my knapsack with the other finds. The lead ball could have been one of Catlett Stride's bullets, I thought. According to Aunt Opal, his sharpshooting had helped win the Battle of Chancellorsville. Union soldiers were larger and easier to see than squirrels, slower than the skittish deer he had hunted in the Ozarks. Later in the war, his sharpshooting ended when he was hit in the eye by a shell

15

fragment. After three months in an Atlanta hospital, Catlett Stride rode back to Arkansas on a mule; he arrived home half blind and close to dead on the day Lee surrendered at Appomattox Courthouse.

After the war, Catlett started to turn strange. He sat on the porch steps with a rifle across his lap and commanded his sons to gather eggs, to feed the cattle. He made them salute him, and at the end of the day he paid them with pieces of orange-slice candy parceled out from a cloth bag. He never shaved, and in murky daguerreotypes his straight gray beard hung to his waist. His face was lopsided and craggy, the right eyelid at half-mast while his good eye stared fiercely enough for two. At night, he heard Union troops in the woods around the First House, gathered for an ambush.

I scraped deep into the ground and found more pieces of glass and some buttons. My stick hit a thick root that oozed orange sap. I reached down and tugged at a round rock but the root held it like a strong brown finger.

Long shadows fell on the ground where I lay with one arm reaching into the hole, struggling to pull the rock loose. I was supposed to be waiting at the Second House when my father got home from work, and I was still far away. The rock felt cool and dry beneath my fingers, which rubbed along cracks that zigzagged like coarsely sewn stitches. I thought it might be a fossil that I could add to the trilobites and pieces of ancient shells I had collected along the riverbank. When I pulled as hard as I could the rock moved a little more, then came loose from the ground with a small sound, gentle as a sigh.

I sat up and scraped the dirt-crusted chunk with my fingernails. As the soil fell away, it seemed too light to be made of stone. More dirt fell away and revealed two eye sockets with a hollow place between them and a row of jagged teeth below. I couldn't tell whether it was a dog or 'possum skull. I rubbed away with my T-shirt, then stopped when I realized that I had found something more strange and rare. A gold-capped front tooth glimmered at me in the late-afternoon sun.

I held the blackened skull of Catlett Franklin Stride in my damp hand. It was time for me to go, but I stared at the skull with its shining tooth and familiar smell, like a fireplace on a rainy day. A trickle of sweat trailed down my side. I would be late for dinner again but I wouldn't say why. I left the clearing with the skull hidden deep in my knapsack, promising never to tell anyone where I had been, what I had found there.

1

THE QUIET BAR

No one in the Quiet Bar talked, smoked, or even moved very much, and the room was tranquil as an aquarium. A few businessmen read newspapers in pale pools of lamplight and swirled their drinks with glass swizzle sticks that resembled rectal thermometers. Even the crunch of almonds between my teeth seemed to violate the hush created by plush couches and indirect lighting. My waitress whispered when she took my order—a whiskey, neat, like the bar.

I struck a match and cringed at the roar. Heads swiveled to stare at the thin plume of blue smoke that stretched from my cigarette to the ceiling. Smoking was a moral felony in Cambridge. Who knew what I might do next? I could be inconsiderate enough to cough, sneeze, laugh. It had been my friend Tucker's idea to meet here for our monthly drink.

Through the window a bloated Humpty-Dumpty sun perched on the horizon, its rays falling on the crooked streets and white frame houses clustered along the shores of the Charles. Harvard was back in session and every day the streets were clogged with more anxious parents and U-Hauls from Connecticut. Harvard Square belonged to the students now. They stumbled through it late at night as if they had just learned to walk. They lay reading in the aisles of bookstores, played guitars on the Common all afternoon, turned restaurants into cafeterias.

I cracked an almond noisily between my teeth and wiped my dusty fingers on the couch. Across the bar, I saw Tucker, his suit immaculate, as if he'd removed it and sat at his desk all day in boxer shorts. He glided across the thick beige carpet with a flash of gold cuff links at the wrists and the gentle creak of wing tips. His eyebrows were thick, his lips too full to be delicate, and his dark hair coarse and slick with hair tonic. But these rough edges gave him only more credibility, more power, hinting that he could be as brutal as any lawyer needed to be.

"Hey. Guess you didn't have to wait for a table." Tucker sat across from me. As usual, he was right on time.

I cupped my hand behind my ear. "Can't hear you. Too much noise from the crowd."

"Admit it, you're starting to like it here." Tucker came to the Quiet Bar for the same reasons I didn't. It was clean and quiet, a place without history. He signaled the waitress with a glance and a curt nod.

"It's not the Elysium." We had spent most of our undergraduate careers in the Elysium Tap Room, a seedy beer hall thick with Cambridge cops, drunks, and Harvard students.

"Come on," Tucker said. "We'd be a couple of seriously hurting puppies if we were still regulars at that dump." He was right. In college, hanging out at the Elysium was like a field trip to a theme park—Drunk World, Six Flags over Misery. At some point I quit being interested in dives, tired of their desperate aura, the cumulative sadness of a thousand lonely beers.

"Remember the grapes?" I said.

"The what?"

"You know. The grapes." The Elysium's walls had been covered with a faded arbor of dusty vines which we defoliated of their bountiful plastic harvest. We used the grapes to lob at dozing drunks.

19

"I can't remember any grapes, except maybe in the wine."

Our waitress stood by, a polite shadow. "White or red?" she asked.

"Actually, I'll have a mineral water," Tucker said.

"With lime?" The waitress looked concerned, as if citrus fruit mattered a great deal to her.

"With lime." As the waitress moved away, I wondered what kind of medication kept her so peaceful. An irritable Viking woman had served as the Elysium's bartender and bouncer. At the end of many drunken nights, a shove from her meaty paw had sent us sprawling down the narrow stairs, sticky as flypaper from beer and other fluids.

"Kind of a boring drink," I said.

"I'm kind of boring, in case you haven't noticed."

"No comment."

"Anyway, my trainer says a drink a day adds up to twenty pounds in a year. Did you know a beer has as many calories as a slice of bread?"

"No. I didn't know that." If I had my way, I'd eat fried chicken three times a day.

"You ought to join a health club or something. You'd feel a lot better," Tucker said. Although I admired his self-control, he had grown a little evangelical about fitness lately. I already got enough healthful hints from my wife, Laura, who jogged and worked out three times a week at the Joy of Self Center.

"You know, you remind me of a guy I went to school with," I said. "I think he was from Virginia."

Tucker shook his head. "Don't start that ancient-history stuff. What's new? Let me know what you did at work today. What movie I should rent tonight." The waitress delivered his drink and a second bowl of almonds, which Tucker pushed toward me.

"In fact," I persisted, "come to think of it, he had exactly the same name as you—Tucker Stimson. Isn't that what they call you?"

"You must have me confused with someone else." At Harvard, Tucker had been the leader of our contingent of malcontent southerners, a group as exclusive as any of Harvard's finals clubs but not nearly as polite. I came from Arkansas. Tucker was from Richmond. We had Florida crackers, Texas shit-kickers, and string-bean Okies. Like Noah's Ark, Harvard wanted at least two of each species on board.

"He used to get knee-walking drunk every night and recite poetry in French at the top of his lungs and take home a new girl every—"

"Enough about college," Tucker interrupted. "It makes me kind of sad." Tucker and I were the only two of our group still around Cambridge, meeting for a monthly drink or the occasional dinner with our wives at Tucker's huge house on Brattle Street.

"What was so sad about it? We had a good time, did a lot of stupid things."

"It makes me think about Ash, okay? I don't want to think about Ash right now." Tucker gave me a look that told me the subject was closed.

"I'm sorry," I said, but Tucker just stared out the window at an empty patio. "I'm sorry, really."

The waitress delivered our drinks and Tucker waited for her to leave. "It's funny," he said. "I was just thinking today about how long ago that was, the Elysium, all that."

"Twelfth class reunion this spring."

"Won't catch me there. It's like they say: 'You can't put your arms around a memory.' "

"Who said that?"

"Jackie Gleason, I think." Tucker shook his head. "I wrote a three-hundred-page thesis on the French Symbolists, and now I'm quoting Jackie Gleason."

I laughed, the sound unnoticed now that the Quiet Bar had filled up with more businessmen. They had come into the bar and headed toward their regular tables, then settled into the couches. They were stunned by their release from office captivity, and their eyes were glazed like mine from staring at computer screens. A drink started them talking about whatever good luck the day had brought them—a new client, a government contract, better software architecture.

"To success happiness a woman with four tits and the time to enjoy them." I delivered our standard toast in a quick jumble, a witticism that had ceased being witty a long time before. I raised my glass and took a sip of sour mash, the hillbilly cousin of the scotch and sodas being nursed by others in the bar.

"Right back at you." Tucker drank his mineral water. "Big weekend?"

"Tonight we're going to a cookout someone from Laura's office is having. Otherwise, the usual chores."

"Michelle and the kids are on the Cape with her parents for a week."

"A bachelor weekend. Don't tell me. You've got nubile young paralegals in tube tops lashed to the Ping-Pong table. Used rubbers hanging all over the banister." I watched a blush spread above the neck of his white button-down.

"The shit you say. Honestly."

"C'mon," I said. "You and Ash used to be such lady-killers."

"I'll tell you the truth," Tucker said. "I don't even think about other women. I miss Michelle and the kids every night. Can't wait until they get back. And I can't imagine ever being without them." Tucker's wife worked in the financial district and was a far cry from any of his college girlfriends, who tended to be moody poetesses of the clove cigarette school.

"You're lucky," I said, and if luck meant money and security, Tucker had it.

"You ought to have yourself a couple of rug rats. They're a whole lot of fun. Tax deductible too, I might point out as your lawyer."

"I want to. We're thinking about next year." Actually, we were thinking about never. Laura didn't want to bring children into an imperfect world. I wanted kids in the same way I sometimes wanted a motorcycle; they seemed kind of exciting, but dangerous and impractical.

"So Laura's finally made an honest man of you?" Tucker asked with a smile.

"That's right. An honest man." I stirred my drink and dug my fingers into the soft arm of the couch as I thought of my lovely wife. I looked at the clock on the wall of the Quiet Bar. Laura was home now. I took a last sip and placed my sweating glass on the wooden table so it would leave a ring.

"You need to relax. Ought to try to take a little time off," Tucker said.

"I don't have time." I had plenty.

"I know what you mean. I hardly have time to do what I'm supposed to, much less what I want to."

"Same."

"Maybe you should think about getting out of the consulting business." Tucker took out his wallet and put down a twenty, shaking his head at me when I reached for my pocket. "From what I read in the papers, it's time to pack up and leave Massachusetts."

"Can't get out. I'm making too much money."

"At least you have something to show for it. You know, the book. I always thought I'd do trial work, but lately all I do is shuffle around papers so the real estate market won't collapse."

"Could be worse."

"Sometimes when I get the right client in my office, I tell him I went to college with the guy who wrote *Sell Straight to the Top*. Scores me big points."

"I'm flattered," I said. "Make sure they buy my next one." Being a management consultant had its advantages. Two years earlier, my boss, the legendary entrepreneur J. C. "Davy" Crockett, had asked me to turn one of my training programs into a slim book, a minor hit among sales and marketing managers.

"There's more to come," I said. "Davy's letting me cut back

on client work for six months so I can work on another book."

"I haven't read the first one yet. Looks good on my shelf, though."

"Don't bother."

Tucker got up, stretched his arms over his head, and did one of the quick, stress-reducing isometric neck stretches Laura was always trying to show me. I put on my suit coat and took a final look around the bar. I didn't recognize anyone here, but they all looked familiar, as if we were all part of a weary club that convened on the shuttle from New York, in corporate atriums, in places like the Quiet Bar.

I followed Tucker down the stairs and we spun through a revolving door into the end of a beautiful afternoon.

When we got to the edge of Harvard Square, he stopped and turned to me. "Listen. I've been thinking about something."

"What?"

"When did you move back to Cambridge?"

"About five years ago."

"And we've been meeting for a drink every month, right?"

"Right."

"I was thinking we should do something else, something new," Tucker said.

Our monthly drink had become a habit by now. "Like what?"

"I don't know. Play squash. Hear some jazz. Go to Chuckle-head's."

"I don't know how to play squash," I said. "Jazz makes me fall asleep. And you know I wouldn't be caught dead in a comedy club."

"I know, I know. Those were just ideas," he said. "Call me at the office when you come up with something you want to do."

"I will." I watched Tucker's face for any sign that he was mad at me, but found none. "I didn't mean to bring up Ash, it's just that I . . ."

"Don't worry about it." Tucker's eyes roamed along the sidewalk. "Like I said, that's just ancient history."

24

"See you next month," I said, not sure that I would.

"Right," Tucker said, then we walked off in separate directions, Tucker toward his car, me bound for the bus stop since Laura had the Volvo today. After a few yards, I turned to watch him fade into the crowd of walkers heading home from work. I could feel the warmth radiating from the bricks beneath my shoes. I wondered if Tucker and I would still keep getting together, or if our friendship would begin to falter, dismantled by neglect like so many others. I knew I shouldn't have brought up our friend Ash again, but every time we got together I found myself wanting to talk about him, the missing point on our triangle.

A few years before, Tucker had just made partner, I was working at the Crockett Company, and Ash was in Tuscaloosa, still hanging around in bars. He had a smart mouth that served him well up north but didn't find favor back home. Late one night, he had said something critical about the Crimson Tide in a roadhouse that featured a mural of God creating Coach Bear Bryant. After four years studying philosophy at Harvard, Ash ended up fighting rednecks in a gravel parking lot. The police said the blow to the head that killed him came from an axe handle or a ball bat, they didn't know for sure. Tucker and I helped carry his coffin, watched his mother drop roses into his grave one by one.

At some point, everyone quits taking chances. Some quit too soon, others not soon enough. We came back to Cambridge and bought in; Ash died and cashed out. As I walked toward the bus stop, I wondered whether Tucker would see it this way, or if he'd say it was all just ancient history.

2

HOME FIRES BURNING

A DOG LEFT in an empty field will soon wear a dirt trail from one side to the other and never stray. I had found my own path through Harvard Square and it became more well-worn every day. I passed a small lot at the back of the square where the city had planted thin, bandaged trees to create a version of a park. These trees never seemed to grow, although they changed color punctually from the first pale green spring buds to these curled, speckled leaves. Maybe city workers glued on new foliage late at night when no one was watching.

The park was filled with the usual assortment of smart people, students, businessmen, and lost *individuals* that could be found in any public space in Cambridge. Copper-tinted winos lay like war dead on the lawn, their bottle and can collections buzzing with bees. Sitting on the grass near them, a young woman with wide-set eyes and a shaved head pulled aside the flap of her black leather jacket and cupped an ample, pink-tipped breast nonchalantly in one hand to suckle a squirming child in her lap. No one gave her a second glance.

The bus stop was just ahead, past the low brick post office. I bought a *Boston Herald* and turned to the horoscope. Capricorn.

The position of the planets marked the beginning of a period of change. I should move forward with caution in any business or personal endeavors. One of Cambridge's army of psychotherapists would have charged me thousands of dollars for this information. At a quarter and a dime, the *Herald* was a bargain. I folded the paper under my arm and took my usual place among the other men in nice suits.

Suddenly I sensed someone's gaze like an urgent tap on my shoulder. My eyes scanned the crowd of people waiting for the bus, all of them oblivious to each other. I looked up the street but didn't find anyone unusual. Then I turned and saw a woman leaning against the brick wall of the post office. She stared right at me, and when our eyes met she kept staring, even now that she had been discovered.

The last light spilled along the horizon and bathed the woman in the amber glow of the sinking afternoon. She wore jeans, a simple black blouse, and a man's coat, baggy and gray, that almost reached her knees. Pale skin set off the watching brown eyes behind tortoiseshell glasses. She was attractive in a way that seemed more natural than calculated, her dark hair shoulder length and slightly untended.

Unlike most people in Cambridge, I liked fitting in. I wore no odd accessories, no attention-getting haircut. It had taken me a long time to get it right, and now that I blended in with the crowd, I didn't want to be singled out. But it was too late. The woman walked toward me, her eyes never straying. She reached into the pocket of her jeans and took out a small black pouch, the kind old men use for pipe tobacco. She unzipped it slowly. When we were just a few feet apart, she spoke in a voice so inviting I half expected her to ask me to dance.

"Do you have change for the bus?"

I had forgotten how to distinguish a meaningful glance from one to determine if I was the kind of helpful, courteous guy who carried around extra change.

"I think so." I reached into my pocket and handed her two

quarters, small and warm between my fingers. The woman held out a crumpled dollar bill. Then I noticed something strange. The pouch bulged with a numismatic mother lode of pennies, nickels, dimes, quarters. Even a few Susan B. Anthony dollars. She saw me looking at the coins and zipped up her pouch, but if she was embarrassed at getting caught in a lie it didn't show.

She held out the dollar. "Here you go."

"No, really. The quarters are on me. It's fine. I insist."

"Thanks. I don't know how I would have gotten home without them." She smiled and I saw a small space between her front teeth, just big enough to pass a matchbook cover between.

"Do you live in Watertown?" My voice sounded as if the words floated up through a sewer drain clogged with leaves.

The woman moved closer. "What?"

"Do you live in Watertown?" A dumb question. We were all waiting for the Watertown bus. It didn't go anywhere else.

"Yes, I do. On Palfrey Street." This name reminded me of the word *paltry*, but from her lips it had a gentle twang nothing like the honking Boston accent.

"Where're you from?" I knew it had to be somewhere far from Boston, the Hub of the Universe.

"Charleston. Charleston, South Carolina."

"I was going to guess Virginia."

"Really?"

"Some of my college friends were from there. I sort of got used to the accent."

She smiled again. "Then we'll have to talk some more." Now that I knew where she came from, I was inclined to think her friendliness might be natural too. When I went back to Arkansas, people said hello, drivers used their turn signals. It took days for me to remember how to be polite again.

"My name's Larkin Stride," I said. "I'm not from here either. I'm from Arkansas."

"Mariah," she said. "Mariah Callahan." We shook hands, a strange formality. I let go a little too fast.

"I asked you for change because you looked friendlier than they do." She nodded toward the other men who waited for the bus. Tan raincoats draped over their arms, they studied their copies of the *Globe* as if there would be a quiz later.

"I wonder if they know that they all look almost exactly alike," she said.

"It's a uniform. They give you one of those raincoats when you graduate from business school."

She laughed. "How convenient."

"When I was in college, I never thought I'd wind up like that. And now, here I am." I hadn't meant the last part to sound so bitter, but seeing Tucker had made me worried that I had strayed too far down the path to respectability. Soon I'd be playing squash, chuckling at some comedy club.

"Don't worry, you don't look a thing like them," she said. "They look like they're ready to explode." Thanks to my job, I was pretty wound up myself, but this stranger didn't seem to notice. I looked at the clump of businessmen. Some checked their watches. Others paced in circles like toy soldiers. The bus was late.

"You just met me. You don't know me from Adam." I was still suspicious. Even if Mariah was from the South, it didn't mean she could go around being nice to everyone she met.

"I know lots of other things about you," she said.

"Really?"

"You notice things, like me watching you. Like my accent." She gave me a coy smile. "And the coins in my purse. Those guys over there wouldn't notice me if I ran up and kicked them, which I might just do sometime."

"Don't let me stop you." In a recurring daydream, I ran wild in Harvard Square, kicked mimes, broke the instruments of inept street musicians.

We stood together and waited for the bus. Our conversation lulled but I was still very aware of her standing close, of her scent, sweet and chemical. I decided I wouldn't tell Laura about meeting this woman. It wasn't important. Mariah probably met someone new at the bus stop every day.

The bus lurched from the tunnel beneath the square and the waiting crowd moved toward the street. Mariah took my arm and held it lightly as we got on the bus. In Harvard Square, the only strangers who touched me tended to be recently deinstitutionalized, so I almost pulled away. We found two seats together near the back and sat down. Mariah let go of my arm as casually as she had taken it, and my suspicions faded. Some people were just friendly and maybe Mariah was one of them.

The bus moved slowly through Cambridge and I watched the familiar landmarks go by—Longfellow's house, a bend in the river, some towers of luxury condominiums, a hospital. We passed the cast-iron gates of Mount Auburn Cemetery, where transcendentalists and robber barons were nestled together beneath the dogwoods. From the gardens, a perfume delicate as the memory of flowers drifted in the open window and spread through the stale bus.

"Do you smell that?" I said. Mariah closed her eyes, then opened them.

"Yes. It smells like spring, doesn't it? I was right about you. You do notice things."

"A good sense of smell doesn't mean much," I said.

"I read somewhere that the whole brain grows out of the olfactory nerve, the one for smell. Did you know that?"

"No."

"It's true. Smell is the most primitive of the senses. The one that's supposed to help you survive." Mariah seemed like the kind of person who collected interesting facts, waiting for the right conversation. Thirteen baby 'possums fit in a spoon. An ordinary man would weigh nine pounds on Pluto.

"It takes more than a good nose to survive," I said.

"Maybe, but it's a start."

"A job might help too."

"That depends. You're in business or something . . . ?"

"Consulting." I never liked calling myself a consultant, a title that meant nothing compared with real jobs like farmer, fisherman, truck driver.

"Sounds interesting."

"Not really. Just common sense in an expensive wrapper." I'd used this phrase so much it had become my slogan.

"There's nothing common about sense," she said. "I've been enough places to know that." Mariah smiled and shook her head. We left Cambridge at a fork in the road where a liquor store's gigantic blue neon sign flashed. Despite its name, there wasn't much water in Watertown, where the Charles River turned into a puny stream. The town did have more than its share of funeral homes and rug dealers, so Stiffsville or Rugtown would have been a more accurate name, if not as quaint.

"So what do you do?" I asked. The bus stopped for a moment and Mariah looked out the window. People tripped out and walked away, bent forward as if pulled home by powerful magnets.

"I'm a photographer. I take pictures of corporate headquarters, CEOs, manufacturing plants, that sort of thing. For annual reports mostly."

"Must be exciting. Being a photographer, I mean."

"No, not really. But I can't complain. It's a living, and I still do my own work on the side when I have the time."

"Your own work?"

"I take photos, more creative stuff. I've always done it, but I decided that the starving-artist routine was a lot of crap, so now I take the kind of pictures that . . ."

"That pay the bills," I said.

"Yeah." Mariah looked carefully at me, and I wondered if she saw someone else beneath the thin consultant veneer.

As the bus got closer to Watertown Square we came to Little Armenia, a neighborhood of Armenians and Greeks. When Laura and I first moved here, we had gone to the small stores cluttered with delicacies I had never heard of, much less tasted—sour olives, pickled okra, black currant syrup, flat breads, dark coffees. We never bought much, since nothing was marked in English and we didn't want to end up eating a can of fish eyes. Besides, the clerks didn't like us. We were strangers here, young, successful strangers.

"Have you been in these stores?" I asked.

"I do my grocery shopping here. The vegetables are cheap, and they always give me a little extra."

"All they ever give me is the evil eye."

"One time an old guy—he must have been about ninety—tried to kiss me when I was going through a box of melons." Mariah laughed. If someone tried to kiss Laura in a store she'd file suit for harassment.

I said nothing and Mariah's words hung in the air. I strained to see her out of the corner of my eye, tried to memorize her face.

"I'm glad I had to go into Cambridge today," she said as we passed the Greek Orthodox church and a butcher shop that sold only blood sausages from a wooden bin. "I hardly ever meet anyone interesting on the bus."

"Maybe you still haven't."

"Not true."

The bus turned and headed down a hill lined with large houses. We passed the Armenian Benevolent Society, an elaborate wedding cake of a building overdecorated with gables, balconies, and tricolored Armenian flags. I wanted to say something else to Mariah. My stop was next. I stood up.

"I'm getting off here. Nice to meet you, Mariah."

"Callahan," she said. We shook hands again. "Like the Callahan Tunnel, the one that goes to the airport. Call me sometime if you want to. I'm in the book." This was no ordinary woman. No one was this friendly.

"If I know . . . Yes, it would . . ." All day, I spoke clearly and articulately to my clients and coworkers, but now English seemed to have become my second language.

"If I have a sudden urge to take the bus, I will. Call, that is," I said. After one last look, I sidled to the front and stepped out on the sidewalk. The bus swayed slowly toward Watertown Square, the end of the line. Mariah waved from the open window.

"I owe you fifty cents," she said.

I flailed for words as the bus picked up speed. "Forget it. Really." I wished I had managed to say something better, but by then the bus was on its way to Palfrey Street. It disappeared around a slight curve at the boarded-up American Legion hall. Sparks dropped from the electric lines overhead and sizzled on the pavement as I turned and walked home.

Our house sat docked off to the side of the street, a Victorian steamboat parting waves of juniper. Bright blue with white trim, it seemed proud, almost courageous, with a chimney rising on the left and a wide porch that swept around to the right. The porch had drawn me to this condo in the first place. It reminded me of the one at the Second House, where my relatives sat and talked about the weather, about our Strides long dead. But the porch was empty now, the wicker chairs stored for the winter. The maintenance people had raked the lawn that afternoon and trimmed back the hedges and rosebushes.

The sky had faded to gray except for a few clouds that drifted slowly by, pink smoke signals in the west. Laura was home from work and I could see the campfire glow of the living room lights. Our house looked perfect, a very realistic advertisement for home. Perfect, but as I stared at the house, blue as a robin's egg, I wondered for an instant what it would look like if it were on fire. How would it feel to douse the front porch with gasoline and toss in a match?

At the front door, I fumbled in my pocket for my keys, then unlocked the door and stepped on our mail. Even though she usually got home first, Laura left it downstairs for me. For years, my address had changed every few months. Even if there were just bills, I liked to see that little pile of mail waiting for me. I reached down and flipped through it quickly—an American Express bill, two bank statements, a couple of magazines, more fund-raising letters from Harvard, more antinuclear propaganda from Laura's mother.

I climbed the stairs two at a time, since I didn't want to run into the Thompsons, our first-floor neighbors. Just a few inches separated our lives, but we avoided any sort of interaction, abiding by the unwritten condo code. Every once in a while I saw them on their way to work in the morning. We passed without a word.

At the second-floor landing, I unlocked our apartment door and went inside, where I paused for a moment and listened to Laura in the bedroom. Careful not to make noise, I continued down the hall using the Indian Walk I had learned in grade school one Thanksgiving, touching my toes to the ground first, then my heels. Toe, heel. Toe, heel.

The bedroom door was half open and I could see Laura bent over, her pale, cleft bottom pointed at me. Her hair, wet from the shower, clung in dark strands to her shoulders. She pulled her panties up from around her ankles, causing her breasts to sway with a slow pendular motion, a delicate geometry that made me ache. It wasn't right to spy on my own wife but I didn't really want to stop. Laura seemed so much more relaxed when she was alone. She moved from the bed to the closet, hummed softly as she dressed. I could see her private constellation of moles and freckles, the red line around her waist from where her skirt had cut into her skin all day. Her business clothes lay in crumpled heaps around her. She kicked them toward the laundry hamper with one foot, then disappeared into the walk-in closet.

Aerobics and jogging kept Laura healthy and strong, virtually unchanged from when we first met. She was solid, "a full-figured gal" as the bra commercials would say. The small women I had known were untrustworthy, prone to tantrums and late-night arguments. Laura was rational. She rarely shouted. I used to find these qualities soothing.

I slipped quietly inside the bedroom. Laura had put on a pair of jeans and a white rayon blouse that she buttoned with her back toward me. She turned and inhaled sharply with a reverse scream when she saw me at the door.

"I didn't hear you get in," she said. "How long have you been home?"

"You're wearing the panties with little blue flowers on them."

"You're mighty sneaky." Laura buttoned her blouse almost up to her neck.

"Not sneaky. Just quiet." I kissed her lightly on the forehead and tasted the salt from her skin, smelled the all-natural spearmint toothpaste on her breath.

"Wait. I'm not done yet," she said. She picked out some socks from her dresser.

"Neither am I." I ran my hand lightly across her back. "I love you," I whispered into her warm neck. She turned and kissed me on the cheek, then rubbed her hair with a towel.

"So how was work?" This question had developed its own four-note melody, a descant that rose slightly in the middle.

"Fine," I said. "Nothing special. How was your day?" We didn't talk much during work hours. But every evening we had our daily debriefing, going through the same questions and answers like prayers.

"Okay. Cliff's being a real pain, but what else is new?" Laura put on a pair of boots I had bought her to round out her decidedly corporate footwear selections—low-heeled pumps and the Nikes she wore to work before changing into her good shoes. Wearing business clothes with gray, scuffed sneakers every morning seemed practical to her, although I still considered it kind of goofy.

"I thought he was going on vacation soon."

"Cliff's always on vacation," she said, kneeling down to tie the laces. "Sometimes I think he retired and forgot to tell anyone about it." Laura worked in Boston at DataTech, a company that sold law texts, insurance handbooks, and all the other dull reference books that businesses needed. The company made mil-

lions. Laura supervised about a hundred telemarketers in a thinly
disguised sweatshop that she did her best to improve. Everyone
loved her except her boss, Cliff, the vice-president of operations,
who had once told her that the two reasons she kept getting
promoted could both be found in her bra.

We talked on and unwound like balls of rubber bands, getting
rid of a week's worth of tension lodged in our necks, stomachs,
brains. I hung up my suit coat and took off my tie while Laura
finished dressing, and then we went into the living room and
watched the news. It was the usual stuff—gang violence in Mat-
tapan, another Irish crime figure indicted, unemployment up.
But it would be a nice weekend, the weatherman said, perfect
fall weather. After the forecast, I got up to take a shower.

"Remember, we have to be at Robert's by eight," Laura said.
Robert managed a separate group of telemarketers for Data-
Tech's periodicals division. They competed like coaches for the
highest monthly sales figures, the best employees. "And I think
we should bring some wine."

"To a cookout?"

"You know how these things are."

I sure did. I nodded and walked down the hall to the bathroom.
Laura had been worrying about Robert's annual end-of-summer
cookout for weeks now, afraid that it might earn him more points
than her carefully planned July Fourth harbor cruise, a huge
success with her minions.

I took a quick shower, trying to wash away the scent that had
built up at the office. Not too many years before, I had worked
as a dishwasher at a barbecue. The job covered me with the
thick smell of cooked meat, as if I had been basted in pork fat
all day. I rarely ate, content just to wear the scent of food like
a coat. Now I carried home a more professional but still unap-
petizing perfume at the end of the day—a mixture of sour sweat,
cigarettes, and take-out Chinese food.

I noticed that some of the grout had chipped from the Spanish
tiles around the antique claw-footed bathtub, and I reminded

myself to make this one of my weekend projects. Some people had children; we had a nice condo, a six-figure baby that we'd be paying off well into the next century. The previous tenant was an old Armenian woman who had kept a dozen cats in the living room. She cooked on a hot plate and dropped her garbage out the bedroom window into the backyard. When we bought the place it was a wreck. We gutted it and started over, erasing any memory of its past.

We had been married only a couple of months when the demolition began, and I was impressed by the way Laura directed the battalions of contractors, paying attention to even the smallest details of the renovation. She sent carpenters deep into the four corners of the condo to rip up, repair, or replace nearly every unacceptable square inch. Her attention to detail included choosing the right sanding compound for the floors, the right varnish for the woodwork. The dumpster in front of the house mounded higher and higher, a monument to gentrification made from old hunks of plaster, broken windows, and frayed wiring. We found angry notes in a spidery octogenarian scrawl tucked under the Volvo's windshield wiper. "You're ruining that beautiful old house," said one, while another reminded us, "You are not wanted here in Watertown." Our neighbors were jealous and suspicious as we barged in, children in their eyes, and laid out a fortune to live in an apartment big enough for a family.

When it was all over I was proud of our place. I rushed home from work just to sit in the living room with Laura and decide what kind of drapes to buy, what furniture we needed. We were close, a team. Whole weekends passed without our ever leaving home except to buy furnishings. We fed the apartment purchases one after another, but it was insatiable, swallowing up handmade Chinese rugs, Art Deco torchères, glass-windowed corner cabinets, a walnut English armoire.

I got out of the shower and dried off. Wiping away the steam from the mirror, I surveyed the familiar landscape of my face. My Cherokee blood showed in a few lingering traces—I had

37

almost no beard, high cheekbones, narrow eyes. My father looked Indian, particularly when he was younger, with hair as black as crankcase oil, eyes shiny and dark. But my hair was lighter and my eyes were green like my mother's.

I was aging à la carte, one feature at a time. My sideburns had started to turn gray a couple of years before, and the corners of my eyes were cross-hatched with smile lines that were beginning to look permanent. My last pimple was more than a decade past, but now the skin under my eyes sagged and turned the color of raw oysters if I didn't get at least eight hours of sleep a night. My hair had backed up a little when I was in my twenties but seemed to be holding steady, despite the yanking I gave it all day at work. My teeth were stained from Marlboros—now Marlboro Lights, a concession to Laura—my lower teeth yellowed like old piano keys.

Maybe I should have quit smoking. I should also have laid off beer and wine, even the good stuff. And I should probably have gotten my cholesterol checked, although I was scared to find out what my bad habits had done. For years I had lived at a different speed, accumulated extra mileage. Now it was starting to show.

The mirror fogged up again and I let it, bored with my own face. I wrapped a towel around my waist, walked into the bedroom, and put on a pair of old pants and a striped shirt. By now, I had almost forgotten about work. The muscles at the base of my spine loosened slowly like a fist unfolding to become an ordinary hand.

I finished dressing and walked into the kitchen, where Laura shook paprika over the largest bowl of guacamole I had ever seen. A bushel-sized salad sat on the counter next to her along with smaller bowls of salsa, both red and *verde*, from Farsabian's, a pricey gourmet place in Cambridge.

"Looks great." I took a fingerful of salsa when Laura wasn't looking.

"Robert asked me to bring a few side dishes." Laura covered

the guacamole carefully with plastic wrap. I thought these preparations seemed a little excessive but didn't mention it.

"Need help?"

"Sure. Why don't you slice green pepper for the top of the
salad." She handed me a colander of bell peppers. As I chopped,
Laura made her vinaigrette dressing, stirring in extra-virgin olive
oil drop by drop with a whisk. The tomatoes were still red and
juicy although every day we moved closer to winter, season of
the flavorless, pink-skinned pincushion.

When I finished slicing the peppers, I opened the liquor cabinet and looked through the bottles of wine I had bought at
Violette Wine Cellars, one of the few Cambridge stores I liked.
The owner was a tall, gentle guy who looked more like an English
professor than a wine merchant. He offered me samples and
urged me to find the hint of hazelnuts or raspberries I could
never taste, hard as I tried. Wine was as mysterious as alchemy
to me and I spent a couple hundred dollars there every month
trying to figure it out. Italian wines should be fine, I thought,
reluctantly choosing an Orvieto and two Amarones I had been
saving. Not everyone at Robert's would notice the wine was good,
but if Laura wanted to send a message that she could blow a lot
of money on a cookout, then I'd do my part.

3

DAMAGE CONTROL

I DROVE EXTRA CAREFULLY on the way to Wellesley, but Laura cringed at every bump, concerned that the guacamole was sloshing over in the trunk.

"Listen, if you want to drive, I'll be glad to switch," I said.

"I just want everything to get there in one piece."

"It will, I promise."

We spun down a winding road lined with tidy maples. It was dark and the lights from the houses were far apart. Now and then I caught a glimpse of a big house set back from the road by a rolling lawn.

"Nice neighborhood," I said.

"Robert's got family money."

"It figures."

"Jealous?"

"No." From Harvard, I knew that family money didn't do anyone any favors. Robert didn't seem particularly happy, at least the few times I had met him. He was nice enough, but he tried too hard to please, like a candidate for student council president. Laura was pretty sure Robert was gay but hiding it to keep his prospects open with DataTech's unenlightened management.

"It's this mailbox," Laura said. I turned in the driveway and the Volvo's tires crunched on gravel, sliding a little as we took the corner.

"Go slower."

"We're here. El Rancho Roberto." I pointed to a large modern house with a backyard lit by the glow of torches. *"Jealous?"*

Laura was keeping score tonight and Robert's house already put her a few points behind. He had lined the driveway with flickering *luminarias*, oiled paper bags filled with sand and a carefully placed candle. The environmentally correct used these things for tasteful, energy-efficient Christmas decorations, but Robert had gone all out. On the gentle slope of the roof, he had carefully placed bags so they spelled out "DataTech" and the company logo, a stack of books with a dollar sign on top.

"Shit," Laura said.

"I guess Robert's cornered the market in the ass-kissing department."

"I think he does more than kiss them, if the truth were told."

A kid in overalls and a straw hat waved me forward with a flashlight, and I steered the Volvo into a field off to the side of the house. At least a couple hundred cars were parked in the grass, cropped short as a putting green.

We parked and got the food from the trunk. With no small satisfaction, I saw that everything had arrived safely. Voices and laughter drifted toward us as we carried our bowls of food toward the backyard. "Sounds like quite a party," I said.

"Don't start." Laura said.

"Start what?"

"You know what I mean." I knew that tonight Laura would take any compliments of Robert as criticism of her ability to pull her way up the DataTech corporate ladder. I didn't point out how ridiculous this thinking was; Laura was in no mood for logic. The voices grew louder and louder as we rounded the side of the house. Tall torches circled the yard and made the gathering seem a little primitive, as if we had come here to walk on hot coals, to sacrifice a couple of secretaries to the gods of telemarketing. The cool night air was warmed by four grills that sizzled with barbecued chicken and hamburgers tended by fry cooks in overalls. Big as it was, the backyard was packed. By the flickering lights, we jostled our way through the crowd and put our offerings on a table already laden with vegetables, dips, and enough hors d'oeuvres for a wedding.

"Robert told me this was going to be a little country cookout, not a medieval feast," Laura said. "Why did he tell me to bring a salad? Was he trying to embarrass me?"

"Why don't you ask him yourself?" I said. Our host emerged from the crowd with his hand out, ready to shake.

"Laura! Larkin! So glad you could come." Robert squeezed my fingers and gave Laura a carefully executed peck on the cheek. He wore a black shirt, pleated black trousers, and a silver bolo inlaid with turquoise. "Flagler and Jones came by," he whispered, loud enough so everyone around us could hear. "Can you believe it? And I heard that Lobell may even show up later for a brief appearance." Robert had the frantic glow of a maître d' whose restaurant was suddenly crowded with celebrities, although I didn't consider middle management prime gossip-column material.

"Looks like you've got plenty of food," Laura said through clenched teeth. Even our giant bowl of guacamole looked Barbie-sized next to Robert's deluxe spread.

"I had it catered by J and T's. Have you heard of it?" I nodded. Jack and Tim's was a take-out place in Boston that sold would-be southern home cooking to people who didn't know much about the South, cooking, or home for that matter. It charged ten dollars for a piece of meatloaf slathered with supermarket hot sauce.

"Be sure to try a Cajun ravioli. They're fantastic," Robert said, pivoting to intercept a reptilian man in a brown suit. More handshaking and small talk followed as Robert worked the crowd like a Kennedy.

"That's Flagler. I've got to go do some damage control,"

Laura said, peering into the crowd. "Be a sweetie, will you? Get me a glass of white wine." And then with a quick kiss, Laura slid into the crowd to dispense corporate greetings. I wandered over to the bar, a rough set of planks nailed together to look like a hillbilly shack, presided over by yet another skinny guy in overalls. A jug band warmed up nearby. The Unreconstructed South didn't seem like much of a party theme to me, but I supposed Robert considered it clever. I got a Budweiser longneck and a pint bottle of wino wine with a twist-off cap from the ersatz moonshiner, who pointed out that the wine was known as hillbilly champagne.

I wandered through Robert's backyard for about half an hour looking for Laura. The crowd had grown larger and the band launched into a de-twanged rendition of "Rocky Top." People stood four deep at the grills, even more milled around the moon-shine shack.

At the center of some of Laura's telemarketers, I recognized Hank, the DataTech nice guy. Every company had one. After he got off the fast track, for whatever reason, the company nice guy settled for protecting his job by being everyone's friend. Hank finished a joke and the group around him laughed politely, all wondering what they had to do to avoid ending up like him.

"Hello, Larkin!" Hank walked away from his audience, which took this opportunity to scatter.

"Hi, Hank. What's up?"

"The usual. Just keeping the troops entertained."

"Looks like you're doing a good job."

"Maybe. But they're starting to look younger and younger. Some of them aren't much older than my own kids. Of course, we're not getting any younger either. Know what I mean?"

"Yes," I said. Hank was in his forties, but he had the red-lined eyes of a serious juicer.

"You know, I think Laura's got it in the bag. Tell her she doesn't have to worry about tonight. Robert's all smoke and

mirrors. Lobell can see through this . . . this cowpoke shit."
Hank swept a hand toward the crowded lawn.

"What do you mean?"

"I mean the guy's using his money to impress everyone. But
that's not what really matters. With Cliff out, we're going to
need a real team player like Laura."

"Cliff's quitting?" Laura hadn't said anything about her nem-
esis leaving.

"This is just between you, me, and the fence post, right?"

"Right."

"Rumor has it that Cliff's out at the end of the year. Not
quitting. Fired. Lobell's sending out feelers for a new director of
operations. Laura or Robert are the frontrunners."

"Think she'll get it?"

"Sure. How can anyone take Robert seriously?" Hank leaned
toward me, and his breath smelled like wine and breath mints.
"Be sure to try a Cajun ravioli. They're *fantastic,*" he said in a
flawless imitation of Robert, then walked unsteadily toward the
moonshine shack.

"Larkin!" A young man with a goatee waved at me.

"It's me, Jerry Klepner," he said. I stared, puzzled.

"I didn't used to have the beard," he said. Then it clicked. I
had talked to Jerry at the DataTech Christmas party the year
before. Jerry had been flailing around Boston, jobless, when the
prospect of regular work, albeit lowly, cropped up in the form
of DataTech's ever-present ad in the Sunday *Globe* seeking
"talented, ambitious, growth-oriented individuals dedicated
to achieving excellence." I didn't find Jerry very ambitious, but
he was certainly an individual. I hadn't seen a goatee in a
long time, even in Harvard Square, a haven for aberrant hair-
styles.

"Hi," I said, moving Laura's pint of wine to my back pocket
so I could shake his hand.

"Nice party, huh?"

"It's something."

"Don't drink that wine. I think it's supposed to be a joke."

"Thanks."

"Is Laura here?"

"She's around somewhere." The wavering torchlight made it hard to recognize anyone.

"Did she tell you my band was playing later?" Jerry said. A lot of Laura's employees were part-time musicians. Making phone calls all day beat working at a restaurant or record store.

"No. I didn't know you played country music."

"I don't. We play free-form improv. It's a couple of other guys from work and me. We're called Decon."

"Like the bug spray?"

"No, like deconstruction. We take jazz standards and turn them inside out," Jerry said, more than a little impressed with himself. I hoped Laura and I could leave soon.

"So what else is new?" Talking with Jerry was part of my role as dutiful husband. If Laura saw me, I could earn valuable points of my own. Maybe this evening wouldn't be a total wash.

"Not much. Still working for DataTech, but I've got to make more money. I've got a Visa bill that you wouldn't believe. Listen, I know you do some consulting work . . ." At parties, doctors heard about aches and pains. Consultants always got hit up by people who wanted more money.

"So you want some advice?"

"Sure. If you don't mind."

"No problem. First, how much do you sell books for, on average?" I started the process the Crockett Company called Individual Competency Assessment, which basically came down to asking questions for a while.

"Well, most of the insurance books I sell go for about twenty-five dollars."

"And how much commission do you get?"

"Five dollars," Jerry said. Twenty percent wasn't bad, but deceptive, since telemarketing was a hard way to sell anything, the modern version of going door to door in a strange neighborhood. Even if Jerry made a hundred calls an hour, which was physically impossible, he'd be lucky to sell two sets of books. So he came out of the whole deal making little more than minimum wage.

"Here's a tip," I said. "If you like sales, try selling something that costs more. Expensive books, or cars or something. At least then you'll be earning a big commission every once in a while instead of a little one every hour."

Jerry looked off into the distance and nodded his head as he considered my lame advice, a revelation to him.

"So you really think I should sell something else?"

"If you want a breakthrough in performance, you need to start with a breakthrough in thinking," I said, quoting the Crockett Company's latest marketing materials.

"I thought I might transfer into Periodicals."

"I'm not telling you what to do. It's just advice."

"No, you've got a point there." A smile spread above his goatee. "Yeah. Thanks. Thanks a lot."

"Sure. Anytime." I walked across the lawn toward the house, looking for a place to hide from the jug band's annoying scratch and pluck. If Laura wanted her wine, she could come and get it.

Inside, guests sat on leather furniture so white it looked bleached. Indian pottery, Navaho rugs, and unidentifiably rusty artifacts from the Southwest filled floor-to-ceiling shelves at one end of the living room, each collectible illuminated by a carefully aimed arrow of light shot from above. Robert's house seemed more like an art gallery than a home—a comment I'm sure he would have taken as a compliment.

At the far end of the living room, two women in high-necked silk blouses sat on a couch looking every bit as bleary and dull as any of DataTech's male managers, a sad version of equality. Empty pints of wine lined the coffee table in front of them, and as I walked closer, I could see their half-eaten carrot spears and lipstick-coated cigarette butts floating in pools of viscous dip.

"My advice is, don't get the uniform until he's had a chance to really decide if he's going to stick with it," one said.

"But he says he's got to have the uniform to take karate classes," said the other, her hair in a painful bun.

"Wait until he goes three times in his gym clothes, *then* buy the uniform. Otherwise you're throwing eighty bucks down the toilet. Mark my words. The thing will be hanging in your closet for years. They don't even make very good bathrobes. Believe me, I know." As she passed on this tidbit of suburban wisdom, the first woman shook her head and snuffed out another cigarette in the dip.

I wandered on through the house, which was much larger than our condo and an embarrassing amount of space for one person. The sun room was filled with ferns and bonsai trees on a long white shelf. It was hard not to feel sorry for the dwarfed shrubs, trapped in perpetual adolescence like teen pop stars. I looked around, then plucked a small red blossom and tossed it in my mouth. The flower didn't taste like anything but it was nice and crunchy. I had another. As I chewed, I looked out the window at the crowd gathered in Robert's backyard. They danced with the rhythmless shrugs perfected by clumsy white people at company parties.

A bunch of damn fools.

I heard Catlett Franklin Stride's thick backwoods drawl whispering from behind the plants.

"You got that right," I said. I had read somewhere that the ancient Greeks actually heard their consciences speak to them. I had listened to my great-great-grandfather's voice since I pulled his charred skull from the ruins of the First House twenty years before. The skull was now hidden deep in the hall closet, where no one would ever find it, but the voice was as familiar as my own.

I opened the side door and walked around to the front steps, where I sat down to smoke a cigarette. I searched my pockets for matches. A great rustling came from the woods and what sounded like a bear thrashed through the undergrowth. In the dusky light, I saw a pale bald man emerge from the trees, swatting at a cloud of bugs around his head. He walked toward the house and sat down next to me on the steps, panting.

"Do you have another cigarette?" he said. I handed him one. He deftly snapped off the filter and lit the butt hungrily with a butane lighter from the pocket of his windbreaker. In the flickering light I could see he was about forty, with eyes watery as egg whites. His straight, thin hair fell in damp hanks along his forehead, pale and glazed with sweat.

"Orioles," he said.

"What?"

"Baltimore orioles. Hear 'em?" he pointed toward the woods. I couldn't hear anything over the band's breakneck version of "Will the Circle Be Unbroken."

"No."

"They're black and orange. Like Halloween. I've been watching them."

"My name's Larkin."

"Hal," he said. "Hal Capshaw." We shook hands. .

"Do you work at DataTech?" Unlike everyone else at the party, Hal didn't seem anxious to complain about work.

"No, I'm a podiatrist. You know. Foot doctor." We smoked through a pause as I tried to think of something else to say, but he beat me to the punch.

"I'm Robert's neighbor. We live over the hill there. My wife thought it would be a nice gesture for me to stop by, so here I am." Hal seemed about as glad to be here as I did.

"Been back to the party?"

"No. You know, when he cleared out that backyard all the orioles migrated to a pond about a hundred yards through the woods. It's kind of hard to get to but it's worth the trip. I tape them. Got sixty-three hours of Baltimore orioles on digital audiotape."

"What do you do with the tapes?" I humored Hal, a strange bird himself.

"I listen to them. What the hell else would I do with them?" he blurted angrily.

"I'm sure that those tapes must be worth something. I mean, to bird-watchers or someone." I wanted to say the right thing to avoid setting him off again.

"Hell no! They're worthless. A waste of time. I make them as an excuse to stay in the woods all night. My wife drinks too much and I can't stand her after about nine." The things people told strangers always surprised me.

"I know what you mean," I said.

"Does your wife tip a few?" Hal leaned toward me.

"Not enough. To be a problem, I mean." Alcohol wasn't healthy, so Laura drank only the occasional glass of wine. Coffee gave her cluster headaches so we drank decaf. Red meat kept her constipated, so we ate vegetables. Sex made her sleepy at work, so we waited until the weekend. She had discipline.

Hal jabbed out his cigarette as Laura swooped through the front door, the screen door slamming behind her. She was half-way down the stairs before she noticed me. "Uh-oh," Hal said, "here comes a live one."

"We're leaving," she said tersely as she passed. I wondered what Robert had done to get her so angry.

"This is Hal, Robert's neighbor," I said to Laura's back.

"Good luck," Hal whispered. He stood up and walked quickly toward the woods.

Laura stared at Hal tromping through the underbrush like Bigfoot. "You *would* end up talking with the strangest guy at the party."

"We didn't have much of a conversation, really. He's a po-diatrist. And an ornithologist, I think." I followed Laura down the sidewalk, staying a few paces behind. She spun around to face me.

"You think you're better than anyone else, don't you?" she said.

"What do you mean? I was just sitting on the porch smoking a cigarette with some guy who likes birds."

"That's just it. Robert's got all my telemarketers wrapped around his little finger, and you're talking to the only person at the party who doesn't even work for DataTech."

"That's not true, I talked to Hank, and to a guy from your department for a while. The one with the beard. Larry?"

"Jerry. Jerry Klepner. The guy you told to go sell cars? Thanks a lot, Larkin."

"I didn't tell him that. He asked me for advice. Anyway, if you paid your people a little more you wouldn't have to worry about how to hold on to them."

"I don't want to talk about it. And I don't want you telling me how to do my job." Laura stomped toward the car. I reached back and felt the pint of wine that had been growing warm in my pocket. I tossed it deep into the woods, where it ripped through the leaves and landed on some rocks with a satisfying smash.

"What was that?"

"Hillbilly champagne." We walked down the rows of cars until we got to the Volvo, the hood still warm from the drive out.

"Why stop now?" Laura said in the car. "Why don't you just break some windshields or something? You know, like in the good old days when you were wild and free." I started the car and backed out, the wheels spinning a little in the dew-covered grass.

"Here we go," Laura said. "If you're going to drive like that you can let me out now."

"Let's just go home, Laura, okay? Don't get so bent out of shape. No one's grading you on how well you schmooze, you know."

"You just don't get it, Larkin. You never have. I can't count the times I've had to make excuses for you. 'Larkin's been working really hard, that's why he's off smoking in the parking lot.' 'Larkin doesn't like parties, that's why we left early.' 'Larkin doesn't like people, so . . .' "

"Knock it off, okay?" I turned onto the main street that led us past Wellesley College. We drove for a while in edgy silence through the empty town.

"Oh, no!" Laura sat bolt upright in the passenger seat.

"What?" I swerved onto the shoulder and then steered the Volvo back on the road.

"We have to turn around. I left the salad bowl at Robert's."

"Just get it on Monday," I said.

"But I like that salad bowl." Laura wanted everything in its place. To her, a misplaced salad bowl was like a lost child.

"So do I, but I'm not driving back to get it. It's no big deal. Call Robert tomorrow and he can bring it in to work." It was just an old wooden bowl, not even one of the Dansk ones we had gotten as wedding presents.

"I'm not calling Robert. You call him. And while you're at it, you can apologize for being so rude."

"I'm not the one who's being rude."

We didn't talk for the rest of the drive, standard postparty behavior for all company events we'd been to lately. These parties had taken on an impossible weight, but now that Hank had told me about Laura's being up for promotion at least I knew why.

I parked in the driveway. Laura jumped out and walked to the front door with her keys jingling, then ran up the stairs of the dark house. As I locked the car, I watched the lights go on in our apartment room by room as Laura checked for maniacs. She was convinced that we would be robbed. Our theft coverage had been raised so many times the insurance agent wouldn't even return my calls.

When I got upstairs, the lights were off again except for the dim hallway sconce. Laura had put on a T-shirt and crawled into bed, where she pretended to be asleep, although I could almost hear the gears click in her head as she tabulated tonight's score. Robert had won, Laura had lost, and I hadn't even been in the game. I took off my clothes and got under the covers, careful not to nudge Laura. It had been a long day, and the bus ride home this afternoon seemed years away. I remembered the woman I had met, Mariah, and wondered what she was doing now in her house just a few blocks away. I stared out the bedroom window and watched a jet move like a slow comet across the black sky. By the time it had faded into the distance, Laura was asleep, as always, on the side of the bed she had long ago claimed as her own.

4

A HILLBILLY AT HARVARD

MORNING LIGHT the color of apricots flickered on the bedroom walls, a good omen for the start of the day. I was surprised to find that I was alone, since Laura usually slept until noon on Saturdays. I got up and put on jeans and an old white shirt with cuffs too frayed to wear to client meetings. As I dressed, I heard a husky laugh from the living room and realized with a sinking feeling that Tammy and Kendra were here. So much for good omens.

In the kitchen, I made myself a cup of instant coffee since the coffeemaker was full of decaf. Two gigantic backpacks were parked on the table, overflowing with videotapes and books. I thought about sneaking back to the bedroom, but it was too late.

"Larkin? Are you up?" Laura walked into the kitchen wearing a sweatshirt and running pants.

I didn't say anything, just kept stirring my coffee. The non-dairy creamer Laura insisted on using turned it gray and soapy.

"Look, I'm sorry I got so upset last night." She came up behind me and put her arms around me. "Work's been a real problem lately."

"Don't worry about it." For now, I was willing to let work take the blame for everything.

"Come say hi to Tammy and Kendra." She tugged on my shirt.

"I thought they were coming over next Saturday." I usually managed to be somewhere else during their visits.

"It's only once a month," Laura whispered. "Just say hi."

"I don't want to bother you guys when you're working," I said, spooning more sugar into my coffee.

"No problem, we were just starting." As we walked into the living room, I worked up a viable smile for our two guests. Kendra ran the Red Star Bookstore, a radical bookshop not far from the apartment she, Tammy, and Laura used to share. Her hair tied in a blue kerchief, Kendra rummaged through a pile of videotapes on the couch while Tammy sat yoga style on the rug and wrote on a legal pad.

"Hi," I said. "What's up?"

"Oh, the usual." Kendra smiled wearily. "Political oppression. Destruction of the rain forests. The myth of patriarchy."

"Larkin, you don't have a Beta machine, do you? Some of these tapes are old," Tammy said without looking at me. Laura had gone to Smith with Tammy, a skinny woman with her black hair shorn in a POW haircut. I squinted at the photograph on her T-shirt. Carlos Santana, I thought, then moved a little closer. Nope. Che Guevara.

"Sorry, just the regular VCR," I said. When she was twenty-one, Tammy had inherited a lot of money in a family trust established by an ancestor who had made his fortune selling ostrich-plume hats to Beacon Hill Brahmins. Tammy could have bought all the home electronics equipment she wanted, but chose instead to use her money to bankroll Kendra's store. She drove a cab and claimed to be writing a book about her experiences as a radical feminist cab driver. Everyone in Cambridge was writing a book about something.

"No Beta machine? I thought you had everything," Kendra said. When she smiled, she looked like a plump, evil elf.

"Be nice," Laura said, giving my arm a reassuring squeeze.

She walked over to the couch and started stacking videotapes. I leaned on the doorway and wondered how long I had to stand here to be considered polite.

"How's the apartment?" I said. A feeble attempt at small talk that Kendra ignored. Back when I was dating Laura, I had to hang out in their Spartan digs, which they described as an on-going socialist living experiment. They posted the house rules at the front door—no shoes, no remarks that might be construed as sexist or racist, no meat, no smoking, no alcohol, and no media. Books were subject to Kendra's approval. The chore wheel taped to the refrigerator mentioned organic gardening, recycling, neighborhood safety patrols, and wheat-pasting political leaflets all over town.

I tried again. "So. Still living in Inman Square?"

"Yes," Kendra said firmly. "They're putting up condos in the vacant lot, but we're ready for them." Kendra turned to Tammy and she gave a conspiratorial nod, ready to fight the good fight. I pitied their neighbors. Kendra had been furious when Laura finally tired of paramilitary living conditions, stewed lentils, false poverty. When Laura moved out, Kendra had issued a rambling manifesto urging her to "refuse to give in to the socialized pressure toward capitalism and enforced heterosexual monogamy." I still saw tattered copies of it stuck on abandoned buildings in Cambridge now and then.

"Look," said Tammy, holding up a videotape. "Here's one on Debs."

"Debutantes?" I said.

"No. Eugene Debs. The socialist," Kendra said with a small shake of her head. To Kendra, I was just a penis thruster, a missile launcher.

Now that Red Star had a video library, Tammy and Kendra descended on our home to screen the new tapes they had received, since under the no-media rule they couldn't own a television or VCR.

"These are holistic health." Laura pointed to stack after stack.

"These are personal and spiritual growth. And these are world religions, ancient arts, and tribal rituals." Laura might not agree with Tammy and Kendra's politics anymore, but she sure was organized.

"How about action and adventure?" I said, backing slowly through the door.

"How about the covert actions *your* government is carrying on right now all over the other Americas," Kendra said, but I pretended not to hear. In the kitchen, I poured my coffee into a plastic no-spill mug, a free gift from the last time I filled the tank at Texaco. Laura walked in to get the backpacks of tapes.

"Didn't mean to break up the fun," I said.

"They like you. It's just that they have problems with men."

"Right. You know what? For Christmas this year, let's get them one of those little portable video players. They don't have to bring it in their apartment. They can leave it in the car or something."

"Be nice. They're still my friends." Kendra and Tammy treated Laura as if she had gone temporarily insane and would return some day to Inman Square and resume her place on the chore wheel.

I picked up my keys from the kitchen table. "With friends like that, who needs friends?"

"They'll hear you," Laura whispered.

"I'm going to go to the office for a while to work on the book."

"You're just going there to get away from them."

"Not true. I've got to interview some guy at ten."

"Will you be back by dinner? I thought we might get Thai food or something."

"Whatever." I kissed Laura on the forehead. We walked back into the living room, where Tammy and Kendra were watching a video.

"You really should see this one, Laura," Kendra said. "It's about that new disorder I told you about, post-stress sleep syndrome. You know, PSSS. I think you may have it already."

"I do not," Laura said. But in fact, she slept more than anyone

I knew. When work was really getting to her she went into all-weekend hibernation. I could kiss her lips, rub her forehead with my fingertips, even run my hand along her stomach without waking her. She claimed she never had dreams, or at least never remembered them. If in dreams we were free to do what we really wanted, Laura chose to do nothing.

"They say PSSS could affect fifty percent of the professional workforce," Tammy said, unprofessional and proud of it. She reached into her backpack and pulled out a bag of Styrofoam chunks. She offered me one. "Puffed-rice cake?" I shook my head.

"And there's absolutely nothing you can do about it," Kendra said. Laura went over to the couch and sat down, her eyes fixed on the screen. Her doctor had told her she didn't have anything a good vacation couldn't cure, but now Kendra had her convinced she had some kind of syndrome. I took this chance to head for the door.

Outside, leaves rustled around my feet as I walked toward the Volvo. Soon winter would blacken any remaining patches of green with a killing frost and sweep the neighborhood clean, but in the glow of Indian summer the morning ripened and decayed. Beneath our apple tree, oily crows pecked at splotched yellow fruit that sent out a sweet rot. The air was thick with the droning of honeybees.

I got in the car and drove to the corner, where a few crimson dahlias bowed their wilting heads next to a chain-link fence. Out on Mount Auburn Street, the front yard of the Armenian Benevolent Society blazed with blood-red leaves. I steered with one hand and held the coffee mug in the other; it was a habit Laura always criticized even though I had perfected it over the years. Only a few cars were out on this quiet morning, so I could weave across both lanes. In Little Armenia, the boys from the produce market sat on the curb, tossing rotten tomatoes at the Captain's Anchorage Pub across the street. I watched in the rearview mirror as a tomato splattered just behind the Volvo.

The flatiron-shaped liquor store that guarded the Watertown–

Cambridge border was closed now, its neon sign unblinking in the morning light. Ahead, the Charles River sparkled and a couple of rowers skimmed along its mercury surface like water-bugs. In a couple of months it would be a ribbon of black ice.

I steered the Volvo down Memorial Drive toward Harvard Square, through the tunnel of gray sycamores so old they seemed to have been extruded from the earth's core. Fresh-looking Harvard students jogged along the path next to the river in thigh-squeezing neon outfits, trying to burn off all their anxieties and frustrated sexual yearnings. My father would call them "unre-sourceful," one of his strongest curses, reserved only for fools who did ridiculous things like run when no one was chasing them.

The brick towers and painted domes of Harvard poked through the trees. For generations, higher education had proved elusive to the Stride family. Most struggled through a few years at the University of Arkansas and left without finishing. A mandatory French course did in my grandfather. My father dropped out to fight in Korea. Given this record, I figured I should try college somewhere else. I got into Harvard because of good test scores, a promising future as a member of the track team, and because only a few other students from Arkansas applied that year. I drove halfway across the country to Cambridge in a red Chevelle purchased from my father and customized during the summer with chrome exhausts, a four-barrel carburetor, deluxe wheel rims. Now, although more than a decade had passed, the fall air and winding river road triggered memories of the first lonely days, when I discovered that ignorance wasn't bliss, that ignorance was no fun at all.

On a chilly September night I had watched my classmates go through a time-honored freshman tradition that involved burning old furniture, running around in jockstraps, and drinking a lot of draft beer. They seemed possessed as they rushed across Harvard yard like roving bands of Indians, yelling at each other in the firelight.

It hadn't taken me long to realize that I didn't belong to any of these tribes from Exeter, Andover, St. Paul's, Groton. I was a tribe of one, a public school student from Dogpatch, USA, green as a kitchen appliance. I had never lived in a dorm, played lacrosse, or worn a school tie. I did my best to make friends in a naive, down-home way, but my twangy mumbling rendered me unintelligible to most of the other students, who talked quickly through their noses like nervous geese. Harvard yard was filled with the best and the brightest young snobs in training. My fascination with them had worn off after a couple of days and now I hated them, not just out of jealousy but out of something more biological, the way a dog hated squirrels.

The fire from the burning furniture had cast a strange glow over the yard, filled with haze and smoke. Off to one side, a row of shining beer kegs wallowed in a mud puddle, and most of the freshman class shuffled around in the muck. Others jumped from second-floor windows clad only in baggy boxer shorts, the kind of underwear worn in prep school. Occasionally, drunken revelers ran out into Harvard Square, where, I hoped, they would be run over by buses. Others crowned the somber statue of John Harvard with a pair of lace panties. The *Crimson* would report this exciting news event beneath a banner headline—"Freshmen Frolic!"

I was not frolicking. In a dim corner of the yard, I stood next to an upholstered chair that had been thrown from a dorm room so my classmates could burn it.

Suddenly, the chair spoke to me.

"I'm so glad to be back where people have heard of Goethe," it said. I squinted, my eyes watering from the smoke. It wasn't a chair after all, but a large girl wearing some sort of garment woven from feed sacks.

"Me too!" I lied. Freshmen were supposed to be enthusiastic.

"I forgot how silly Freshman Week was," she said. "Can you believe these are the future leaders of major corporations?" She delivered this last phrase with a knowing contempt, as if she somehow sensed my own disgust.

"Sure. I mean, no."

"My name is Patina Napolitano," said the girl-chair as she reached her hand from beneath her sack. Looking more closely, I saw an intricate embroidery of spirals and diamonds. It was a strange costume, something like a magician's cape, but at least it wasn't another tattered St. Paul's sweatshirt.

I bent forward in a brief bow. "Larkin Stride," I said, always serious and polite during introductions. "Glad to meet you." We shook hands.

"You're a freshman?" she said.

"Yes. Aren't you?"

"No. A junior. But I took a year off to travel in Africa. I got in a few days early. It feels so strange to be back here." We watched as roving gangs of student firewalkers jumped through the dying flames. Yes, it was strange.

"What did you do in Africa?"

"Research. I'm an anthro major. And then I just traveled around. I worked for a while at a market in Nairobi. Have you been to Kenya?"

I laughed. "I haven't been anywhere like that."

"You must have been somewhere. I can tell you're not from around here." I wondered what made people spot me as a stranger almost instantly. My unstylish sideburns, shaggy and pointy like those of latter-period Elvis? My jean jacket with the dirty sheepskin lining? My brown cowboy boots? More than likely it had little to do with any piece of clothing. Even in their clothes, I would still stand out—the something that was wrong with this picture.

"I'm from Arkansas. We used to go to Texas or Oklahoma in the summer to visit relatives, but that's about it."

"I've never been to Arkansas. You'll have to tell me all about it." She smiled. So far, Patina was the only person I had met at Harvard who seemed remotely interested in me. The longer I looked at her, the more attractive she became. Her face lit up when she smiled, which was often, and I could imagine staring into her chestnut eyes for a long time.

"It looks like this is about over." I nodded at the smoky courtyard. "Do you want to go somewhere?" Somewhere? Certainly not Pennypacker Hall, where I shared a tiny double with a pimply guy from New Jersey. I held my breath as I watched her face, waiting for an answer.

"Why don't we go back to Adams House for a drink," she said. "I've got some wine in my room."

I nodded, relieved, excited. We weren't just going somewhere; the Adams House indoor pool was renowned as a late-night undergraduate spawning ground. Patina and I walked away from the hazy remnants of Freshman Week, and for the first time since I arrived in Cambridge, I was happy.

Just a few blocks and about fifteen years away, I parked the Volvo and locked it. Charlesview Place, our office building, loomed up ahead, a large, red brick structure topped by a stubby smokestack. In the last century, it had been a shoe factory; it had been converted into office space a few years ago. The windows were rimmed in a green that reminded me of cabbage. The cornices along the top of the building were painted pink. A white concrete circle crowned the center of the roof, a clock with no hands, no hours, no reason to be there. A statue of an angel, wings folded, perched next to the circle and stared down at the small courtyard.

I passed two marble benches so conspicuous that no one ever sat on them unless they had no choice. In the center of the courtyard was a small flower garden, raked clean now, ringed by a circle of sidewalk we called the Career Path, since our boss, Davy, liked to bring his employees down here for serious discussions about the future. To get to the front entrance, I had to walk beneath an arch supported by two white pillars, a larger version of something a four-year-old might build with blocks. The arch served no purpose except to "define the space," as the architect would argue. To me, it just defined how silly a building could be. I looked up every time I walked under this arch, worried that it might fall on me. It would be an embarrassing way to go, crushed by a piece of postmodern architectural whimsy.

Other office buildings in the square had gone under or were half filled with struggling companies, but Charlesview Place was at maximum occupancy, with a waiting list of potential tenants who had proved more resistant to the economic virus that was going around. The names of the building's occupants were painted in large gold letters on a faux-marble panel in the foyer. Most ended in the word "Associates," which said that these companies were start-up businesses with one leader and a few followers straight from Harvard B School. Above them all stood the Crockett Company, serious and respected, filling the whole top floor.

I decided not to take the back stairway, which had aerobic value but smelled of the piss of a hundred pea-bladdered couriers. In the elevator, I saw my reflection in the brass doors and gave it the finger.

Our floor was empty, airless as a closet. I turned on the fluorescent overhead lights and then turned them off quickly when I saw the empty desks, blank computer screens, glass-enclosed conference room. Dim light filtered from beneath office doors and through venetian blinds. The management offices had all the windows, and when we shut our doors and closed our blinds the center cluster of cubicles—the bullpen, we called it—was dark as a cellar. Like hothouse plants, senior consultants were rewarded with sunlight.

In my office waited the familiar desk, bookshelves, and computer stand. I hung up my coat, then looked down on the lower side of Harvard Square, lined with bookstores and expensive ice cream places. Students gathered on street corners like balls of crimson and gray lint, walked stiffly through the square as though their parents were watching. The boys had short hair and their faces looked rosy and healthy, even from my window. The girls were blond and most wore tan pants and sweaters covered by light fall jackets.

Patina would have stuck out in her dark outfits, pieced together from visits to the Salvation Army and stores that sold only clothes from developing nations. I stood at the window until I realized that the old girlfriend I was looking for in the crowd had been gone for a long time. I sat down at my desk, turned on my computer, and shuffled papers like a pro.

At a little before ten, I started looking through the background materials for my interview with Dave Dahlgrin, president of National Timeclock, "the company that brought the computer chip to the time-recording industry," according to the company's latest annual report. Thanks to National Timeclock, it was virtually impossible for employees to falsify their time cards, and this saved companies millions of dollars and made thousands of hourly workers feel like robots.

I looked through the press releases and company newsletters, then decided to wing the interview. Nothing was more boring than being prepared. I reached into my top desk drawer and rummaged through half-empty bags of candy, the high-octane-sugar brands favored by kids in their single digits—Chompers, Runts, Sprees, Fruitsters. I chewed a handful of Smarties for motivation.

Being an efficient executive, Dahlgrin had set up this interview for Saturday so it wouldn't interfere with his normal managerial duties. I called his number precisely at ten, just as we had planned. He answered on the second ring.

"Dave Dahlgrin."

"Mr. Dahlgrin. This is Larkin Stride calling from the Crockett Company in Cambridge."

"Yes?"

"Did you get the copy of my book, *Sell Straight to the Top,* that I sent you?"

"No, I did not." He sounded kind of annoyed. I must have forgotten to ask the secretary to send it out.

"Well, as we discussed last week, I'm working on a new book,

Strategies for Success, that takes a look at field-tested management strategies from the country's top executives," I said, reading from the brief, ingratiating paragraph of boilerplate I'd prepared for my interviewees. "I want to include interviews with leaders like yourself who have risen to the top of their respective industries. First, let me start with a little background."

"Okay."

With the introduction out of the way, I was on my own. I stared at my empty notepad and waited for a question to pop into my head, then wrote Dahlgrin's name at the top of the page. "Right. From looking at your company's materials, I see you started out at Rand."

"Mead."

"Exactly. And when you took over National Timeclock, it was just a minor player in the time-recording industry."

"Actually, it was already the industry leader in terms of dollar volume."

I hit a few keys on the computer to make convincing sound effects, hoping to bolster my crumbling credibility.

"How did you bring National Timeclock to its current level of success?" I paused, having finally come up with an open-ended question that would get Dahlgrin talking.

"I'm not sure I know what you're getting at. Do you mean in terms of restructuring the organization? Or our commitment to R-and-D?"

I floundered. "Uh. Both."

"That's discussed in this year's report to the stockholders, pages ten through twenty-five."

"I'll read it," I said.

"For now, I'll cut to the chase." Dahlgrin's staccato delivery reminded me of an angry drill sergeant. "The Japs and Koreans were beating our butt. I got a piece of legislation shoved through that put temporary trade restrictions on time clock imports. That bought us time to can the management deadwood and do a little blue-skying about a new marketing plan. And do you know what I found?"

"What?"

"I'm not going to tell you," Dahlgrin said. "So far this has been the worst interview I've ever given. If there's one thing that pisses me off, it's inefficiency. First of all, you were supposed to call at ten."

"I called at ten," I said.

"Here in California, it's only seven, and I'm in the middle of my morning workout."

"I'm real sorry." I made a mental note to check for those pesky time differences.

"And I hate it when you smart-ass consultants act like you know everything. You don't know jackshit about time-recording."

"It's a very complicated industry," I countered, feeling my face get hot.

"Then start doing your homework. If you fax me ten questions on Monday I'll respond to them in writing sometime in the fourth quarter. But as for now, this interview is officially over."

I heard a click; then I dropped my receiver back on the phone console and held it down for a moment to make sure Dahlgrin was really gone.

"Shit."

I stood up and stalked around the office, then lit a cigarette. My ears burned as if I had been scolded by the school principal. I was already way behind on the book and the last thing I needed was another delay. Dave Dahlgrin was right about one thing: I didn't know anything about time clocks and my interest in learning about them was at an all-time low.

I looked out my office window and watched couples walking along the riverbank, soaking up the last warmth of the season. Cars were spinning along on both sides of the Charles, windshields and chrome bumpers shining in the sun. Why was I in the office on a beautiful fall day instead of home, spending time with my wife? The botched interview made me question more than my weekend plans. It made me wonder what I was doing in this business in the first place.

* * *

My classmates left Harvard with good jobs, connections, or at least plans for a summer in Italy. I graduated with even less of an idea of what I wanted to do than when I had gotten there. Back in Arkansas, I spent most of my time at the kitchen table with the help-wanted section of the *Little Rock Traveler* in front of me. I couldn't concentrate with my stepmother placing complicated bets on baseball games by phone, repeating the word "honey" like a mantra. Janine didn't seem quite like what a mother—or even a stepmother—should be. She was in her late thirties, still attractive but getting a little thick around the middle from beer. All summer she wore a white terry-cloth robe over a pink one-piece bathing suit. Her wavy blond hair looked bleached and her skin was tanned from lying on the patio in a refrigerator box lined with foil.

My father had met Janine at a building-materials trade show in Topeka, where she was modeling for a brick siding company. She stood in front of its display wearing a red bikini and a banner—"Built Like a Brick House." My father fell in love with this brick house and traveled around the country to see her at car shows and shopping mall dedications.

His persistence prevailed and Janine agreed to move to Arkansas. They married secretly in Reno a few months later, and called me from the hotel afterward. My father told me he didn't want his second wedding to be a big deal. He didn't want me to come all the way home from college—a consideration that didn't hold much water. Actually, I think he knew that the Stride family wouldn't approve of Janine, whom he called Top Shelf; the nickname referred both to her fondness for high-quality liquor and to her most prominent feature, a bosom that could accommodate a small card game.

We were polite to each other but not exactly friendly. Top Shelf had been around. She had dealt blackjack in Vegas, sold real estate in Florida. She had even been married once before. I thought she was after my father's money, the little that he had left after the recent flurry of home renovations.

Love made a middle-aged building contractor do strange things. The Second House had been empty since my grandfather died. Over the years, he hadn't been able to take care of the sprawling house with its tin roof, gabled upstairs windows, and legendary front porch. Top Shelf went crazy about the place and my father turned it into a hillbilly Versailles with his new bride installed as queen. He fixed the foundation, tore out some walls, and put in air conditioning. He cleared the backyard of all the broken farm machinery I used to play on, dredged our swampy pond and placed a fountain of Venus on its banks. As a tribute to Top Shelf, the former Miss Brick House, he even put fake-brick siding on our old home, now converted into a guest house.

One morning, after finishing her phone calls, Top Shelf sat down at the table next to me with the sports section. After a quick glance at the scores, she put down the paper. "You a Red Sox fan?"

"No," I said.

"I can't imagine going all that way to Boston and not taking the time to see Fenway." She shook her head. "It's one of the last old-time ball parks."

Top Shelf was not impressed with me or my education, and at this point I was not impressive. I slept until noon, read magazines, or hung around the kitchen. On a particularly ambitious day I might take a long walk to the ruins of the First House, completely overgrown now. I had looked up my old girlfriends, hoping to use some of the sexual knowledge I had learned from Patina and other college girlfriends, but most were married now, some with kids.

Top Shelf turned to me after a while. "What time did your daddy say he'd be home?"

"Around seven."

"He sure is a hardworking man. Up at the crack of dawn." She put on her reading glasses and started working the word jumble. Top Shelf's last comment hit a nerve. Was she saying that I wasn't hardworking, that I wasn't a man?

I threw down the paper and pushed my chair back hard enough to shake the table and spill Top Shelf's Tab.

"God damn it! What're you getting all creased about?" She sopped up the mess with a *Parade* magazine.

"Nothing."

"Yeah, nothing. You've been pissed ever since you got home from school, and I think it's high time we came to an understanding." Top Shelf tossed the soaked magazine in the trash. "And I was going to read that later."

"I'm worried about getting a job," I said. "That's all."

"About finding one, or about having one?" Janine came back to the table with two Buds from the refrigerator. "Want a beer?"

I took the can and opened it. We faced each other with the checkered tablecloth between us, reminding me of the chess masters I used to see in Harvard Square. I never thought I'd miss Cambridge, but it beat sitting here in Pine Bluff without a job, a career, or even a clue.

"What do you mean? I want a job. I just haven't found one yet."

"Look at this," Top Shelf said. She picked up the help-wanted section I should have been reading. "Here's a bunch of jobs. Manufacturer's sales representative. Line cook. Bartender. Outdoor pool installation crew chief. Foreign car mechanic. You're good with cars, aren't you?"

"Yeah, but . . ."

"But nothing. Work's work. If you really wanted a job, you'd have got one lined up before you graduated. You can't tell me all that smart stuff you learned at Harvard couldn't land you something sweet."

"Maybe that's not what I'm looking for."

"Then just what *are* you looking for?" Top Shelf had me stumped, but I didn't want her to know.

"I'm going to Tulsa." The words popped out of my mouth. "I've got some friends there. Maybe I'll get a job in the oilfields."

"Now, that's a different story," Top Shelf said. "What brought on this big decision?"

"I always wanted to live in Tulsa." This wasn't true. I did not like Tulsa, a flat city where summers were hot as the inside of a kiln.

"When do you plan on heading out?"

"Tomorrow morning." I said.

Top Shelf paused for a moment, registering this change, which meant I'd be out of the kitchen finally. "Then we'll have to have ourselves a little party tonight." She walked over to the refrigerator, opened the freezer door, and looked in through clouds of frost. "I'll call your father and have him pick up some ribeyes on the way home." Top Shelf seemed to move with new energy.

"You don't need to do anything special," I said. I walked toward my room to pack.

"I know that," she said. "I just want to."

"I appreciate it."

"I know you don't like me very much right now, and I don't blame you. I'm not your mother and I never can be. But I can be your friend. And I will be someday if you don't watch out." Top Shelf stuck her tongue out at me and laughed as she walked outside to drop a trash bag into the shiny aluminum garbage cans instead of dumping it over the fence for the cows to eat, like we used to.

I packed, not exactly sure why I was going to Tulsa, but glad that I had a purpose to my life again, or at least a destination.

That night, Top Shelf cooked an incredible dinner—steaks, baked potatoes topped with bacon and cheese, fried okra, fresh tomatoes covered with pepper and sugar, corn on the cob, blackberry pie with ice cream. We drank beer, cheap champagne, and Jack Daniel's with fresh mint from the garden. Before she turned in, Top Shelf gave me a rib-crushing hug, and I knew that she was right. I would be her friend. After she left the room, my father slid five one-hundred-dollar bills across the table, then gave me some advice worth a good deal more.

"I don't know what they taught you out at Harvard," he said, drilling into me with his Cherokee eyes, still clear after the whiskey. "And I don't exactly like the idea of you running off like this. But no matter what you end up doing—even if it's shoveling shit—you got to do it better because you're a Stride. You're from damn good breeding stock. And don't you forget it."

Shoveling shit wasn't such a bad description of what I was doing at the Crockett Company on a Saturday morning. I started working on a list of questions to fax Dave Dahlgrin but gave up. It could wait until Monday. For now, I wanted to go home and rake leaves, change the oil, or do some other stupid chore that would make me forget the guillotine click of Dave Dahlgrin signing off.

I picked up the phone to call Laura, hoping Tammy and Kendra were gone by now. But as I reached toward the console to press the button programmed for home, I decided to call information instead.

"What city please?"

"In Watertown," I said.

"Yes?"

"Callahan. On Palfrey Street. Mariah Callahan."

5

THE LOST YEARS

AT NOON, I left the office and walked along the river toward the address Mariah had given me. Clouds had moved in all morning and now the air was heavy and smelled of pond water. I thought of the raincoat I kept in the office for just such a change in the weather. But I didn't want Mariah to think I was just another businessman in a tan London Fog. What I wanted her to think wasn't so clear.

The wind had raised a chop on the dirty emerald surface of the Charles, driving away the rowers. My freshman year, I had jumped into the river on a hot day and floated downstream beneath bridges and past electric plants, kicking along with the current that pulled me toward the harbor. The Charles seemed like a fine river to me at the time, winding through Cambridge with the same graceful bends that I remembered from the Ouachita back home. Even if the day hadn't turned cooler, I knew too much to jump in now. Most people considered the Charles toxic; rowers who fell in were given shots.

On the other side of the river, Boston looked tired and empty— The City That Always Sleeps. The rows of expensive Back Bay brownstones were no more inviting than housing projects.

71

In the distance, the gilded orb of the State House cupola rose over the clutter of Beacon Hill, and beyond it the nameless slabs of the financial district stared vacantly across the water. I tried to picture this low knob of land as the Pilgrims first saw it, the woods unmarked by cattle paths, the lowlands flooded, the harbor empty and waiting.

I walked past MIT, then cut away from the river toward Kendall Square, where rotting textile mills and shoe factories had been resurrected as software developers and biotech companies. The streets were deserted, the corner restaurants closed, and the whole area looked like an abandoned stage set.

When I called, Mariah had invited me to meet her at One Technology Centre, a tall building designed to look like a giant microchip, its sides etched with silver lines that connected each of the narrow windows as in a complex pattern of circuitry. At the base of this computer monolith, I saw Mariah talking to a man in a leather trench coat. I walked across the breezy plaza past groups of people unloading equipment from a van or drinking coffee.

"Larkin! Glad you could make it." Mariah reached out and gave my hand a squeeze.

"Hi," I said. The leather trench coat guy gave me a wary look. He was in his forties, with a droopy gray moustache and a narrow face that made him look like a frumpy rabbit. The frames of his glasses were the color of red licorice.

He turned to Mariah. "Who's he?"

"This is my friend Larkin," she said. "He's a consultant. Larkin, this is Alan."

Alan dropped the smoking filter of a cigarette to the concrete and ground it beneath his gray Italian shoe. He turned toward me. "Are you billing us for this? Because if you are, I need to get an estimate okayed by Purchasing before you start."

"No," I said. "I'm just a visitor."

"We're on a budget here. The bean counters back at the shop will have my hide if this shoot doesn't go right." He lit another cigarette. "Look at me. I'm a nervous wreck. If we don't get this baby on press in a week, Nimbus may jump ship or I may jump off a cliff. Maybe both." I nodded, but wasn't sure why. "Whatever you do here, Larker, just make sure it isn't billable, promise, tiger?"

"I promise."

"Let me know when you're ready to shoot, babycakes," he said to Mariah. "I'm going to go make sure our boy has his tie on straight." Alan trudged toward some men in suits gathered at the entrance to the building.

"I didn't think there'd be so many people," I said.

"This is nothing." Mariah knelt down and opened an aluminum case.

"I don't want to get in your way. Are you sure I'm allowed to be here?"

She stood up and pushed her hair out of her face. "I'm the one who told you to stop by if you wanted to, remember? Having someone new around always makes things more exciting."

"Exciting?"

"Sure. I've done about fifty shoots with Alan this year. He's one of the best art directors in town, but he's really getting on my nerves." She took cameras and lenses out of the case and put them together quickly. "We've had to cancel a couple times because of weather. It drives him crazy when God keeps getting in the way of Nimbus Computer's annual report."

Nimbus was the Apple Computer of the East Coast, a phenomenally successful company that had sprung up during the booming "Massachusetts Miracle" days. Over at the entrance of One Technology Centre, I recognized the founder, Jack Briggs, from business magazines. A tall man with a craggy, tanned face and a shock of unruly blond hair, Briggs sent a confident, charismatic aura out over the other executives around him. In different clothes, they could have been a baseball team, fighter pilots, a wilderness expedition.

"Is he a nice guy?" I asked Mariah, who wore a camera around her neck. She attached a larger, more complicated camera to a tripod.

"Jack? About the same as the rest. He wants to look good but he won't let us put any makeup on him. But yeah, he seems all right."

I thought about going up and handing him my business card, asking if I could interview him for my book. Nimbus was the kind of success story Davy wanted me to get. But I was only a guest.

"Move those lights more to the right, Michael," Mariah shouted over at a guy with a ponytail who raised what looked like a glowing pup tent at the end of a long aluminum pole. On the concrete plaza, assistants plugged in cables, adjusted reflective panels, and fiddled with complicated equipment.

"Do all these people work for you?"

"I hired some assistants and a stylist for the day." Mariah loaded the cameras with film. "Those guys in suits are from Nimbus. Everyone else is from the ad agency, except Alan, who's from Mars. I mean, the guy has ten pairs of matching glasses and suspenders."

Alan walked back toward us, a cigarette in his mouth and one in his hand, smoking behavior that even I found a little beyond the pale. Behind him, the other businessmen headed toward the sidelines and left Jack Briggs alone on the steps. A woman in a pink rain jacket stroked his charcoal-gray suit with a lint brush.

Mariah turned to me. "I'm going to be busy for a little bit, then we can talk."

"Fine," I said. She looked through the viewfinder of the camera.

"Start shooting before God smites us again," Alan said. "It's going to rain. I feel it in my tootsies. And it was so beautiful before. So many lumens."

"Lumens?" I said.

Alan walked over and stood next to me. "Itty-bitty pieces of light, like fireflies," he said. "Lumens are my life."

"Well, the light meter says the lumens are history," Mariah said. "We'll have to use the tents." She reached down at her feet and hit a button on a black box that looked like a car battery. Suddenly lights blazed like safety flares, shifting the cloudy day to high noon.

"Attention!" Alan shouted. "We're shooting. Everyone quiet on the set."

"Alan, we're taking a photograph, not shooting a feature film," Mariah said. "Who do you think you are, Werner Herzog or something?"

"Just having a little fun, lambchop." Alan winked at me. "Take me a Polaroid."

Mariah pressed on the end of a cable, and the camera clicked. She pulled a piece of film from the camera, looked at her watch for a little bit, then peeled away a photo and handed it to Alan. We looked at the greenish shot of Jack Briggs, who stood in front of his company and glared at the camera.

"Oh my. He looks a little too mean. Might scare the stock-holders," Alan said. "Can't you make him look a little warmer and fuzzier? Do a little magic on him. We need some fresh creative here."

"All right, Alan." Mariah walked to the steps and spoke with Briggs for a minute. He started to laugh, then draped his arm across her shoulder. Although Mariah wasn't short, she looked like a girl next to the lanky CEO. She leaned up and whispered something to him, but we were too far away to hear.

"I wonder if she's talking dirty," Alan muttered.

"I hope not," I said, surprising myself.

"I bet she is." Alan winked at me, then lit another cigarette.

Mariah came back and looked through the camera again. Briggs smiled now, scanning the horizon as if he liked what he saw there. Mariah clicked the shutter a few times, then looked up at the gray sky over Nimbus Computer. She reached down and turned off the lights.

"I'm going to go with natural light," she said.

"It'll be underexposed," Alan said tersely. "We've got about three more minutes before he flies to Hong Kong, and you don't have a shot yet. Come on!"

"Just cool out, Alan," Mariah said softly, without turning around.

The low clouds began to part a little and a few brilliant rays of sunlight—*lumens,* I guess—pierced through the gray sky, arcing down to light the circuitry etched on One Technology Centre. As Mariah clicked the shutter faster and faster, Briggs stood like Moses of the Microchip, his company lit by the heavens for a moment before it faded back to become another gray office building.

"Got it!" Mariah said. The assistants applauded and Nimbus executives rushed forward to whisk Briggs into a limo waiting in the company parking lot. Alan knelt in front of Mariah and hugged her knees.

"Alan, could you stop acting like a poodle?" Mariah said. "You're embarrassing me in front of my new friend."

"Just tell me what you said to him to get that look. Tell me it didn't have anything to do with getting naked."

"When we were setting up the shot, all he wanted to talk about was golf," Mariah said. "So I told him to pretend he was standing on the golf course on a beautiful spring morning, watching his shot bounce toward the flag for a hole in one."

"Dullsville." Alan got up and dusted his pants with one hand, unleashing a squall of cigarette ashes, then wandered off across the plaza.

Stockholders would see the picture of Briggs on the cover of the annual report and assume that he was confident about the company, about the future, about increasing dividends. Only Alan, Mariah, and I would know he was really inspired by golf.

"Come on," she said. "Let's go for a little walk while they pack up."

We strolled side by side, almost touching. As we headed back toward the river, I listened to the space between her steps, a new rhythm.

"I didn't mean to surprise you on the phone," I said. "I'm not really sure why I called."

Mariah's dark hair fell on the shoulders of her green hound's-tooth jacket. She wasn't wearing glasses now, and I could see that her eyes weren't as dark as I remembered, but the color of coffee with extra cream.

"I'm glad you did. A few minutes later and I would have been out the door. So what do you think?"

"About what?"

"About the shoot," Mariah said.

"I think you're good at it." I remembered how she had moved with a practiced grace as she made adjustments to the camera, each motion of her hands deft, precise.

"Good enough."

"But I have a feeling you don't like doing it much." I waited, hoping I had guessed right. She scrunched up her mouth a little.

"It's not that I don't like it," she said. "Anything you do too many times gets boring. I set up the shot, talk to the subject, make sure the client is happy. Then take the picture. Click." Mariah lowered her thumb on an invisible cable release.

"It's got to be more complicated than that."

"Everything's more complicated than it sounds," she said. "But now that I've got the routine down, I don't want to do it anymore. I don't want to take pictures when there're so many people around. It makes me feel like a juggler or something."

"Better a juggler than a clown." I remembered the interview with Dave Dahlgrin.

"What?"

"I mean, I know what you mean." I couldn't believe how stupid I sounded. Once again, Mariah rendered me tongue-tied.

We crossed Memorial Drive and walked along the jogging path next to the river. Near one of the boathouses was a grassy alcove hidden by a low hill and a grove of trees. When I was a student, I had slept in the sheltering weeds a few times on lush spring nights when I couldn't manage to find my way home from the Elysium. I had been guiding Mariah here ever since we left

Kendall Square. We sat down on a wooden park bench, finally alone.

"So," she said, "can I take your picture?" She got up from the bench, backed away, and raised the camera she still wore around her neck, not waiting for me to answer.

"Oh, you don't have to do that," I said.

"Come on, don't be shy." She lowered the camera.

"I'm not. It's just that I'm part Cherokee. We Indians have this thing about photos. You know. Something about how they steal your soul," I laughed, but in my heart I thought there was probably something to it.

"You look about as much like an Indian as I do," she said. "Anyway, I just want to use up this film. Nimbus Computer's paying for it."

The grove smelled dusty and old, as if books moldered beneath the mat of fallen leaves. I watched Mariah crouch and focus, then heard the click of the shutter. She stepped back, and as she took another photo I heard a whisper.

Look temptation in the eye.

Catlett Stride's words blended with the rattle of sycamore branches in the breeze, the click of Mariah's Nikon. Temptation was everywhere, and my ancestor's warning couldn't stop it any more than I could.

"Stop looking so serious," Mariah said. "You look like a consultant."

I thought about the Crockett Company offices nearby, sickly with fluorescent lights. I shivered involuntarily at the thought of leaving our bench to go back there.

"I'm not. It's just a job," I said. "I did lots of things before this."

"Like what?"

"After college, I worked in Oklahoma. In the oilfields."

"Did you like it?" The camera clicked and whirred, recording me.

"It paid a lot, but having crude oil spraying in my face all day took the fun out of being a roughneck."

"I can imagine."

"Then I drove a delivery truck for a caterer in Dallas."

"Any better?" Mariah stalked around the grove for different angles.

"Cleaner, but it didn't pay and I didn't like setting up chairs for birthday parties and Kiwanis Club luncheons. So I worked in a hardware store in Galveston for a year. You might say I hadn't found my true calling."

Mariah stopped taking pictures and stared at me with the same intensity as she had at the bus stop." Go on," she said.

"Then I landed my favorite job. I washed dishes at a barbecue in Kansas City for a couple of years."

"A lateral career move?" Mariah came back to the bench and sat down close to me.

"Exactly. I was looking for a way to advance myself. It takes a lot of skill to spray barbecue sauce off plates."

"Somehow, I can't imagine you washing dishes," Mariah said. No one at work knew about my real résumé, a catalogue of waywardness.

"I'm sure you had your share of jobs. Everyone has." I looked at her full lower lip, the hollow of her delicate neck.

"The usual. Waitress. Receptionist. I worked in a bank for a while. But once I started making money from photography, that was it. I don't miss those days at all."

"I was happier then," I said. "I honestly think I was happier then." I neglected to mention that my boots were always wet and rank with splattered food, that paying rent at the end of the month meant putting pennies in wrappers.

Mariah stood up and pulled her jacket around her. I hoped I hadn't bored her.

"I better be getting back, before they take off with my equipment," she said.

"Right."

"You'll have to tell me more, sometime."

"About what?"

"About working at the barbecue. About everything."

"I will." I wanted to tell Mariah that I liked how she squinted her brown eyes at me without her glasses, that I liked the way the air around her felt. More: I wanted to kiss her. But instead, we walked to the edge of our quiet grove, the dull roar of Memorial Drive traffic growing louder.

"So," Mariah said, "will I see you again soon?"

"We could have lunch sometime," I said: a scary idea.

"I've got to go down to New York next week for a job. But call me Thursday. If you want."

"I want," I said. "I mean, I will."

"See you," she said, backing slowly away from me. She smiled and waved, a quick trill of her fingers that made me laugh.

"Thanks," I said.

"For what?"

"For inviting me."

"Next time I'll make you earn your keep," she said, then turned and retraced our path back to Kendall Square.

As I walked back to the office, the jitters got hold of me and made me laugh out loud, made my hands shake. I had a new friend, a new secret.

In Harvard Square, I dodged through the crowd, my reflection speeding along next to me in store windows. Pedestrians kept getting in my way. I slipped through a clump of people watching a blind guy play Beatles tunes on an electric dulcimer. A fat man with a backpack plodded down the middle of the sidewalk, belting out an Irish folk song at the top of his lungs. A kid with dreadlocks sideswiped me, then joined a pack of skinheads huddled at the subway stop like scalping victims.

I cut into the alley next to the shoe repair shop, taking my shortcut back to the office, one that avoided the main streets and anybody who might distract my thoughts from Mariah. The passageway was so narrow I had to shuffle sideways, my boots crunching on broken beer bottles. Unlike clean, quaint Brattle Street, this alley smelled of bum piss and beery vomit. Yellow milk dripped from a restaurant dumpster and a few rats lapped at its surface, then scurried away when I got closer. I came out in a parking lot just a block away from the Crockett Company building.

"Larkin! Larkin Stride?"

I stopped, paralyzed as a jacklit deer, then turned to find a man in a shapeless tweed coat with leather elbow patches. His small head was topped with a brown derby. None of my friends would wear such a dumb hat. His complexion was pale as chicken skin left in water, broken by thin lips and wispy nostrils. A pair of beady eyes stared at me, magnified by thick gold-rimmed glasses. I tried hard to come up with this stranger's name, but he was a riddle I couldn't solve.

"It's me. Sheffy Grey." He pointed to himself with a stubby finger.

Then I remembered. This was Sheffield *Firestone* Grey, barely recognizable from when we both ate at the Freshman Union. In all, we probably spent a total of an hour talking during a year's worth of dinners. From the looks of Sheffy's paunch, he'd done more eating than talking lately.

"Sheffy. Hi. What a surprise," I lied. Despite my shortcuts, I ran into my classmates almost every day, but I had hoped that this would be a day without alumni. I wondered if I should turn and run.

"Back for a visit?" he said, moving closer. Too much money at an early age had buffed the edges from Sheffy's features. Even naked, he wouldn't stand out in a crowd. Sheffy reached out and I shook his hand, lifeless as wood.

"No. I live here."

"Still hanging around Harvard Square, eh?" A hint of wistfulness. Sheffy's eyes misted behind his glasses.

"I've been working here for a few years now," I said. "I'm a consultant." I looked off toward the Crockett Company offices, so close. I wanted to work on my book, make paper clips into a little chain.

"How have you been, you old wanker you?" *Wanker?* At some point shortly after birth, Sheffy had adopted British ways. By the time I met him in college, he had them down so well that I assumed he was a transfer student from Oxford or Cambridge, the real one. It would have flattered him to hear this. In fact, Sheffy was the second cousin to a gasoline fortune. "Some of the Firestones had tires, but all we got was *gas*," he had said breezily at dinner, many times. I knew a dozen like him, men burdened by their inheritance, the trust funds that dwindled down from grandfather to grandson until someone had to start over from scratch. Ashes to ashes, trusts to dust.

"Fine, Sheffy. I've been fine. Really good."

"Didn't hear much from you after graduation, Larkin. Where did you go? Graduate school?"

"I traveled for a while."

"In America, or abroad?" Sheffy had always been vaguely amused by my accent and the fact that most of my family did funny things like raise cattle or work for a living. I started to lie.

"Mostly in the South and Midwest. I was on a Rockefeller."

"Oh? A grant!" Sheffy leaned forward, interested now, ears perking up at the mention of lucre.

I continued the whopper, reinventing my history to suit my needs. "I did research for five years, on and off."

"What were you studying?"

"The effects of numbing manual labor on the nation's under-class." Fabricating on the fly was kind of intoxicating. "I interviewed about a thousand waitresses and dishwashers. The foundation is still compiling the data in New York. The study should be out in a couple of years. PBS is interested."

"Marvelous! Some fun! And I read something about you in *Harvard Magazine* not too long ago. You wrote some book . . . about sailing, was it?"

"It was about sales. *Sell Straight to the Top*," I said. A group of drunk students ran by with a keg of beer sloshing in a tub. For a moment I thought there might be hope for today's youth. As we watched them go by, Sheffy's eyes clouded up again.

"It must be great living here in Cambridge."

"Yeah. Great," I said. Gray sky reflected in Sheffy's glasses. His bloodless face reminded me of the old men who ate lunch alone in dim corners of the Harvard Club. Did I look this old?

"Listen, Sheffy. I'd better get back to work," I said. "Have a good visit."

"Nice to see you, Larkin, really. And good luck," he said, tipping his dumb hat. I watched Sheffy toddle down Brattle Street by himself, then I headed straight back to work, my blinders firmly in place, eyes on the crooked bricks in front of my boots.

I took the elevator up to the Crockett Company, where some associate consultants were preparing for an important client presentation. I nodded to them and walked quickly to my office, as though I were anxious to get back to my own project. Then I looked out between the blinds, watching the young consultants stare intensely at a computer screen. Davy valued this kind of dedication. Like them, I used to work hard to identify the key strategies that might solve our clients' problems. We might recommend more training for the sales force, a corporate restructuring, or a host of other antidotes. But now I knew it didn't really make much difference, that trying to change a corporation was like trying to change the weather.

I liked the other consultants but I was never that friendly to them. They reminded me that I didn't fit in here any better than I had at Harvard. As I peered out into the bright office at my hardworking coworkers, I doubted if they harbored any secrets, at least not the kind I did.

One winter night in Kansas City, I had come home late from washing dinner dishes at the K & M Barbeque. As I sat in my kitchenless studio apartment and read the paper, the noises started up, the way they did every night from four floors of retirees and illegal aliens. A lonely chorus echoed down the narrow halls. Dishes rattled in sinks. Television channels switched abruptly. An old man yelled at his cat in Spanish. The apartment house and its occupants seemed strangely out of place in Kansas—the Sunflower State—with its sunny fields of golden wheat.

I grabbed a can of chicken soup from the top of my dresser and headed down the narrow hallway. Splintered green wainscotting lined the walls, and dim bulbs dotted the ceiling every few yards. Eight lights would bring me to the apartment of Mrs. Weingarten, an old woman who let me use her stove in exchange for my doing some small chores—taking out the trash, collecting her mail from the downstairs lobby. She must have been almost ninety, happy but confused, her mind like a house being shut down room by room. I rang the buzzer.

No one answered. Figuring Mrs. Weingarten must be at her son's house for the night, I let myself in with the key from under the doormat. In the dim kitchen I swatted for the light cord, and glare from the bulb fell on Mrs. Weingarten, curled up like a child on the floor. I stood still for a moment, staring at the first dead person I had ever seen. Mrs. Weingarten seemed to have been turned off like a flashlight, her eyes unmoving and vacant. I did what I had seen in movies. I put my hand over her eyes and tried to lower her eyelids, but they rose back up slowly like a doll's. I checked for a pulse but found none, her skin cool as watermelon rind beneath my fingers.

My legs started to shake, at first a little and then more, so much that I had to sit down on the sticky kitchen floor just a few feet from Mrs. Weingarten. When I found Catlett Stride's skull, I wasn't afraid, since it seemed familiar, a piece of family history. When my mother died, my father made sure I was far away. But now, tears ran down my face as I sat on the floor next to Death, everyone's worst fear. I knew that I could end up lonely and dead, and it was this vision of the future that scared me and made me shake.

I drifted through the apartment in a fog, looking at the pictures of smiling grandchildren taped to a mirror, the family of ceramic dogs on the dusty mantel. I opened a desk drawer but then shoved it back in, and wiped my fingerprints from the handle with my sleeve.

In the bedroom, the nightstand was cluttered with prescription medications and stuffed animals from recent hospital stays. A tiger that wore a small T-shirt that said "I Love You, Grandma!" A stuffed white kitty with pink whiskers. Next to the kitty was a shoe box with its lid half open. I lifted the lid and saw that the box was full of green peas, dried green peas. I picked one up and it started to come apart in my hand. Looking closer in the pale light from the nightstand lamp, I could see that it wasn't a pea at all, but a dollar bill compressed down into a tiny green wad no bigger than the spitballs we used to shoot when I was in school. Mrs. Weingarten must have spent hours compacting her money into tiny balls. Maybe she had planned to eat them, hide them, plant them in the ground. Whatever she intended, it was lost now. All that remained were hundreds of tiny green pellets.

I opened another and found a five, then two singles, then a twenty. It didn't seem like money to me, but more like something I might find in a fortune cookie. I closed the box and put it under my arm, then turned and walked quietly out of the bedroom. The kitchen light had been off when I came in, so I pulled the string quickly without looking down at the bent body. I stepped into the hallway, closed the door and locked it, and made sure no one was watching as I put the key back under the doormat. The Meals on Wheels volunteer would find her in the morning.

I sat at my table and unwadded almost two thousand dollars in cash. Several times I thought about sneaking back to return the money, but I didn't. Instead, I looked around my grotty apartment as if for the first time. The ceiling was cracked and the walls were covered with shadows from pictures long gone. It looked more like a hotel room than a home, since I owned almost nothing.

It's time to go.

The words came up the ventilation shaft from deep inside the building. Catlett Stride's message didn't surprise me. I knew that I had to leave, and not for another apartment like this, not for another job that would embarrass my family. Catlett Stride had fought in the Civil War with Stonewall Jackson. I washed dishes and thought I was being brave. No one cared that I didn't own a suit or work in an office. My foolishness became obvious, as if a spotlight had singled out my tiny room and lit it for my ancestors to judge.

At work the next night, I paid back the waitresses I owed with some of the money from the pellets, my bankroll. I bought everyone a round of drinks after my shift was over and silently raised my glass to Mrs. Weingarten. After I said good-bye, I hung up the plastic apron with "Larkin" stenciled on the front, and left the restaurant for good. In the parking lot, my Chevelle waited with everything I owned packed in a battered leather suitcase in the trunk. I drove away, headed back to Cambridge to start a new life, one that I—and all the other Strides—could be proud of. I would quit taking chances. I would find a good job and make money. I would get married.

I got home around six but Laura was out running. The mail didn't look very good today, just a couple of catalogues and more bills. In the kitchen, there were a few remnants of Kendra and Tammy's visit—a crusty bowl of hummus on the table next to some flyers for a rally to ban condos in Cambridge. I tossed them into the trash along with the catalogues. I wanted to call Mariah to tell her it was good seeing her today, to hear her voice again. But it was almost Saturday night and she was probably getting ready to go out. I didn't want to bother her.

The front door slammed and I heard Laura clomping up the stairs. I sat at the kitchen table and pretended to be deeply interested in the business section.

"You're back," she said. "Get a lot done?"

"Enough." I kissed Laura's damp forehead. "How far did you go?"

"Seven miles." Laura bent over and did a few quick stretches. "I called you in the afternoon to see if you wanted to meet in the square for dinner. They said you were out."

"Had to go to the post office."

"I thought it closed at noon on Saturday."

"I just dropped some things in the box." I needed to change the subject before Laura saw a tiny Mariah frozen in my eye like a bee in amber. "There's something I wanted to ask you about."

"What?"

"Last night, Hank said you were up for vice-president of operations. Why didn't you say anything to me?"

"Because that's just complete conjecture at this point." Laura shook her head. "Cliff's fighting it and I don't think they'll be able to get rid of him. He's got seniority."

"Hank said Cliff was on his way out."

"Hank likes to talk." Laura pulled her sweatshirt over her head to reveal a gray sports bra underneath, a straitjacket for her generous breasts. She wadded up the sweatshirt and held it under her arm.

"But why didn't you tell me about it?"

"I didn't know you liked to hear all the gossip from work."

"I do if it's important." Not true. I didn't care that much about Laura's job.

"I'll tell you if anything important happens. Right now, I don't want to jinx it."

"You sound almost superstitious," I said. Laura thought it was ridiculous to read horoscopes, to look for omens.

"I'm just being realistic. Right now I'd really like to go take a bath."

Laura walked down the hall, and then I heard the tub running. I had come home one sunny Saturday in the spring and heard splashes from the bathroom. When I pushed open the door quietly, I had found Laura lying on her back in the claw-footed tub, her eyes closed tightly as she whirled a washcloth between her legs. From that afternoon on, I knew that sex—among other things—was a solitary pleasure for Laura.

I could still walk to the bedroom and dial Mariah's number while the water ran. Laura wouldn't hear me tell Mariah that I had been thinking about her since the afternoon and that I wanted to see her again soon. From the kitchen window, I looked out toward Palfrey Street and wondered what Mariah was doing, if she was alone.

6

THE VELVET COFFIN

WHIRLWINDS OF TRASH danced in the dusty grass along Memorial Drive, where I was stuck in traffic less than a mile from the office. In the rearview mirror I could see a line of cars that stretched back to Watertown. Each car contained a man or woman going to work. And within each man or woman was a long tube that spoke at one end, excreted at the other. It was this primal tube that made us go to work to make money to keep it fed. Why else would we sit in our cars every morning, performing this tedious ballet of ill-tempered business commuters?

The driver ahead of me had slammed his seat belt in the door and I watched it drag on the road, limp, useless. We jostled forward when the light turned green, then stopped a few seconds later when it turned red again.

An idea came to me. Before it faded I shifted into first and pulled the Volvo over the curb and onto the jogging path, then touched the gas pedal slightly and sped forward, honking to scatter joggers. Unsmiling men in BMWs and Saabs stared wide-eyed, shocked that someone would be rude enough to drive on the sacred jogging trail. The speedometer edged upward as I shifted into third.

The Volvo picked up speed on the flat stretch that led to Harvard Square. I cut over into the intersection just as a dinky Toyota entered from the other direction. Its driver saw me barreling toward it and stopped. I punched the gas and leaned on the horn, since under Boston's unwritten driving rules intimidation was the appropriate response to indecision. Just before we collided, I caught a glimpse of the other driver, a woman with braids and large glasses, the kind that looked as if they were on upside down. Her face turned tranquil as she raised her chin, closed her eyes, and prepared to go to Secretary Hell, a vast plain strewn with jammed photocopiers and telephones that kept ringing no matter what.

I cut to the right and heard a sharp *clink* as I clipped off the Toyota's mirror, then careened toward the Weld boathouse. I pulled back to the left and fishtailed into my lane, tires squealing, plowing on unscathed.

My heart pounded and sweat trickled down the undersides of my arms as I spun down Memorial Drive at about sixty, turned off into the Crockett Company parking lot, and pulled into my reserved space. I slapped the wheel and laughed so hard my eyes watered. Even a minor traffic infraction seemed daring compared with my normal morning routine. But in the car, the engine ticked and the thrill faded. I got out and checked for damage, running my fingers along a small crease in the Volvo's shiny black fender, definitely below my deductible. The day had just started and I was already down a couple hundred dollars in body work. But it was worth it.

I walked toward the Crockett Company, my velvet coffin, a comfy place for dead people. I shuddered as I walked past the Career Path and entered the familiar lobby with its incense of coffee and shampoo, its smothering crush of velvet.

"Good morning, the Crockett Company. Business is our business." Our secretary answered the phones and murmured the Crockett Creed into the kind of high-tech headset favored by astronauts and rock drummers. I walked to my office past consultants who twitched at their desks, so addled by coffee that they could only stare at their computers or scan *The Wall Street Journal*. Everyone was in the usual holding pattern for our morning meeting.

Through the glass panels that faced the bullpen, I could see our leader, Davy, in his corner office. He yelled into his red cordless phone and exhaled smoke from a thin cigar into the receiver. As he paced, he reached down to punch numbers into a calculator and hit a key on his computer.

I pitied the person on the other end of the line. Davy started his days at a furious pace inspired by the Crockett Company's staggering overhead, which required monthly billings that could support a small town. With more and more money as his goal, every minute of Davy's day had a purpose, every week had a quota. I envied the simplicity of this equation, although I found Davy hard to believe, a little too figured out, like a furniture showroom.

Davy had always been an entrepreneur, an incubator of dozens of schemes, all profitable. Back in the sixties, someone had written a book about him, *Davy Crockett, American Business Pioneer*, complete with a cover photo of a much thinner man standing in a boardroom wearing a brown three-piece suit, coonskin cap, and snaggled smile. Davy proved that it wasn't important what you knew, how much experience you had, or how smart you were. What really mattered was how everyone else perceived you. Now that he was a respected management guru, Davy wouldn't be caught dead posing in a coonskin hat, and his teeth had been capped long ago.

While I waited for our meeting to start I watched my coworkers in their offices, looking busy even if all they were doing was cleaning up. Davy liked to see intensity, action, rolled-up sleeves. I guess that was what he liked about me when I joined the company—I worked hard, and just in case being from good breeding stock wasn't enough, I had lied during my job interview, telling Davy I had an MBA from Wharton. After three years, I believed in the lie as much as he did.

Just before nine-thirty, I walked to the conference room, where a few consultants were gathered around the polished walnut table. Davy entered carrying the cordless phone, still hustling as he sat down. He had a phone in his car, one in his boat, and even a mobile unit that he could carry around in a special backpack. I had read that Mary Baker Eddy, the founder of the Christian Science Church, was buried with a working phone in Mount Auburn Cemetery. Given the chance, Davy would probably keep drumming up new business from the grave. Bert, our accountant, sat next to Davy and typed something into a laptop computer. Jack "Puffy" McCormick sat on Davy's other side. McCormick was one of Davy's pals from the old days, an Irishman with a pink, broiled face.

Ellen Atkins walked in last, looking schoolmarmish in a prim blue dress with white lapels. Like me, she was a senior consultant. Unlike me, she worked so conscientiously that she always seemed on the verge of collapse. She had helped me out when I first joined the company, a dishwasher in an Armani suit bought with Mrs. Weingarten's money pellets. Ellen dropped a stack of papers on the table and sat down with a sigh, then took a white plastic spoon from her purse and dug into a container of blueberry yogurt.

Davy put down the phone and the meeting began.

"I'd like to point out that I lost five hundred bucks on the playoffs this weekend, so you'll all have to work extra hard today." McCormick wheezed, his version of laughing. Davy always began things with a light touch, a joke to warm up his audience. Then he got down to business.

"We've got five people from Digital coming in for a presentation at three. Everyone look smart, and they'll pay us a couple hundred thousand to do a Competency Assessment Profile of their line managers." Davy lit a little cigar and its burnt smell filled the conference room. "Avery is handling the presentation, but he may be asking the rest of you to help out. Right?"

A voice came from the other end of the conference table. "Actually, I think I'm covered." In his late twenties, a couple years out of the B School, Avery Gillman always seemed a little damp and unformed, as if still in a larval stage. He held up a thick binder I recognized from his last presentation.

"I pulled some slides this weekend and put together this package of information," he said. But I knew for a fact that Gillman never came in on weekends. What a weasel.

"Should be a no-brainer," Davy said.

"Picked the right man for the job," McCormick muttered.

Gillman blushed and twitched his head to one side, sending his dark hair tumbling, curling inward on his forehead like quotation marks. He probably thought McCormick's comment meant that he liked him. In fact, McCormick didn't like anyone.

"Gillman's got everyone's support for his meeting," Davy said. "Am I right or am I right?"

"You're right," we said.

"On to the next item on the agenda. The good news and the bad news. Who's getting paid, who's getting laid."

Bert pulled out his reading glasses and read from a spread sheet. These meetings were like going to church when I was a kid. I let my mind wander while I feigned interest in the report from Bert, bald as a hard-boiled egg and about half as exciting. While he droned on about accounts payable and accounts receivable, I stared at my hands and noticed that one weird hair stuck out from beneath my watchband. The hair looked gray as steel wool, but maybe it was just the lights.

"We made our budget numbers for September by a good margin. Fall's been slow, but historically things tend to pick up around the end of the quarter. If we keep our vendor expenses low and a couple big jobs come through, we'll end the year with forty-percent growth." Bert peered over his glasses and looked around the table. "Not bad at all." I wrote "40" on my pad and looked for that hair again. It was definitely gray. Since when did my arm hair start turning gray?

"One last thing," Bert said. "If you're using Styrofoam coffee cups, don't throw them away so quickly. You should be able to get a week out of one cup. They're durable, and we're spending about three thousand dollars on cups annually." I wrote "cups" on my pad and crossed it out, then put my hand under the table.

"You're kidding," McCormick said.

"Really. Three thousand dollars." Bert nodded gravely.

"No, I mean the part about saving our coffee cups. Why don't we start saving little pieces of string too?" McCormick served as the company's goodwill ambassador. With his huge expense account, he kept box seats at Fenway Park, took clients to dinner at Biba's, rented suites at the Ritz-Carlton. McCormick's antennae went up when anyone mentioned belt-tightening, in his case a physical impossibility.

"Bert's right," Davy said. "We've got to stay lean and mean. For you, Puffy, just mean will do. Everyone drink directly from the coffeepot." McCormick leaned back in his chair and stared at the ceiling tiles.

"Next. Lillivale, a marketing update, please." Tom Lillivale stood—the affectation made Ellen roll her eyes. Like Gillman, he was fresh out of business school, where someone had taught him that standing up during a presentation generated a more positive audience response. So here he was, in an informal meeting, stiff as a choirboy but not so innocent. His face looked tight and his eyes were small, gray, and humorless. His short blond hair, perfect nose, and tiny earlobes made him look like a poster child for the master race.

"Our new Total Quality Improvement brochure went out to a thousand CEOs in the Midwest last Friday," Lillivale said. "Ellen and I'll start following up with phone calls next week and turn over the leads as they come in. I'm also looking for a new market niche to go after. Any input?"

"The Sox," McCormick said. "With a little consulting, maybe they won't choke again next year."

"We could do a mailing to hospitals and health plans," Ellen said. "They're pretty huge, and I'm sure they have organizational problems. I mean, I spent about an hour waiting for a booster shot last Saturday."

"I could go for a shot right about now," McCormick said. No one laughed.

"McIvy Consulting has health care in the bag," Davy said. "Plus hospitals are full of sick people. We want to deal with healthy clients with big healthy budgets. Fortune One Hundred or better."

"How about going after more government contracts?" Gillman said, pushing his hair out of his eyes again. Under the table, I had my own hair situation to deal with. No matter how hard I yanked, the gray aberration on my wrist seemed firmly rooted. As I tugged, my eyes started to water from the pain.

"Apt Associates has that one wrapped around its little fat pinkie," Davy said. Having made careful note of everyone's input, Lillivale sat down. Good boy. Consulting was strange. We were making more money than ever now that business was bad. In desperation, our clients paid us huge amounts of money to shuffle their personnel and tinker with their marketing plans. If things didn't go as we said they would, we could always find a way to shift the blame. Anyway, it was too late; we already had their money. Who really cared if a corporation made a couple million less? We were in the business of pretending to care while always covering our butts. On Judgment Day, the seven consultants around the conference table would find it hard to point to one good work we had performed.

Davy turned his attention to me.

"You look kind of funny, Larkin. Feel all right?" I gave the hair one last tug that wrenched it out by the root. I stifled a small scream.

"Fine," I said, blinking. "I'm fine."

"How's the book going?"

"Good. Really good." Lillivale and Gillman skewered me with sharpened stares, pissed that Davy had let me reduce my client load to write another book.

"How many contacts did you say you were going to make?" Lillivale said, implying that I wasn't doing enough research.

"I'm contacting one hundred CEOs. So far I've wrapped up some key interviews," I said. "I should have the rest finalized soon."

"Wouldn't it be better to talk to five hundred contacts, maybe get some interns to do the interviews? It might give you a more accurate database." Every time Lillivale had a suggestion it meant more work for me.

"I don't think an intern could do these interviews," I said. It was true. Even I couldn't do them. I had no intention of calling any more Dave Dahlgrins.

"I look forward to seeing your research." Lillivale showed his teeth the way animals do before they lunge. "When will we see a draft?"

"Early February."

"We sent an outline and a sample chapter to Briefcase Press and it looks like they're going to take the book," Davy said to everyone. "Should be a hefty advance, paperback rights, international distribution, the whole nine yards. Plus lots of free publicity for us."

"Sounds good," Bert said. Anything free sounded good to him.

"That should be about it." Davy reached over and dropped his cigar in a coffee mug with a sizzle. "Unless anyone has something to add." Davy paused and we sat still for a moment listening to the hum of the heating system, the phones ringing in the next room.

"That's it, then. Today's going to be an over-quota day. Am I right or am I right?"

"You're right," we said. McCormick struggled out of his chair as the leaders of the Crockett Company filed out of the conference room. I hoped today would be a quiet day.

Sticky yellow post-ums clustered on my computer like evil butterflies—a couple of calls from clients and, to my surprise, one from my old friend Dan Holsapple. We had gone to high school together back in Pine Bluff, and now he worked in an auto body shop in Bloomington, Indiana.

I punched Dan's number into my phone console and the line rang with a grating series of clicks. I imagined Dan here in our suite of offices or me in his garage; each seemed equally impossible. When I asked for Dan, a woman connected me to the service department.

"Dan. Hi. It's Larkin." I heard a delay, either from the connection or from Dan. I couldn't tell.

He spoke just above a whisper, as if his boss stood near him, listening. "I knew you'd call back. How are you?"

"Okay," I said. "Good."

"Working hard or hardly working?" In the background I could hear shouting and the hiss of hydraulic tools.

"A little of both. Sounds busy."

"We're taking an engine out of a Camaro. Some high school kid smashed it into a tree last night. You ought to see it. We found a big chunk of his scalp stuck on the windshield. You're part redskin, you want I should send it to you?"

"Thanks but no thanks," I said.

"I'll save it for Christmas. This may be just the thing for the man who has everything," Dan said with an unwarranted touch of envy.

Dan got back in touch at odd times. His call was a sign, like cattle sitting down in a field before a rain. He had been my best man at our wedding, showing up in a red Porsche just in time for the ceremony but leaving before the reception. I found out later he had to get back to Indiana to return the car, stolen from an orthodontist.

"How's Laura?" he asked.

"There's a lot going on." I resisted the urge to tell Dan about Mariah. She had to stay my secret.

"What's up?"

"Laura's all worried about her job. She's acting kind of

strange," I lied. Despite her worries, Laura always acted about the same.

"Women are all crazy," he said. "If the moon made your pecker bleed once a month you'd be crazy too."

"Thanks for that insight." Dan had always treated women as though they were radioactive, too dangerous to stay close to for long.

"Anytime."

"Laura's too smart to be crazy."

"You weren't planning on hanging around with waitresses for the rest of your life, were you?"

"No. I'm just bored, that's all." Right away, I regretted saying it. I sounded like a spoiled whiner, tired of his expensive toys.

"So what?" Dan said. "Why don't you and Laura move out here? You could live like a king on the kind of money you make." I tried to imagine us in Indiana but couldn't picture it.

"I'm stuck here for a while," I said, then looked around the office to make sure no one could hear me. This wasn't what a team player for the Crockett Company would say.

"Then make the most of it," Dan said. "Boston's supposed to be a great place, not that I've ever been there. Lots of lobsters. If I were you, I'd do something new."

"Like what?"

"I don't know. Rob a liquor store or something." At least Dan's recommendation sounded better than Tucker telling me to go to a comedy club or play squash. A few years back, Dan had held up a QuikStop in Indianapolis. He told me armed robbery had a way of making all your other problems seem insignificant.

"But I like liquor stores," I said. I thought of my wine store, where the owner tucked away special bottles of wine for me, gave me an open line of credit.

"I tell you what. Let's trade jobs for a month. A worker exchange program. You come out here and fix this Camaro, and I'll come to Boston and do whatever it is you do. I got a suit somewhere." It wasn't such a bad idea. Working on cars was honest labor.

"You'd hate it here. The people are no good."

"People are the same wherever you go. You can't go blaming your problems on where you are," Dan said. "If you're bored with your wife, find someone else. If you're bored with your job, quit. If you hate Boston so much, move. If you're tired of being rich, give me all your money. No one's making you do anything."

I couldn't come up with a clever response. I looked down from my window and watched students march through the square.

"Hey. Don't get pissed off," he said.

"I'm not."

"I'm just a little worked up lately. Makes me talk too much."

"How are things out there?" So far, the conversation had been about me.

"It's my father. That's why I called," Dan said. "He's dying. They had him in for prostate surgery and they found the cancer had spread all the way up to his rib cage."

"Jesus," I said. "I'm sorry. I had no idea. I can't imagine your father being sick." I had met Old Man Holsapple a few times, a tough country lawyer, the kind whose clients paid in cattle and produce. He told me once that he had made love to a thousand women but killed only three men. He considered that a pretty good ratio, and I didn't question his math.

"It showed up real quick a couple months ago. The doctors thought they had it in transmission, but they didn't," he said quietly. "Now he weighs about ninety pounds. I pick him up and carry him around, but he don't even know it's me."

"You okay?" What could I say? I heard Dan's unsteady breathing and behind it the sound of metal scraping metal.

"Yeah. I'm fine. Sure," he said.

"Listen. Is there anything I can do?"

"I suppose you can help me bury him when he dies."

"These things are unpredictable. Sometimes people get better when it seems like there's no chance," I said, uncertainty being the only meager antidote I could offer. "Is he in the hospital?"

"Yeah. In Little Rock."

"You should go there. Having family around can help a lot."

"Can't go," Dan said. "This Camaro's all bashed up, and the kid's father wants it fixed so when the little fucker's head heals he can wreck it again. There's a Grand Prix that needs a new engine. And a Charger with a leaky oil pan. And a Nova that got mashed by a semi . . ."

"They can wait."

"It's not just that. My boss won't give me any extra time off and I can't afford to take a couple weeks without pay. I've been thinking about doing a little job. I got my eye on a U-Tote-Um outside of town."

"Don't. I'll send you some money. How much do you need?"

"Five hundred dollars would really help out. I'll pay you off when I can, but it'll have to be sometime next year."

"Consider it paid," I said. "You can fix my car sometime for free."

"A Volvo 240DL, right? The way you drive, the head gasket'll blow at about sixty thousand, mark my words. Drive it out here and I'll fix it up."

"I'll send you a check today."

"Thanks, Larkin. I really appreciate it."

"I hope we'll see you in a couple months. You going back to Pine Bluff for the holidays?"

"Maybe. I hope so." The hiss of an arc welder grew louder. "Got to go."

"Good-bye." I put the receiver down gently, then reached for the leather checkbook in my top desk drawer. I wrote Dan a check for two thousand dollars, addressed the envelope, then put it with the stack of bills to mail on the way to lunch with Mariah.

7
DOING LUNCH

MARIAH AND I sat in the Café Tangier next to a peeling mural of Ali Baba and the Forty Thieves. Fez-topped thieves popped out of olive jars, ducked into alleys, ran down narrow streets. A thief also ran the restaurant, which served overpriced Middle Eastern food. I hadn't brought Mariah here for the ambience. The uneven tables were jammed closely together. The service was miserable. Someone on hallucinogens had done the decorating. But no one from the Crockett Company ever came to the Café Tangier, since it didn't take American Express— meaning no expense-account lunches.

"It's good to see you again," I said. An understatement. A little more than a week had passed, and every day had tilted toward this lunch date.

"Thanks," she said. "Sorry we didn't have more time to talk at the shoot, but I was kind of preoccupied."

"How did the photos come out?"

"The ones for Nimbus? They were fine," she said. "Everyone's happy." Mariah wore a loose-fitting navy dress. Her dark hair was carefully controlled by a simple mother-of-pearl barrette.

"Here," she said. "I brought you a present." She reached

inside her black leather satchel and placed a manila envelope between us. I tore open the flap, watching Mariah for some clue, then reached in and pulled out some photos.

"You do good work." I leafed through the silvery black-and-white photos of me sitting on the bench next to the river.

"Now you can forget that stuff about photos stealing your soul."

"Maybe not." In one photo, I looked at the camera with such obvious desire that it made me cringe. I never had much of a poker face.

"I think you're photogenic," she said. "Lots of character."

The waiter came and we ordered drinks—a vodka and tonic for me, a glass of Chardonnay for Mariah. We sat in our quiet eddy while other conversations flowed around us. Mariah seemed completely comfortable, but I felt my throat tighten and my shoulders hunch.

"You weren't quiet last time I saw you," she said.

"I was about to say the same about you."

"But you didn't."

"That's because I'm so *quiet*." I smiled. "Plus this time you have to do the talking." I didn't want to get going on the old stories again.

"I told a friend of mine I was having lunch with a man I met waiting for the bus," Mariah said.

"And?"

"And she said it was the most romantic thing she'd ever heard. She said things like that weren't supposed to happen anymore. You know, meeting strangers."

"There's only one thing that bothers me," I said.

"What's that?" She leaned forward, concerned. Her smile faded as though I were about to tell her something bad. That my wife wouldn't approve. That this would be our first and last lunch.

"I'm not really a stranger anymore."

Mariah reached across the table and for a brief moment I felt the soft weight of her hand on mine. But then other conversations

102

closed in, especially from the next table, where an older couple fussed over plates of falafel. I would never eat anything that rhymed with *awful*, or so closely resembled balls of camel dung. I looked over when their honkings became really annoying, hoping that a sharp glance might quiet them down. But it didn't.

"I don't know where he got such an idea," the woman shrieked. "It's preposterous!" She looked medieval—ye olde goode womyn of Cambridge—with her gray hair tied in a ponytail and a brass medallion as big as a sundial around her neck. The tarnished metal faded into her sweater, brown and lumpy, woven from natural fibers and old birds' nests. My educated guess put her at Radcliffe in the late fifties or early sixties.

"So what else did Richard say?" she asked. Divorced or widowed, she had some money of her own now, enough for summers in Provincetown, life-enriching evening classes, a therapist, a Saab. I seemed forever doomed to run into these creatures, who spouted a running commentary during movies, and eyed my medical thrillers with disdain at the Harvard Book Store.

"He said he expects to see a *tour de farce*," said her lunch companion, a tweedy old fart with a crimson bow tie knotted tight as a tourniquet. He looked familiar. Maybe I had taken a course from him at Harvard, but I couldn't remember. His gray eyebrows twitched like the pill bugs I used to catch in the woodpile when I was a kid, poking them with sticks until they rolled up into little balls. I was easily amused back then.

I watched Mariah and tried to guess her opinion of these two. For people who liked Cambridge, academic wittiness was part of the attraction.

"Well . . . just think of it as background music," she said.

I laughed. "It's not music."

"They come with the territory. If you can't stand the heat, stay out of the kitchen. Or at least out of restaurants like this."

"It's not the heat. It's the stupidity," I whispered. Mariah and I hunched over the tiny table, our foreheads only inches apart. We turned toward our neighbors.

"I mean, if he wanted a lighter approach, then why didn't he just say so?" the woman said, flailing her arms like a swimmer with cramps. Everyone within a ten-table radius turned and stared. I had met dogs with better voices.

Our waiter arrived, placed a cocktail napkin carefully on the table in front of me, and set down my drink.

"Your hand's shaking," Mariah said to him.

"It's a side effect of my medication," the waiter said. "I'm on lithium."

"Really?" Mariah shook her head and winked at me as the waiter walked to the other side of the table.

"But it's better than the mood swings I used to get," he said.

Back in Pine Bluff, no one would confide secrets like this to strangers. But Cambridge was ruled by part Yankee honesty, part affectation.

The waiter was about twenty-two, with cropped dark hair, adobe skin, and deep brown eyes rimmed by long lashes. A small gold earring glinted from his earlobe. The cuffs of his white linen trousers broke gently over black Italian shoes that cost more than a week's tips.

"The specials today are the lamb kabob with fava beans, and beef kabob with rice pilaf and grilled baby vegetables." He enunciated each word like an Elizabethan, and probably harbored the fierce but unfocused creative aspirations that made most waiters unhappy. When I worked in restaurants, I never met a waiter who had any talent beyond the ability to total a bar tab. Some couldn't even do that. As far as I could tell, the struggling-waiter/artist route to success was an insidious lie restaurant owners used to snare fresh recruits into a life of menial labor.

"I'll have the grilled chicken and rice with baby vegetables," Mariah said.

"The beef on a stick for me," I said. "Does that come with fries?"

"I'm sorry, we don't serve anything fried."

"Rice pilaf, then," I said. I wanted to stand up and shake this guy, tell him to lighten up a little. As he gathered up the menus and headed toward the kitchen, I pitied the dishwasher who had to deal with him. Mariah shook her head. I wondered if she regretted going to lunch with me yet.

"It's all part of life's rich pageant," Mariah said, lifting her wine. "This isn't Arkansas anymore."

"I know. Believe me. I know that."

We clinked glasses and I drank my vodka and tonic. The season for this drink had ended months before, but I didn't care.

"So what are you doing here?" I didn't intend the question to sound as blunt as it did. The voice booming from the next table made me jumpy, or maybe it was Mariah again. "Not here, I mean. I mean here in Cambridge." She took a steel Zippo from her purse and lit a Winston, breaking the restaurant's no-smoking rule with a nonchalance I admired.

"I came up north to get out of Charleston," Mariah said, snapping the lighter closed. "You don't know what it's like to be a woman there. They treat you like a queen, but if you actually try to do something, they think you're a witch."

"You mean something besides going to debutante balls?"

"Exactly. All my friends from high school are raising kids and going to club meetings in the afternoon."

"All mine are raising pigs and playing pool in bars." I knew this wasn't true, but it sounded good.

"Could be fun," she said. "Why did you leave?"

I leaned forward and looked both ways before I spoke. "Because I'm scared of pigs." Mariah laughed. I was trying to amuse her, to win her over as I had women in college.

"No, really. Why are you here if you don't like it?" It was a good question, the kind without an answer.

"I came here because I wanted to be civilized," I said, looking over at the table next to us. "Can you imagine that?" We watched as the loud woman handed over a thick manuscript to her eager-fingered companion, who cradled the binder as delicately as if it were Baby Jesus.

"I think you'll like the new play," she said. "I've set it in

Guatemala. Turn of the century. A remote town in the mountains. The female lead is a nun who arrives from England to teach the gospel. But she falls in love with a gentle native. From there it gets rather, well, *racy*."

Our waiter paused at their table, carrying our food on a faux-marble tray shaped like a fish. He broke into a dreamy drug smile.

"It sounds wonderful," he said to them. "I'm fascinated by theater. Do you know Peter Sellars? The director, not the Pink Panther guy. He used to eat here a lot, you know, back when he was at Harvard. He had the wildest haircut!"

I held back a laugh until I began to gasp for air.

"Larkin, what is it?"

"Nothing. Nothing, really," I said. I tried to swallow but gargled my drink instead. I wiped my eyes with a napkin.

The couple looked up from reading the manuscript, finally noticing me. The fussy professor turned bright red and opened his mouth to say something, but nothing came out. Being laughed at was cause for apoplexy at the Café Tangier, where everyone—waiters and all—insisted on being taken very, very seriously.

"Larkin. Are you okay?" Mariah looked concerned, then started to laugh with me. The restaurant was ridiculous, and it was easy to imagine everyone around us sprouting clown suits, big floppy shoes, and orange wigs.

Our waiter brought over our food—premature vegetables arranged carefully on a plate, tiny cubes of meat charred on a stick. Clown food. We laughed harder.

"Sorry about the delay," he said, setting the plates on our table with his shaky hand. Personally, I'd take the mood swings.

"Listen," I said. "The food looks great. In fact, it would be a crime to eat it. Just run it back into the kitchen. Tell the cook we had to go."

"Really?"

"Really. Right now." I pressed fifty dollars into the waiter's damp palm. Perplexed, he took the money. We stood up and I grabbed our coats from the rack behind us, Mariah shaking with laughter. From a distance, it might look as if we were having an argument, the kind that ended with two lovers walking quickly across a restaurant with blotchy faces.

The woman at the next table spoke loudly at our backs as we left, almost running now. "Incredibly rude young couple. Imagine, eavesdropping on our conversation!" When we reached the door, I looked back at the restaurant, packed full of clowns chewing, clowns talking. I flipped Cambridge Woman the finger from under one arm so only she could see it. Her eyes grew wide, as if I had waggled my pecker at her.

The chef came out of the kitchen, a bear-sized man in a clean white smock. He waved to us, the couple who had paid him the ultimate compliment by not even touching his beautiful food. The chef could believe whatever he wanted. The truth was extremely flexible. One size fit all.

Mariah and I left the Café Tangier with the cook weeping, the waiter shaking, and Cambridge Woman gaping. It was the best lunch I'd had in months.

I was not drunk, so I could not blame what happened next on that. Mariah and I did not part ways with a peck on the cheek and promises to call each other. We walked through the cold streets, the afternoon already faded to a cloudy half-light. Pulled onward by an unspecified gravity, we stopped for a cup of coffee at the Oar House, a dumb pub with oars mounted on the walls. I called work from a pay phone and told the secretary I felt sick and wouldn't be coming back in for the rest of the day.

Then we walked down by the river, crossing the Western Bridge to the Boston side. Mariah reached out and took my hand as though it were the most natural thing on earth to do. As we walked, I told her about my family back in Arkansas, about coming to Harvard, about working at the barbecue in Kansas City. We stopped under a bare-branched tree and I moved toward Mariah to light her cigarette. But instead, she let the cigarette drop, leaned forward, and kissed me on the lips until the match burned my fingers and brought me back to the chilly riverbank.

"Do you want a ride home?" I said.

"That would be nice. It's cold for October." We kissed again.

"Yes, that's true." The long winter approaching didn't fill me with the usual dread.

We walked to where I had left the car at lunch, days ago, it seemed. Mariah said it was too early to go home, that we should drive along the river. When we passed the Riverside Motel, a seedy place in Brighton, she joked that we should stop in. I said that sounded like a good idea. Or was it Mariah?

I walked into the motel office, where the desk clerk mumbled about regular rooms with double beds, larger rooms with twin beds, business suites with two rooms, cable TVs, and minibars. He was a pale, froggy man with thinning hair who reminded me of Lee Harvey Oswald. I slid five twenties across the desk and he handed me a key with a knowing look that told me he had seen afternoon visitors before.

We locked the door to our room and drew the blinds without turning on the lights. Then we added our own brief history of deceit to the unwritten register of the Riverside Motel, the one recorded on rented sheets, overheard through thin walls. In a few quick motions, I undressed Mariah, her skin warm beneath her blue dress, which slid quietly to the floor. Weak light leaked through the curtains and gave the room a greenish tint. Together, we moved slowly backward to the bed, the sheets scratchy and smelling of Pine-Sol. I touched her in the dark, lingered on the back of her neck, ran my fingers up her thighs. She pulled me closer, and in a moment I was inside her with a sigh that seemed to come from us both. We made love quickly, Mariah arching her back to fill whatever small space was left between us. We couldn't stop now for guilt or indecision. The motel walls echoed with one small cry, then another, quieter sound, and finally only the distant hum of cars on the turnpike as we held each other, shaking.

Our clothes covered the pale shag carpet as though blown there by a strong wind. We had overturned a desk chair and its spindle legs pointed at the ceiling. The dry air burned my throat. When my heart finally slowed down, I rolled onto my side and pressed my ear between Mariah's breasts, small and firm as persimmons. I listened to her heart beating quickly as a bird's. This would have been the point when I remembered my wife, but I didn't.

Mariah whispered into my ear. "I want you."

"You have me." I kissed her lips, and her tongue slid across my teeth.

"I mean inside me again. I want you to make love to me over and over."

With Laura, making love was as complicated as a phone call to Japan; if I didn't press all the buttons in the right order, we didn't connect. We made love a few times a month. I couldn't imagine twice in an afternoon.

But slowly, much to my surprise, I pushed into Mariah again and again, like back in college when sex was new and most of it just practice. We stopped finally, delirious, stuck together with sweat. When I shut my eyes I could see flashes of light from passing comets, sexual hallucinations I hadn't had in years.

My throat was parched, my lips cracked. What I really wanted was a postcoital Pepsi. I got out of bed and stumbled across the room, hand over my crotch though no one was watching as I high-stepped across the cool carpet, dodging furniture and piles of clothes. I pulled the bathroom door closed behind me, fumbled for the light switch, clicked it on. The overhead light blazed down on white tiles. I squinted and turned on the tap, sucking the water down as it filled my cupped hands.

A man's heart can burn like wood.

Catlett Stride's voice reverberated through the white room.

109

But I wasn't that concerned about my heart; it could stand a little more heat.

"I know what I'm doing," I said. "Anyway, you're the one who set fires." I pictured Catlett Stride's drooping eye, long beard, hollow cheeks like gray cloth placed on sharp rocks. My own wet face and bloodshot eyes stared from the steamy mirror. I smelled cigarette smoke from the bedroom, then heard a soft knock on the door.

"Larkin? You okay?"

"Yeah. I'm fine." I dried my face with a towel that smelled of mildew, then turned and opened the door. Mariah stood in the doorway wearing only my T-shirt. I leaned toward her and we kissed, my damp face against hers.

"I heard you say something."

"Must have been from the other room. The walls are thin."

"No. It was you."

"I talk to myself sometimes."

"What did you talk about?"

I reached around and rubbed the small of Mariah's back, her skin warm and smooth. "About how good you made me feel."

She moved closer and put her arms around my waist, then pressed her lips close to my ear. "We made love," she said.

"How could I forget."

"Oh. It was too dark to see this." She traced her finger along the shakily drawn pair of dice tattooed on my right shoulder.

"More evidence of my misspent youth."

"I like it. It reminds me of a cave painting." It reminded me of the night Ash and I got really drunk at Slade's, a bar in Providence that featured an on-premises tattoo parlor. He chose the ace of spades, while I opted for lucky sevens.

Mariah took my hand and led me back into the dim bedroom. "We better get going. It's cold and this place is kind of spooky."

We reached down and gathered our clothes in the dark like blind field hands. When I closed my eyes, I could still see flashes of light, but distant now, fireworks seen from another town.

110

* * *

Raindrops swarmed around the headlights of the Volvo as we drove toward Watertown. I glanced at the dashboard clock and tried to figure out if I'd be able to get home before Laura. By now she had already left work and caught the express bus.

"You don't have to tell her," Mariah said, catching my eye on the clock. "I won't think less of you if you don't. This is our secret."

"What do you mean?"

"I mean your wife. You don't have to tell her you're sleeping with someone else. Not that we did any sleeping. I don't want you to tell her. It's just too predictable, the other woman and all that. I'd like to think we did more than just screw."

"It was much more than that."

"You won't be lying, you know. Think of it as a new way of being honest. It will be our secret." Mariah moved closer and put her hand on my leg as if we had driven together for years.

"A secret's the same as a lie. You just don't tell it."

"Sounds like you know what you're talking about," she said.

"Maybe."

"You wanted me, didn't you?"

"Yes." We crossed the low bridge over the Charles that would take us to Watertown.

"Then doing anything else would have been wrong."

"I suppose that's one way of looking at it," I said. We drove without talking, past a store that sold lawn statuary, each concrete deer glistening with rain. The road was crowded with cars going home, exhaust steaming. Mariah stroked my leg gently. I looked at the dashboard clock again. Six-thirty. On a normal day I would have been home watching the news with Laura.

I turned off at Palfrey Street and Mariah directed me to a yellow frame house. We really were just a few streets apart, even closer through backyards. I parked, then turned toward Mariah, wondering if I should tell her that I loved her, because on that gloomy afternoon she had set something in motion.

111

But Mariah spoke first.

"I want to say something. And it's important for you to re-member." She reached up and put her hand on my cheek. "Whatever you do, don't fall in love with me."

"Why not?" I had heard this before. Sometimes women had told me not to fall in love with them but meant just the opposite. Others really meant it. With Mariah, I couldn't say which was right. In any case, telling people not to fall in love was like telling them not to get older.

"Because I want a different kind of love. One that doesn't follow the old rules. We met at that bus stop because we were supposed to. Do you believe in fate?"

"Yes. I do."

"Well, that's what brought us together. Not love." Mariah said this as if she had thought it over very carefully. "I'm not your girlfriend, or your mistress, or whatever. I'm just a friend. A friend you made love to."

"Can I see you again?"

"Yes. And the next time will be in my bed, not in some creepy motel," she said. She opened the car door and stepped out. The open door buzzed. "Not that I minded, really." She leaned back into the car and kissed me. "I've got you inside me now," she whispered. "Don't forget."

"I couldn't if I wanted to."

"Thanks for lunch, Larkin Stride," she said, closing the door. She walked slowly toward her house, then stopped on the side-walk to search through her purse for her keys. A gentleman would have waited to see that she got in safely, but I didn't have time to be polite. I drove slowly down Palfrey, then floored the gas at the corner. It was almost seven. Even if she had left work late, Laura would have to be home by now. Traffic was light as I sped down Mount Auburn and took the corner, tires squealing.

I could see our house up ahead, every window dark. I slowed down, thankful that Laura had missed her bus or was having a drink with friends from the office. I parked next to the house and sat for a moment catching my breath. Maybe Mariah was right about fate. If the lights had been on, I might have walked upstairs and told Laura what had happened. I pulled on my scarf and smelled Mariah's scent on my fingertips. Upstairs, I would shower and shove my rumpled suit deep in the dry-cleaning hamper.

I walked up the sidewalk toward the dark, silent house and thought about Mariah one last time. Then I tucked all the memories of this afternoon safely away like souvenirs hidden in the back of a desk drawer—Mariah in the Café Tangier, Mariah walking beside the river, Mariah in my arms.

8

PILGRIMS

I TOOK A SWALLOW from a can of Narragansett and watched gigantic inflatable mice and pigs float above the cold New York City streets. If my Indian ancestors could have foretold that Thanksgiving would become a parade and some football games, they might have decided to keep the corn and turkeys to themselves.

Ray, Laura's father, aimed the remote at the TV and pressed the mute button.

"Let me show you something," he said. We walked over to the wall of the study, or "den" in Ray-speak. The basement was the "rec room," the bathrooms were "heads," where Ray went when he needed to "take a bio break."

"I got into stargazing last summer. Snapped this shot of Jupiter with an experimental telescope I borrowed from a guy in the satellite engineering division." Ray pointed to a photo of a green planet as detailed as anything I had seen in *National Geographic*. But he shook his head. "I should have used a faster film. Had to use a long exposure. That accounts for the slight ghosting effect you see here around the outer edges."

"I see," I said, kind of understanding.

"Know what that is?" Ray pointed to a small dot in the upper corner.

"No."

"Guess." Ray never gave an answer without asking for a guess—a habit that reminded me of one of my high school science teachers. It made Laura furious.

"It's a star."

"Guess again."

Ray was bald except for two gray patches along his temples, and his eyebrows arched upward and his forehead became lined with parallel furrows when he was in interrogative mode.

"An alien spacecraft with its high beams on?"

"That's funny," he said, not laughing. "It's Io, one of Jupiter's moons."

"I didn't know that." I could tell Ray wanted to show me more intergalactic photography, but I escaped back toward the recliner, the parade, my beer. Last time we visited, I had spent about four hours down in the basement looking at Ray's fossil collection. Although he put a lot of money into his hobbies, Ray didn't waste much on life's small pleasures. The beer had been in the garage so long it tasted like a mouthful of pennies.

"I bet you can't name the other moons," he said.

"Nope. You got me there." Ray's eyebrows dropped to half-mast and he smiled. I think he liked me because I let him ask the questions, because I admitted I didn't have all the answers.

A dense turkey breeze drifted in from the kitchen. "Something sure smells good," I said.

"Must be Laura doing the cooking." Ray wiped a thick coat of dust from the top of his beer can with his handkerchief. "Helen can't make a decent meal to save her life. Flat-out refuses to learn. We'd starve if it weren't for Lean Cuisine."

It had been Laura's idea to make this a Thanksgiving in the truest sense, a chance to put aside her long-standing grudges with her parents. Besides, she'd read some new holiday recipes in the *Globe*.

115

I tried to watch the parade but kept hearing fragments of conversation from the kitchen.

"I just don't see how it's possible . . . it's not . . . things are different than when . . . Mom." I could barely hear Laura over the sound of pots and pans clanging.

Then I heard Laura's mother, her tongue loosened by several glasses of white Zinfandel. "I was eighteen when I had you and . . . almost twice as old as that."

"Thanks," Laura said.

"It's true . . . needn't get all . . ." Helen said.

"I said . . . about it right now."

Ray pointed the remote control at the screen and brought up the volume to cover their voices. He developed software at Raytheon—Ray from Raytheon—and his vocation spilled over into his craving for order at home. The magazines fanned out chronologically on the coffee table. In the basement, the fossils were nestled in their slots, meticulously labeled. Ray's plans for this holiday weekend were just as organized and did not include arguments.

In a little while, Laura appeared next to my recliner.

"Mom's driving me nuts," she hissed in my ear. "She forgot the oysters for the stuffing. Can I have the car keys?"

"Sure, but I don't think you're going to have much luck finding a store open on Thanksgiving."

"I see you're not willing to try either."

"That's not what I meant. I just don't think it's worth going to a lot of trouble for oysters. Portland's twenty minutes away." If it hadn't been so cold outside, I might have volunteered to make a run into town to get away from Ray for a while.

"You sound like my mother."

"Maybe you should let them decide what kind of stuffing they want."

"If we weren't here they'd be sitting with TV trays and watching Dan Rather."

Laura returned to the kitchen and slammed the door.

116

"So how's the consulting racket, Larkin?" Ray said, selectively deaf to Laura's insults.

"Okay. I'm working on a new project. It's another business book."

"Can't say I've read your last one, but it's up there on the shelf." Ray pointed at *Sell Straight to the Top,* sandwiched on the bookshelf between a ten-volume scientific dictionary and the Time-Life series *Mysteries of the Unknown.*

"It looks good there. I'll send you the next one when it's done."

"Don't bother, I hardly have enough time to get through the magazines we get every month." Ray never worried much about politeness.

He switched channels. The Razorbacks were getting whipped by the Longhorns, in a football rivalry that was probably causing a lot of screaming back in Pine Bluff. I wanted to be home, far from this Down East Thanksgiving, which put the grim in Pilgrim.

"Ray, can I use your telephone for a minute?" I said. "I want to call my folks."

"Sure. Use the one upstairs so you can get some privacy."

Ray and Helen's bedroom was painfully clean, with about as much personality as a Petri dish. A fuzzy orange blanket covered the bed, which was mounted on casters so it could be moved across the beige carpet for easier vacuuming. One bedside table held a complicated digital alarm clock and a foil-stamped techno-thriller about a rampaging computer virus. The other held a book titled *The Nuclear Menace,* a stack of envelopes, and some dried flowers—the only evidence of life in the room. I picked through the letters as I pressed the buttons on the white Princess phone. I recognized the smoking cooling towers of Three Mile Island on an antinuclear mailing that Helen kept sending us as part of her work for Maine Moms Against Atomic Meltdowns.

Top Shelf answered on the first ring, shouting over the television. "Hello?"

"Hey. Happy Thanksgiving!"

Top Shelf covered the phone and whispered. Someone giggled.

"Longhorns suck! Go, Hogs!" I heard about a dozen voices scream, then break into drunken laughter.

"We're having a ball, sweetie," Top Shelf said. "How come you're not here?"

"We're in Maine," I said.

"Let me guess. You're having lobster for Thanksgiving dinner."

"No, don't think so."

"We're having all your favorites. Two turkeys with cornbread stuffing. Fried quail. Honey-glazed ham just to make sure. My biscuits. Aunt Opal's corn fritters and syrup. Green beans with chunks of smoked ham hock. Acorn squash baked with molasses and bacon . . ."

"Stop it," I said.

"And for dessert, there's pecan pie. Pumpkin pie. And lemon pie too."

"I'll be right over."

"Sorry, we're full up. Eighteen people. I put all the leaves in the dining room table this morning." Besides my father and Top Shelf, there would be my uncle Jack, called the Shit King since he ran a fertilizer warehouse; several cousins, no-account farmers who never amounted to much; my great-uncle Bud, an eccentric fisherman with a belly like a watermelon; my great-aunts Lessie, Opal, and Stella; plus assorted children and neighbors.

"Is Dad there?"

"He's out back shelling pecans and shooting the shit with Uncle Bud. Probably more of the latter."

"You tell him I called, okay?"

"I will. And you make sure you and Laura get down here for Christmas."

"We will," I said, knowing that we had already decided to spend Christmas in Maine, New Year's in Arkansas.

After I hung up, I stayed in Helen and Ray's bedroom for a minute and listened to the alarm clock tick. I wondered if they had sex right on the bed where I sat, but it seemed unlikely. Passion didn't exactly come with the territory around here.

We sat in high-backed chairs at the small dining room table and began the meal without saying grace. Ray carved the turkey while Laura sent around bowls of carefully prepared yams, corn, orange-cranberry relish, potatoes roasted with rosemary. The dining room was so bright that every dish shined like the varnished stunt food in the window of a sushi bar.

"I think the bird's a little underdone, Helen." Ray held a pink drumstick on the end of the carving fork.

"It's fine. The little plastic thing popped out. That tells you it's ready." Helen spooned a tiny portion of potatoes onto her plate. Laura stood up and took a closer look at the turkey.

"Dad's right. I think we better put it back in the oven."

"It's fine, really," Helen said. "Larkin, didn't you work at a restaurant once? What do you think?"

I leaned forward and looked at the turkey, still pink inside, undercooked enough to be dangerous. Laura and her parents waited.

"It looks fine," I said.

"Fine? It's raw." Laura grabbed the platter and carried it away.

"Next time, preheat the oven like you're supposed to," she shouted from the kitchen. "I just asked you to do one thing."

Helen helped herself to another glass of white Zinfandel as we sat listening to Laura pound around the kitchen. She turned to me. "So've you changed your mind about nuclear power?" Helen's eyes were gray and hard, and she was dressed in faded jeans, flannel shirt, and hiking boots.

"Don't let's get started on that now," Ray said.

"Did you hear the latest about Squanto?" she said to me, ignoring Ray. Helen spent most of her time working on antinuclear causes now that she had retired from teaching social studies at the high school. The Squanto Nuclear Power Plant was a controversial project just outside of Portland. During our last visit, I had been noncommittal on the issue, which I knew little about.

"They found radiation levels ten times above normal in sea creatures a mile from the cooling ducts. It's a crime." Helen waited for me to say something. Like Laura, she expected nothing but unconditional agreement.

"That must make for some mighty large lobsters," I said, picturing mutated crustaceans crawling from the depths.

"That's funny," Ray said, not laughing.

"Funny?" Helen put down her fork with a clatter. "When they declare a level-two emergency, we'll be the first who have to evacuate."

Laura came back to the table. "Don't even think of coming to stay with us, Mom. We finally got our place all fixed up." I had seen Helen's office upstairs, ankle deep in petitions and overflowing file folders. Laura had inherited her father's penchant for order.

"We're counting on you taking us in during our golden years," Helen said tartly. She carefully weeded every blade of rosemary from her cooling potatoes with her fork.

"No need to as long as Dad's working for the Death People." Laura's voice grew louder as she got angry. "Lots of missile money coming in from the taxpayers."

"Missile money put you through Smith, my dear," said Ray, whose software work had something to do with missile guidance systems. "Pass the yams, please."

"Why are you doing that?" Laura pointed to her mother's plate, where she chopped her naked potatoes.

"I don't like rosemary."

"Then why didn't you tell me that when we were cooking?"

"I didn't want to spoil your recipe."

"You're impossible, Mom. Did anyone ever tell you that?" Laura tossed her napkin on the table and stomped into the kitchen to check on the turkey.

"Yes. You've been telling me that for years." Helen took a minuscule dab of yams and shook salt over them. She drank her white Zinfandel. Ray heaped his plate high with everything and took neat forkfuls from each pile in rotation. He savored each bite, oblivious to his wife and daughter, only a little more aware of me. I could almost see the entry on his mental checklist for today—*6 p.m. Enjoy Thanksgiving dinner.* The three of us ate quietly while Laura banged around pots and pans.

"Happy Thanksgiving!" Ray said as Laura brought in the turkey. She placed the platter on the table, teeth clenched. This dinner hadn't gone the way the *Globe* said it should have.

"I'll carve," I volunteered, glad to do something. I sliced the turkey and passed the plates. The meat was so dry I had to slather it with butter to keep it from lodging in my windpipe. Laura shook her head at me.

"So much for your cholesterol," she said.

"It's a holiday." I shook pepper over my plate, hoping to add some flavor.

"Fooled me."

The dinner continued without a sound track as Ray devoured everything that came around, Helen toyed with a child's portion, and Laura jabbed at her food in a snit. I thought of things to say:

"Laura, I sure do love this Maine hospitality."

"Ray, you must have a hollow leg or something. You really pack it in, for a propeller-head."

"Helen, tell me more about Squanto. Please. Much more."

But I didn't say anything.

Our cranky Yankee Thanksgiving ended abruptly when Laura announced that we would drive back to Boston after dinner instead of staying over as we had planned. She started to clear the table while Ray picked at the bare carcass with his fork. I walked up behind her as she stood at the sink and stacked plates with a vengeance.

"Don't you think you're taking this a little too hard?" I said.

"You don't understand. They always pull stunts like this. It's impossible to do anything here. I want to go."

"All right, but at least be polite to them. They're your parents."

"You be polite."

"I thought I was."

"So polite that you'd eat raw turkey to keep from offending my mother? Frankly, I think that's taking it a little too far."

"Look," I said. "You can't always plan how things are going to go. Just don't take it out on them."

Laura turned off the hot water and dried her hands on a dishtowel. "They just drive me crazy. That's all," she said. In the living room, I heard the TV click on as Helen and Ray sat down to watch Dan Rather from their matching oxblood recliners.

9

A HISTORY
OF THE STRIDES

THANKSGIVING DINNER left a dark cloud and I woke the next morning with my mind full of worries. I got up and walked to the bathroom, where I stood for a long time under the hot shower and ran through the usual causes. Two Narragansetts and a glass of white Zinfandel weren't enough to push me to say or do anything too offensive. Laura and I hadn't argued much on the drive back to Boston. But still, the cloud remained.

I dressed quietly, then went downstairs to get the paper. From the front porch, I could hear a drum beating in the distance with the steady throb of a heart. They were probably having band practice at Watertown High, although it was cold and rainy, a miserable day to be marching around carrying a tuba. Upstairs, I fired up our sinister, matte-black coffeemaker with real coffee, which sent high-octane aromas wafting through the kitchen as I sat reading the paper, or at least turning the pages.

A secret has a way of surfacing, no matter how carefully it has been hidden. At first I thought Mariah was just a diversion from my usual dogpath. Now I wondered what I was getting into. We talked on the phone every day. I slipped out of work to meet her for coffee. I went for walks at night and ended up at Mariah's apartment, where we talked at her kitchen table, made love quickly on her king-sized bed, the couch, the floor. Any horizontal surface was fair game. If I had been a better person, I'd have told Laura what was going on and have faced up to the repercussions. But then again, a better person wouldn't have been doing these things in the first place.

The marching band played louder now, but there were no trumpet fanfares, no flatulent trombones, just a single drum.

Laura came in and poured herself a cup of coffee, took one sip, and poured it in the sink. She sat down at the table. "What's that noise?"

"The coffeemaker?"

"No, outside."

"Marching band. They must be practicing or something."

"You'd think they'd wait until noon." She pulled out the Business section and walked back to the bedroom.

I opened the window to let in some air and saw dozens of people walking down Mount Auburn Street toward Watertown Square. I thought it might be some kind of holiday parade, but there was nothing festive about these walkers. I stuck my head out over our flower box, empty now except for a few dried marigold stalks. Looking closer, I saw tiny gray-haired men in dark raincoats and black felt hats, funeral clothes. I saw an old woman wrapped in a white shawl, her face shriveled as a dried apple. Behind her, two boys carried a sagging banner that read "Freedom for Armenia!" There were others—"Remember the Armenian Genocide," "Watertown for Armenians," and some signs in a language with letters that looked a lot like pieces of elbow macaroni.

I had never heard of Armenia until we moved to Watertown. Now I knew only a little more. Watertown had the largest population of Armenians in the country; that much was obvious from a walk through the square, where every store name ended in -ian, the Armenian suffix—Kashperian Tailors, Horvorkian Florist, Lamjunian Bakery. From what I had seen, the locals

124

weren't very happy about the gentrification of their quiet town. They knew that people like us brought more than expensive stereos, foreign cars, and squash rackets. We brought lots of money. And money meant things would change, that their neighborhood would never be the same again.

They were right. Soon after we moved in, a French bakery replaced the shoe repair shop with the dusty collection of platform boots in its window. A collectibles shop called Maxine's ousted the store that sold bowling trophies. Stellina's Restaurant opened where there used to be a neighborhood bar filled with muttering drunks.

I watched the parade and wondered if the Armenians would understand that I wasn't like the others who crowded the bus from Cambridge every evening. I didn't like these strangers any more than they did. I liked the old, grungy Watertown, where corner stores were still called spas, and no one knew what radicchio was.

The drumbeat grew louder.

"Laura," I shouted back into the empty kitchen. "You have to see this."

"What is it?"

"Something. A parade."

"I'm busy," she said, but I could tell from her sluggish voice that she was already half asleep, still exhausted from the Thanksgiving debacle. She claimed that her parents' house was filled with some kind of sleep-inducing gas that drained her of energy. Kendra's diagnosis of post-stress sleep syndrome sounded more likely.

"It'll just take a minute. Come on," I said.

"All right. All right." A few minutes later, Laura came back into the kitchen.

"You're letting all the heat out," she said. I watched as a formation of boys in beige uniforms walked by, some kind of Armenian Boy Scouts, or Boy Scout*ians*. Rain fell in an invisible mist that ran down their faces. Laura stood next to me and shivered in her T-shirt and panties, her arms crossed in front of her.

"Who are they?"

"Armenians."

"Oh. What's the parade for?"

"It must be the anniversary of something," I said. A lot of awful things had happened to the Armenians, and the signs were all about remembering them—"Remember the Genocide," "Remember the Earthquake," "Remember the Armenian Freedom Fighters." It was a sad parade but I couldn't stop watching it.

"Is this what you wanted me to see?"

"Yes."

"Why don't they mobilize and march on Washington or something?" Laura said, showing a little of her mother's lefty pragmatism. "They could petition their congressman or do something positive. Honestly, I just don't get it."

I put my hand around Laura's waist and slipped two fingers beneath the elastic of her panties.

"Maybe later. I'm really exhausted." Laura moved my hand away gently and walked back to the bedroom.

I stayed at the window and watched as the last stragglers passed, their limp banners held high. At the end of the parade, one last old man in a black raincoat moved slowly, burdened with a huge drum slung from his shoulders by thick leather straps. Two boys ran alongside and took turns hitting the drum with sticks tipped with wadded rags. They walked on and the drumbeat faded, the parade over.

I stood at the window for a few more minutes, a thick sadness settling over me. It wasn't the parade that made me sad, but something Laura and I had lost, something no parade could ever bring back. I closed the window, sat at the kitchen table, and started reading the paper, all of it, hoping that the world's problems would displace my own.

We trudged through the holiday weekend, which should have been long enough for us to relax and have some fun. But this wasn't on our list of things to do. On Sunday, we drove to Conran's in Porter Square and looked at a new platform bed for the guest room. Something about the wood-grain veneer wasn't quite right. We wandered through the store for a while, down aisles of furniture and kitchen supplies, but didn't buy anything.

Then we drove to a couple of antique stores on Hampshire Street, where we saw a Victorian mirror that might look good in the living room. We used to get excited about furnishing the apartment, searching for the lost puzzle piece to complete a room. But now we couldn't seem to find anything that fit. On the drive home, we returned the videos from Saturday night and stopped for frozen yogurt. All the while, Mariah lurked in my mind so clearly that I was afraid I might blurt out her name.

Before dinner, Laura went running while I sat in the living room and paid some bills. I should have gone to the office to get caught up on my book, but it was too dismal a place to spend a rainy Sunday afternoon. Instead, I reached for Aunt Opal's book, *A History of the Strides,* tucked away in the guest bedroom bookshelf. It was typeset by someone with a shaky grasp of spelling and punctuation, photocopied on yellowish paper for an antique look, then bound in fake leather. But it was one of my favorite possessions; just opening it reminded me of home.

Aunt Opal had organized our family history into three sections—Early Years, Work and Achievements, and Death. In photos, various Strides stood in front of the District School in Pine Bluff, the youngest always holding a slate written with the year—1875, 1882, 1901. In other pictures, children sat on reluctant calves, wooden sleds, and sturdy bicycles. They ice skated, played on the lawn of the Second House, held stringers of fish and the lolling heads of deer.

Work and Achievements showed updated views of these children as they grew older and more successful. In one, my uncle Jack the Shit King stood proudly at the entrance of the fertilizer warehouse that would earn him his nickname. In another, my grandfather held the tether to a prize-winning steer. Just back from Korea, my father posed in the front seat of a glimmering black Ford. A clipping from the *Little Rock Traveler* told about my great-uncle Bud's being reelected the county's fish and wildlife commissioner, while another article, "Produce Roundup," mentioned that my cousin Roy had grown the largest watermelon in the county. A photo from *Lone Star* magazine showed a Bill Stride shaking hands with LBJ at the 1961 Texas State Fair. I didn't even know how I was related to this particular Stride.

The last section—Death—had more photos and articles, each dated in Aunt Opal's neat hand. Catlett Franklin Stride, former Confederate sharpshooter and Jefferson County pioneer, perished in a fire (1867). Sterling Stride died in a threshing accident (1912). Thad Stride, a pilot, disappeared over Germany (1943). Carl Stride, coach of the Pine Bluff Pinemen, had a fatal heart attack, leaving a lifetime record of sixty-one wins, twenty-three losses, and five ties (1951). Allison Stride, my mother, died of tuberculosis (1970).

I turned back to Work and Achievements and read the two clippings about me. One announced my acceptance to Harvard, the other my marriage to Laura. I wondered if these would be my only achievements—Harvard, marriage, death. But there were other stories, some of them not so favorable, that wouldn't be found in Aunt Opal's book.

For instance, the book didn't tell how Laura and I had developed cold feet before we got married, both scared to find that we might actually spend the rest of our lives together. A month before the wedding, Laura quit wearing her engagement ring, a diamond solitaire that cost me several Crockett Company bonuses. Kendra had told her the ring was "patriarchy in a glittering package." Meanwhile, I panicked and had a pathetic one-night stand with a salesgirl from Solo, the store in Harvard Square where I bought my ties. Her tight black skirt and come-hither stare had made me think she might be the kind of wild college girl receptive to whatever oats I had left to sow. But instead she spent all night snorting cocaine and talking about the guys she knew from obscure local bands. The sex that we

128

had, if you choose to call it that, was so frighteningly base that it filled me more with fear than with pleasure.

Momentum carried Laura and me inexorably forward. We were married in Arkansas for several reasons, none of them very good. Laura was mad at her parents about not helping her more with the preparations, so she decided to have the wedding in Pine Bluff to spite them. Plus, Top Shelf and my father had been making noises about not wanting to travel all the way to Maine, which seemed as far away as the moon.

On our wedding day, I watched myself go through the ceremony from a couple feet above and behind—an eerie, cinematic vision that I occasionally reencountered during long plane flights when my head howled with migraines.

We stepped through the front door of the Second House after the mercifully short ceremony and unruly reception and emerged to the steaming afternoon, blinded for a moment. Relatives and guests followed, most a little crocked from Uncle Bud's punch, a potent concoction called Ozark Trailblazer. The photographer, a burly roofer who worked for my father, crouched in the dusty driveway waiting for us to quit squinting. And behind him, a chauffeur stood next to a long white Cadillac, ready to take us to the airport. The photographer looked through the viewfinder. Perfect, he said.

Above us we heard the loud wrenching squeal of nails being pulled from a board. The window to one of the attic gables opened slowly for the first time in years. Looking up into the bright sun, we could make out a pair of hands holding something. Then that something grew larger as it hurtled toward us. I pushed Laura back toward the doorway, and with a sickening smash and a yowl, a heavy sack about the size of a laundry bag hit the sidewalk and raised a thick cloud of dust. The bag had missed us by inches but landed on one of the many cats that skulked around the Second House, flattening it beneath a mound of chicken feed. I wondered if having a black cat die in your path was worse luck than having one just cross it.

All we could see was a dirty curtain billowing from the open window. Then the face of Willie Stride emerged, one of my second cousins, a disturbed boy of sixteen whom my father had long before deemed "a couple sandwiches shy of a picnic." Willie smiled and waved a little, surprised to find so many people staring. Then he started to laugh, a shrieking laugh without cause or effect. No one laughed with him.

We found out later that Willie hadn't been able to find any rice to throw at us, and chicken feed was the closest thing he could come up with. It never occurred to him to open the bag first.

Laura and I got in the car and the driver sped us away. I looked back at the crowd gathered around the flattened cat and Top Shelf yelling up at Willie. My father the contractor, always quick with the right tool for the job, had brought a shovel to remove the lifeless kitty and the pile of chicken feed. Even over the roar of the air conditioner and the crunch of the Cadillac's tires on the gravel driveway we could still hear Willie's crazy laughter, louder now, as if he were laughing at us.

Laura started to say something but she was too stunned to finish. She hadn't even had a chance to toss her bouquet, still clutched in her hand. I hadn't delivered the brief speech I planned to give. But more important, it seemed as if we had missed some crucial part of the wedding, the part where we both became joined together as one.

The car drove down the long winding road, gliding by cattle pastures, farms, and other landmarks from my past. Creekbeds where I had hunted snakes. Side roads where Dan Holsapple and I had raced, the dust rising up like tornadoes behind our cars. The brick Texaco station where we used to buy fireworks on the Fourth of July.

Red crepe paper streamed behind the Cadillac like flames. When we passed the watermelon patch near the river, I could see field hands in overalls and white canvas hats waving at us and shouting something I couldn't quite make out, something about good luck, I hoped.

* * *

I took a manila envelope from the back of Aunt Opal's book and opened it. There I was, sitting by the river and staring at the camera with lust in my eyes. I had hidden Mariah's photos here since it was the last place Laura might stumble upon them. As I looked through the photos, I wanted to hear Mariah's voice, to be with her again.

I was still staring at the photos when I heard Laura come in from her run. I shoved them back in the envelope but they wouldn't go in right, so I closed the whole mess inside the book, then jammed it back on the shelf. A few quick steps took me into the living room, where I lay down on the couch and turned on the television with the remote.

"Anything good?" Laura said, her gray sweats splotched at the neck and under the arms.

"Not much. Just the news."

"I'm going to take a bath before dinner."

"Okay."

"Do you want to pick something up . . . ?" Laura did a few quick stretches.

"No, let's just stay in."

"We have some pasta," she said.

"Pasta's good."

"Are you okay?"

"Fine," I said.

"You seem sort of jumpy."

"I've got a client presentation tomorrow. It's important." Actually, I was so out of touch with my clients they probably didn't even remember my name.

"Why don't you go to the office early?"

"I was thinking about going in for a little bit after dinner."

"If you really have to," Laura said.

"I have to," I lied. Laura nodded and headed off for her bath. Tonight was just the latest in a series of late nights at the office, fictional dinner meetings with Davy, and long walks to the store

131

for cigarettes. Deception required imagination, and I knew that eventually I'd need to come up with more excuses, better lies. But I wasn't worried.

Later, with the table cleared and the dinner dishes washed, I sat in the living room and pretended to work on my presentation while Laura read in the bedroom. When Laura clicked off the lamp on her nightstand, I walked into the kitchen and took a Pepsi from the fridge, then looked out the kitchen window and waited for her to fall asleep.

The moon was small, a silver dime that glowed above the Armenian Benevolent Society before luminous clouds quickly consumed it like a magician's hand. I saw a few dim stars and the red lights of three radio towers that blinked slowly on the horizon. These towers always looked forlorn to me, the urban equivalent of a mournful train whistling in the night. Far in the distance, I could see the dome of the Watertown Armenian Church, a gray onion placed gently on the rooftops.

From our kitchen window the trees looked etched into the sky, the houses hand-tinted. In the house next door, I watched our neighbors play cards in the yellow glow from a small kitchen lamp. They were up late for old folks, I thought. I remembered that back in Kansas City, Mrs. Weingarten always had trouble sleeping. It seemed that the older people got, the more they had to remember, until finally their thoughts kept them awake.

The old man dealing the cards was Armenian. Maybe he had been in the parade earlier today. I could see his wife's dark dress, her knitted shawl. She pulled her cards toward her, stacked them carefully, then picked them up. When I was a kid, I had always imagined these were the kinds of things people did when they married—play cards late at night, go for drives in the country.

I stood at the window and finished my Pepsi. In the bedroom, my wife slept a dreamless sleep I envied. Tomorrow would begin like all Monday mornings—another day, another suit from the dry cleaner's. But for now I was free. I got my overcoat from the hall closet and walked to the door.

I turned toward the bedroom. "I'm going into work for a little bit," I said, my voice echoing down the hall. But Laura was fast asleep. I walked downstairs and out the front door. Beneath the streetlights, the Volvo waited like a conspirator to take me away to Mariah.

10

HOLIDAY SPIRITS

"Do you think we should get a tree?" Laura sat at the desk and flipped through a pile of catalogues—J. Crew, Williams-Sonoma, Harrington's, J. Peterman. Light snow fell outside the living room windows.

I looked up from the couch, where I sorted through the day's pile of Christmas cards and bills. "I don't know. Do you want one?"

"Kind of, but they always dry out and drop their needles all over," she said.

"So you don't really want one?"

"Well, I'm not sure yet. I mean, it would look nice over there." Laura pointed to an empty spot between the Biedermeyer desk with its cubbyholes full of stamps and bank statements and the stereo cabinet stacked with components.

"If we decide we want one, the Elks Club is selling them in the square." I had seen the signs of Christmas everywhere—holiday craft fairs, carolers in front of the Coop.

"Or we could go get our own," she said. "There's a place out in Lexington that lets you cut your own tree." After Thanksgiving had failed to match up to its timeworn image, Laura was de-

termined to have an old-fashioned Christmas. If we had a fireplace, we'd be roasting chestnuts by it.

I never really understood the attraction of the "U Pick" farms
to the west of Boston, where you could pick your own apples,
pumpkins, Christmas trees. It seemed strange that my childhood
chores had been turned into weekend entertainment, although
I'd like to see "U Burn Your Own Trash" or "U Emasculate
Your Own Calves."

Laura went back to her catalogues. Tucked in with the red-
enveloped Christmas cards, I found a letter with an Indiana
postmark. I opened it.

> Dear Larkin,
> Thanks for the money. It helped out a lot. I'm writing
> to tell you that my father died last Friday. The old man
> finally gave up. By the end, there wasn't really anything
> they could do. I stayed on a fold-out bed at the hospital
> and watched him check out. You wouldn't have hardly
> recognized him with all those tubes going in and tubes
> going out. He was one tough customer, you know. I kept
> wishing he was a car so I could fix him up and replace
> the broken parts. I guess we all end up like old cars sooner
> or later, full of dents but still running. See you soon maybe.
> Your friend, Dan

I stood up and walked toward the door, my back to Laura,
my eyes shining. "I'm going to start getting ready."

I walked slowly out of the living room and down the hall to
the bathroom, shedding tears for Dan and his father. I turned
the taps of the bathtub, hoping a bath would soothe my mind.
When I lived in crummy apartments, a hot bath was one of the
few luxuries I could afford. Laura liked them too, but for her
own reasons. I tested the water with one hand, then undressed.
In the tub, I took a quick inventory of my physical problems—
shin splints from wearing boots too much, a chronically sore

back, and an unpleasant blossoming in my hindquarters I liked to call asteroids. Dan was right about ending up like an old car.

Laura and I dressed in the bedroom, getting ready for our separate holiday fetes, the boring, stuffy Crockett Company Christmas party in Cambridge and the gigantic DataTech yuletide bash in Boston.

"Do you know how late you're going to want to stay?" I buttoned my shirt. Laura wanted to go alone to her party, which promised to be the latest chapter of the Robert-versus-Laura promotion melodrama.

"Pretty late. I'll take a cab or get Hank to give me a ride." The bed was strewn with a dozen outfits she had tossed aside in a fashion frenzy. This would be Laura's last chance to lobby for the promotion, to shine more brightly than her natty rival. She walked into the bathroom and turned on the water in the sink.

"I should be home around midnight," I said. I heard the medicine cabinet open and a small snap as Laura opened her Valium.

"Try to have a good time," she said.

"I will. You too."

Alone, I walked through Harvard Square; the streetlights were wrapped in greenery and strings of white lights hung across Mass Avenue. Beneath them, couples walked in long overcoats, scarves, and Russian fur hats. When I was a boy, the two weeks before Christmas were so stoked with anticipation I could barely sleep. But now my senses were as frozen as the streets, sent into hibernation for the winter. The faces I passed were pale, lips thin and chapped. My thoughts lately centered on how to get through the gray days when the sun set at four o'clock. Ideas and plans shriveled and dried like gourds.

The bitter December winds had thinned out the lost souls who huddled on heat vents. Those who remained wore greasy down jackets one over another, their legs wrapped in plastic bags, their swollen joints jammed into gloves without fingers. Back in Arkansas my grandfather used to judge the winters by the thickness of caterpillar wool, but in Cambridge these people were the season's true measure.

Near the bank a dark-haired, glowering man known as Paranoid Pete huddled under a blanket, his army jacket scrawled with rambling notes about the Trilateral Commission and government radio waves. I dropped a dollar into a red plastic bucket next to his blanket and he acknowledged it with a shake of his ragged beard. Farther down the sidewalk, Mattress Man had parked his shopping cart stacked high with bedding, just as he had when I was an undergraduate. He looked even smaller than usual in an oversized parka patched with silver duct tape. I placed a dollar in his copper palm. "Gladta see ya. Happy holidays," he said.

Down the street, The Hopper lay in wait, emaciated, hair long and matted as a lion's mane. He walked toward me, then took a Chaplinesque leap backward, his own peculiar two-step. He stared at the dollar I handed him and tried to find the hidden message.

Despite Cambridge's liberal reputation, handouts were few in Harvard Square, where most pedestrians had mastered the urban survival technique of looking away just in time to avoid meeting a stare that came with hooks. I knew that generosity meant much more than money handed to bums, but I did it anyway, as much for me as for them.

I walked through the useless archway that led to Charlesview Place and saw a long figure on a bench, hunched over a pint bottle. The security guard usually kept the courtyard cleared of vagrants. I stopped and looked closer.

The man looked up and laughed. "Got a dollar for me, Larkin?"

"Avery?"

"Yeah." I walked over and sat on the bench next to him. He smelled like a peppermint stick.

"It's a little too cold to visit the Career Path, don't you think?"

137

"Colder up there." He pointed a wavering finger at the top floor of our building, where our offices blazed with lights and a blinking Christmas tree. Silhouettes holding drinks looked out over the Charles.

"What's up?"

"Here. Take this." He handed me a balled-up piece of paper. I unfolded it and found a check for two thousand dollars, made out to him.

I tucked it into his overcoat pocket. "I think you better hang on to this, Avery. You may want it later."

He leaned toward me. "It's an insult," he said, then louder, "it's a fucking insult from the . . . the Crock-of-Shit Company!" Gillman laughed until he started to choke.

"Hey. Calm down. Come on."

Gillman took a deep breath and exhaled a sweet wind of peppermint schnapps. "I'm not that closely aligned with Lillivale, you know. I know you think we're close, but we're not. Not anymore."

"You're kind of drunk, aren't you, Avery?" I already knew the answer. I just wanted to give him the chance to shut up.

"Yes, well, maybe I am. But you would be too if you got a lousy two-grand Christmas bonus while some asshole who worked half as hard got five."

"Lillivale?"

"Uh-huh."

"Don't sweat it. Davy likes you. I can tell. He just likes to keep his best employees a little hungry."

"That so?"

"Yeah. It's just how he does things. You can't let it get to you." To Gillman, money was more than just numbers and decimal points. It was how he measured himself, how he decided whether he was bad or good, a winner or a loser. Like a lot of people at the Crockett Company, Gillman had become addicted to crisp, green dollars, to envelopes with windows.

Gillman reached over and put his hand on my shoulder.

"I appreciate that input, Larkin. I really do," he said. "I know we don't always see eye to eye, but that's not the point now, it really isn't. The point now is . . . the thing I wanted to tell you . . ." His eyes unfocused a little and his lower lip turned slippery with drool.

"I'm going to go on up for a little bit. Why don't you take a cab home, Avery. I'll see you on Monday. We can have lunch and talk if you want to." He looked up at me, startled, a few errant flakes of snow landing on his face.

"Sure. If you really want to. Thanks for stopping by."

I made the rounds upstairs, shaking hands, sipping a glass of champagne.

"Larkin!" Davy walked toward me in a red blazer and a pair of bright green pants. He stopped a few feet from me.

"What do you think?"

"Your tailor is a very clever man. Christmas, right?"

" 'Tis the season." Davy directed me over to a quiet corner of the bullpen and slipped an envelope into my coat pocket with an exaggerated backhand delivery so everyone in the room could see. After all, what good was generosity if no one noticed?

"Here's a little holiday cheer."

"Thanks, Davy."

"Just a little something to tide you over until the book money starts rolling in," he said. "We're looking at a great year coming up, Larkin. Another great year."

"I know," I said, not convinced. McCormick stumbled over to Davy and pressed his florid face against Davy's ear, his way of telling a joke. I walked down the hall to the bathroom, then into a stall, where I ripped open the envelope. My Christmas bonus was ten thousand dollars, a reassuring sign. I put the check in my wallet and pitched the card without reading Davy's long-winded annual thank-you. On the way back from the bathroom, I ran into Ellen, who wore a white knit dress with linebacker-sized shoulder pads.

"Hi," she said, tugging at her dress a little. "Tell me if this looks okay. I couldn't decide what to wear." Ellen looked as good as she could, given her awkward construction.

"You look great," I said. "Maybe take out the shoulder pads."

Ellen rolled her eyes. "There aren't any shoulder pads. I need a second opinion. Where's Laura?"

"Her company party's tonight too."

"That's too bad. We need more women here." Crockett Company gatherings usually degenerated into a lower order, with Davy, McCormick, and a batch of drunk young consultants heading downtown to the Combat Zone strip joints. A couple of years ago I would have been with them.

"You and I have been friends for a while now, right?" Ellen's dark eyebrows scrunched together when she got serious.

"Right," I said. We sat on a small couch in a corner of the office. A waiter came by and offered us a platter of hors d'oeuvres. Ellen picked a few pieces of melon from beneath a pile of prosciutto, and I took a heaping plateful of stuffed mushrooms and scallops wrapped in bacon.

"I've been meaning to talk to you," Ellen said. "You don't seem particularly happy."

"Actually, I'm having a pretty good time. These scallop things are good." I was swooning from the taste of bacon, which Laura had banned from our kitchen.

"I mean in general. You almost fell asleep during yesterday's planning meeting. You leave at the end of the day without saying good-bye. You never stay late for cocktails anymore. Even Lillivale asked me what was up, and he doesn't pay attention to anyone but himself. So what's wrong?"

"I've just had a lot on my mind lately." It was the oldest excuse but it was true. I had quit seeing my friends, even Tucker, so I could spend more time with Mariah.

"Are you having an affair?" Ellen asked with Yankee directness.

I swallowed a mushroom cap whole and it journeyed painfully

down my throat. "As a matter of fact, yes. How the hell did you know?"

"I know you pretty well, Larkin. You've been buying flowers a lot lately, and you told me once Laura was allergic to them. You're on the phone a lot with your door closed. Lots of phone messages from a woman named Maria or something."

"Maybe you should be a private detective instead of a consultant."

Ellen shook her head. "I'm not giving you a hard time. I just wanted to make sure you know what you're doing. So many of my friends end up getting divorced it's enough to make me glad I'm an old maid."

"You're not an old maid and I'm not getting divorced," I said.

"I like Laura, but you're my friend, and I want you to be happy. You know you can talk to me, don't you? When you first came here, you used to talk to me all the time, remember?"

"That's because you were the only one here who would have anything to do with me." The Harvard B School crowd had snubbed me, the stranger from Wharton, actually a career dishwasher without portfolio. Ellen had edited my reports and covered for me more times than I could count.

"So don't forget your old friends," she said.

"I won't," I said. "There's just a lot of things going on right now. I'll be better once I finish this book. I promise."

"I'll hold you to that," she said. We stood up and Ellen kissed my cheek. "See you Monday. I have to talk to you about a downsizing I'm working on at Genetronics."

"Right."

After Ellen disappeared into the crowd, I walked to the front of the office, grabbed my coat, and raced down the staircase.

In the Volvo, I checked the dashboard clock. It was a little before nine, three hours before Laura would be home. I drove through Cambridge, past the blue liquor store, its neon sign blazing in the cold. In front of the Armenian Benevolent Society, a long row of cars lined both sides of the street. I stopped at a red light and looked through the large front windows to where a man in a dark suit spoke from behind a podium, gesturing with one clenched fist in the air.

I parked in my usual safe hiding place—the dark corner of a vacant lot near Mariah's, where no one would recognize my car. Walking quickly up the street, I passed Tuxedo Junction, one of my favorite Watertown landmarks since its window displays were always a little screwed up. I couldn't tell whether it was a joke, sabotage by a bored clerk, or just indifference. Tonight, a bald female mannequin was bound for a Christmas party in a shiny red dress not quite long enough to hide her missing feet. Her date held both hands over his crotch, suffering from a common teen affliction. In the next window, a groom's fingers lay in pieces next to his shiny black shoes. The bride's nose was chipped and her legs were covered with greasy fingerprints.

A dozen small holes pockmarked the windows. Shooting store windows with a pellet gun was the kind of prank I would have pulled when I was a kid if there had been a tuxedo store nearby, which there wasn't since clean overalls were considered formal wear back home. The pellets had left little cones in the glass, a tiny hole in each center. Looking closer, I could see a small tear in the groom's ruffled shirt from a bullet that had struck just above his heart. Not a bad shot. Across the street was a cemetery with a small plaque stating that this site was briefly home to the Continental Congress. Now it was just another hangout for high school kids. I hoped the bullet holes were old.

Palfrey Street was a dark road that rose on the highest hill in Watertown. I started up the hill, out of breath almost immediately. To the left, the land dropped off into a flat neighborhood far below that blinked with Christmas lights. Smoke rose from chimneys, and church spires pointed at snow-filled clouds. In the west, the lights stopped and the first low hills began, the view as peaceful as a Christmas card.

My footsteps echoed as I walked toward the yellow house halfway up the hill. Mariah opened the door mid-knock.

"Come on in out of the cold, stranger," she said. She shut the door behind me, then leaned against it.

"I missed you." I put my arms around her and we kissed. She wore her stained lab coat, vinegary from darkroom chemicals.

"You're right on time." She took off the lab coat and revealed a blue-and-white-checked dress beneath it. "I just finished up in the darkroom."

"Hungry?"

"Starved."

I took a paper bag from my overcoat pocket. "I brought the secret ingredients."

"I think I've got everything else," she said. We walked into the kitchen. My Christmas present to Mariah was a home-cooked dinner. But this wasn't any ordinary dinner. In the paper bag were my great-uncle Bud's special recipe for fried catfish and all the right spices, which I had hunted down in Little Armenia.

I took out a smudged Polaroid of Bud holding up a stringer of fish next to his trailer home, about fifteen miles up the Ouachita from the Second House. "Here's the old guy's picture."

"He doesn't look quite as wild as you said." Mariah seemed a little disappointed. I had told her a lot of stories about Bud, an ornery recluse who used his job as the county's fish and wildlife commissioner as an excuse to avoid people. When I was a boy, a visit to Bud's camp was an adventure, my father and I setting out in a motorboat full of supplies.

"In that trailer home, Uncle Bud has six televisions stacked in the living room," I said. "He likes to watch them all at once."

"Can't blame him for wanting to stay up on current events."

"They're for wrestling and baseball."

"Oh." Mariah took a package of catfish from the fridge and opened it up, then rinsed each fillet under the tap. "Let's see the recipe."

I handed over the oily piece of paper bag where Bud had scrawled the instructions: "Catch fish. Gut and skin it. Take KN peppers, white pepper, and rosemury. Pound them with hammer. Rub on fish. Fry filays in white skillit. Eat. Serves one."

"Not exactly the Frugal Gourmet," she said.

"Do you have a hammer? I think that may be part of his secret."

"Whatever Uncle Bud says." Mariah reached in a drawer and handed me a hammer. I dumped the spices onto the counter and pounded away, creating a dusty cloud that made me sneeze.

"Anything else, chef?"

"A white skillet."

"I don't think I have a white one. Just this." Mariah held up an expensive no-stick skillet. From what I remembered, Bud cooked fish in an oily cast-iron pan, but this would have to do. "I think he may have just meant it has to be white-hot," she said.

"Right. White-hot." I turned the gas on all the way beneath the skillet, then rolled the fish in the spices. I wasn't much of a cook, since my culinary training consisted of dishwashing.

"So tell me more about Uncle Bud." Mariah rubbed her fingers along the back of my neck as she walked by me.

"I loved going there as a kid. He let me drink beer and shoot snakes with the four-ten."

"Sounds like a good role model." Mariah cleared all the photographic gear from the kitchen table and put on a checkered tablecloth. "Maybe someday you can take your kids to meet him."

"Doubtful," I said.

Mariah picked up the picture of Bud and propped it up at the center of the table next to a bowl of salad and a plate of cornbread she had made. "He looks pretty healthy to me." Uncle Bud had a belly big as an outboard motor.

"I expect he'll live to be about a hundred," I said, "but I'm not sure that's long enough to meet any kids of mine."

"Why not?"

I thought of the times Laura and I had talked about having kids. She had her mind made up not to have any. "Kids are completely out of the question," I said.

Mariah stuck a candle in an empty wine bottle, then lit it with her Zippo. "That's too bad."

"For me, or for Uncle Bud?"

"Both," she said.

I stood over the smoking skillet and dropped the fish in, raising a vicious spice cloud that hit me in the face and dropped me to my knees, gagging.

"Did you burn yourself?" Mariah said, then began to choke.

"Open the window," I said. "Fast!"

Mariah had covered her windows with heat-conserving plastic wrap for the winter, but she tore into a section with a fork, ripped it back, and threw open the window. Tears ran down our faces as a cold wind blew through the kitchen.

"This better taste good," she said.

"It will," I said, not so sure as I peered at the stove from a safe distance.

We watched the erupting skillet send noxious smoke signals up to the ceiling. After a few minutes I crept forward, head low, and scraped the fish from the charred surface of the pan. When I flipped the fillets, the pan sent up another menacing peppery cloud. Mariah's smoke detector broke into a fit of shrill chirping. Somehow I never remembered cooking being this exciting. I reached up and unmanned the smoke detector of its batteries.

In a few minutes, I turned off the stove and carved the fish into tar-covered portions. Mariah wiped her eyes with a paper towel.

"I think we may need a beer with this," she said, reaching into the refrigerator. "I don't think Uncle Bud would mind."

It was a dark and stormy meal, nothing like the festive holiday repast I had envisioned. The fish had seared into crusty, over-spiced flanks of fish jerky, and I caught Mariah hiding most of hers beneath some salad. We drank about four beers each to douse the fire on our tongues, but nothing seemed to help. At the end of dinner, Mariah stood up abruptly and made a beeline for the bathroom. The water went on and then I thought I heard retching.

"You okay?" I said when she came out.

"Fine." She looked pale. "Much better. I'm not used to home-cooked meals."

"You can tell me if you didn't like it. I won't be mad. It's Bud's recipe."

"No, really. I liked it. It reminded me of Girl Scouts." She headed for the liquor cabinet. "How about some whiskey with your coffee?"

"That might help," I said.

After a few shots of whiskey, most of the smoke had cleared and we could close the window. I raised my glass toward the big squinting man in the out-of-focus picture.

"To Bud!"

We clinked glasses. "His secret recipe's safe with me," Mariah said.

"Someday I'll tell you what he eats for breakfast."

"Please, not now," she groaned.

"Don't you want to hear more thrilling tales of Arkansas?"

"No, I've had enough excitement for one night."

"You sure?" I reached under the table and ran my hand up Mariah's leg.

"Hold on, I've got a present for you." She walked out of the kitchen and returned a few minutes later wearing her lab coat again. I thought she wanted me to see some new photos; she liked me to look at her work. But instead, Mariah walked to the center of the kitchen, looked directly into my eyes, and let the coat slide slowly over her pale shoulders. Pausing briefly at her nipples, the coat fell to the floor, and Mariah stood naked in front of me. I thought this sort of surprise happened only in the letters columns of men's magazines.

"Merry Christmas," she said.

I moved toward her, unbuttoning my shirt.

We rolled on the sticky kitchen floor among the metal chair legs. Stray matchsticks and spare change stuck to our skin. I ran my hands up and down Mariah's narrow back then licked her chest, tasting her salt. She put her arms behind me and I pushed quickly inside her. For days I had waited for this. Her dark hair fanned out on the kitchen floor, sliding back and forth as we moved slowly together. I touched and kissed and loved with every ounce of energy I had left at ten on a weeknight until finally we lay tangled together on the floor like broken dolls. Exhausted, we slept.

I woke staring up at the sweaty pipes leading to the sink and wondered where I was, how long I had been asleep. Mariah lay next to me, breathing softly. I kissed her on the forehead and she murmured but didn't wake up. I searched through the kitchen for my rumpled clothes. Covering Mariah with the lab coat, I carried her into the bedroom, careful to lift with my legs to avoid having to explain any back injuries. She felt supple and warm in my arms. I wrote a short note and put it on her pillow: "Thanks for the present. Sorry about dinner. I owe you a new frying pan. Your lover, L."

I put on my coat, then closed the front door softly behind me. The cold air burned my face as I walked quickly downhill toward the car, my clothes untucked, dirty, buttoned wrong. I brought Mariah's scent with me on my fingers, my lips. It was past midnight, and along the quiet street the dark houses sheltered peacefully sleeping families. A gray cat crossed in front of me, its legs a blur as it raced under a parked car. My head spun, opiated with sex.

The thought of Mariah made me invincible, weightless. The sky had cleared and I rose above the snowy streets, high above Tuxedo Junction, the brides pointing up at me with their broken fingers. Above the Armenian Benevolent Society, where a few old men sat up late talking, and the cemetery crowded with spirits from the Revolution. Past every landmark, familiar but growing smaller, until I looked down on a toy town where Mariah's house moved closer and closer to our house until they combined like drops of mercury beneath the moonlight.

Then I remembered that this night was rare, that despite her

Christmas present Mariah wasn't really mine to keep. The potion that had held me wore off like cheap bar cocaine and left only a sweet throbbing in my head. I walked along the frozen sidewalk toward the dark lot and my frost-glazed car.

As I drove down our street, I saw the blue house, its windows dark. Inside, Laura slept now, hot beneath layers of blankets. I walked to our front door, keys in hand. The stairs creaked as I passed the Thompsons' door with its cheerless bay-leaf wreath. I stood just inside our doorway for a minute and heard the living room clock tick, the refrigerator hum, the storm windows rattle. In the distance, I could see the radio relay towers pulse in a slow red beat along the deep blue horizon. I paused in the hallway, where moonlight raked in parallel lines across the polished wood floors, then did the Indian Walk back to the bedroom.

11

JERKS AND
ASSHOLES

DAVY OPENED my office door and stuck his smiling face inside.

"Give me the hot buttons. C'mon. C'mon. "Hot buttons" were words that sold, that made money. I looked up from my computer, where I tried to build a chapter around two or three decidedly lukewarm buttons.

"One hundred top executives tell you their success secrets," I said.

"I like it. More."

"Insightful interviews bring you a millennium of management know-how."

"Good. Briefcase wants a warm-up teaser to send to the trades." Ever since Davy had finalized the contract for *Strategies for Success*, he had been checking in each morning to see how the book was going.

"New strategies for the world's oldest profession." I turned back to my computer. I could make up these things for hours.

"Wait a minute. I thought the world's oldest profession was . . ."

"Prostitution. Business. Same difference," I said.

Davy dropped his smile for a minute. "I hope you're joking."

"I'm joking."

"This has got to be serious. Hard-hitting. The kind of book every manager will put on his shelf."

"Davy, this book's so good, motels will put it right next to the Bible."

"That's more like it. Hey. Maybe we should call it *The Executive Bible* instead. What do you think?"

"Catchy."

"You're wrapping it up and it's going to be great. Am I right or am I right?"

"You're right," I said.

Davy was smiling again as he closed the door, his hot button pressed.

All I had to do was write a couple more chapters and edit the whole manuscript. After Davy left, I sat at my desk and stared at the computer screen, listening to the room hum with a low current transmitted across stale air, through thin walls and glass partitions. I used to like my office. My phone rang, my fax machine churned out pages of information, my computer connected me to New York, Los Angeles. These devices used to make my work seem important. But now my office reminded me of a space capsule, with me the monkey waiting for instructions from Earth. Clients called and I talked to them. Other consultants came in and asked for advice, showed me their reports. The cursor blinked, begging for more words, and I typed them in one after another, filling my computer files with business fodder.

I was working on a particularly dumb chapter called "Putting the Man Back in Manager," which profiled a take-charge executive who ruled his insurance company with the subtlety of a pit bull. My favorite anecdote: Needing to cut costs, the CEO invited all the employees to the company lunchroom and handed out envelopes—half got pink slips, the other half got tickets to the Super Bowl. He considered this a nice strategy for "personnel surplus reduction."

When I finished the chapter, I visited Ellen's office as my reward.

"Hi. What's up?" she said. A half-eaten bagel, empty coffee cups, and a yogurt container ringed her computer. A pair of jogging shoes were drying next to the baseboard heater.

"Not much. You?"

"Working on a Potential Appraisal Program for Wegcorp."

"Anything interesting?"

"I'll give you a copy of the report when I'm through. The focus groups showed that eighty percent of the employees hate the company and want to leave."

"Sounds familiar." I walked over to Ellen's bookshelf, loaded with business books about how to be a better manager, how to increase productivity, how to negotiate. Everyone wanted to be better at something. I saw a few of Briefcase Press's best-sellers— *Managing by Doing Nothing, What Color Is Your Overcoat?* and *Teaching the Elephants to Swim with the Sharks.* I took down some old copies of the *Harvard Business Review.* "Hey, can I borrow these for a couple of days?"

"Sure," she said, "but I thought you were finished with research."

"I just want to add a few more footnotes. Davy's worried it won't be serious enough." Down the hall the secretary buzzed my line, but I pretended not to hear.

"I'm sure it's plenty serious," Ellen said. "Davy told me it's going to be great." She pushed off with one foot and spun around slowly in her chair.

"Davy always says things are going to be great. Sunshine and clear skies ahead. The trick is knowing when to believe him."

Ellen's eyes narrowed and her smile faded. "Sit down for a minute," she said. "We have to talk."

I sat on the plush couch. Ellen spent most of her time at the office, so she had turned it into a version of home, with comfortable furniture and plants. "I have to say I'm really worried about you," she said. "Ever since I talked to you at the Christmas party."

"Don't be."

"People are starting to ask me what's wrong with you."

"Tell them I'm just in deep with this book. I'll be done soon," I said. In fact, the book had little to do with my office malaise.

"Maybe you should take a break when you finish up."

I pointed to a framed print that showed a summer day on the Cape Cod seashore, sea oats poking through the sand like thinning hair. "Laura and I are going to the Cape next weekend."

"At this time of year?" she said. "Could be depressing."

"I like the Cape in the winter. It's quiet and there's no one there."

"That sounds like the way you want it here," Ellen said. "Quiet, with no one around."

I shrugged. Yes, that sounded pretty good.

The chair casters squeaked as Ellen scuttled across the carpet toward me. "You told me once that the world was made up of two kinds of people—jerks and assholes," she said.

"I remember that." It was one of the theories about the world I had come up with when I worked at the barbecue. Washing dishes left plenty of time to develop a definitive personal philosophy. "Assholes are bad people but they know it. Jerks are bad but think they're great."

"So which are you now? A jerk or an asshole?"

"An asshole. Definitely an asshole. I know I'm bad."

"Then quit acting like a jerk, okay?" Ellen put her hand on my arm and gave it a little pat, the way she might say hi to a wayward cat.

"I'll have to create a third category for you," I said.

"How about just being my friend again?"

"Jerks, Assholes, and Friends. Sounds like a good name for a consulting firm."

"Now go away. I've got to finish this report." She rolled back over to her desk. "How about lunch sometime after you've miraculously returned to normal?"

"Fine. We'll go the Harvest. You can pay."

Ellen laughed. "You really are a jerk."

I closed my office door and locked it, turned the radio on low to cover the annoying office hum, closed the venetian blinds so I wouldn't look out at the bullpen. There wasn't time for daydreaming now. My yellow legal pad was covered with chicken-scratchings that I had to decipher and turn into platitudes.

Outside, the streets turned a dark gray as the winter sun began to fail. Words hovered on my computer screen like fireflies. I patched together a ratty quilt of lies for the last chapter, "The Future: What's in It for You?"

"In the future," I wrote, "true success will depend not on increasing profitability alone, but on finding brutal new strategies suited for a hostile and changing marketplace. Customer focus and total quality will simply be the cost of admission to a new global arena." I could see businessmen in rumpled white shirts reading my book on weekday commuter flights, experiencing managerial epiphanies at twelve thousand feet. They would nod and underline buzzwords in ballpoint, convinced that I was "talking their language."

I coasted for a few pages. It was easy to lie about the future. I wrote about a world where crafty executives reigned, where competition was vicious and the rewards enormous. What I really envisioned was a catastrophic act of reverse economic alchemy that turned all the money in the world to shit, tawny rivers of it gushing through bank lobbies. Waitresses and dishwashers would inherit the earth while CEOs and middle managers sank to the bottom of this fecal freefall. But I didn't write about that now. That vision of the future wouldn't hit anyone's hot button except my own.

At three, the secretary dropped off my mail, the usual catalogues and training newsletters, plus a neatly wrapped package from Raytheon. I opened it and found a note from Laura's father, saying how nice it was to have had us over Christmas. I had almost managed to forget the visit. Enclosed was a videotape labeled "A Maine Christmas." A better title would have been "A Kabuki Christmas," since Ray had reduced the holidays to a series of ceremonies—the trimming of the tree, opening packages, Christmas dinner—without much room for improvisation or emotion. Looking for any excuse to avoid work, I walked to the empty conference room, turned on the television, and fed the tape into the VCR. Laura came onto the screen, standing at the top of the stairs.

Ray (off camera): "Okay, one more time." He tracked Laura with his ubiquitous video camera as she ran down the stairs, heading toward the Christmas tree and its carefully stacked booty.

Laura: "We do this every year. Can we stop now?" She walked back toward the camera, her face unsmiling, blanched by the glare of the lights.

Ray: "Just one more time to make sure."

Laura walked upstairs. Per Ray's instructions, we were all wearing pajamas, and I spotted myself in the background padding around awkwardly in fuzzy bath slippers two sizes too small. I looked yellow and hung over, although the unpalatable drinking options—Narragansett and white Zinfandel again—had kept the holiday less than festive. Ray, a self-proclaimed "morning person," had summoned us downstairs at six with his traditional trumpet blast.

I looked at the camera and waved feebly.

Ray: "Now let me get a shot of the both of you running down the stairs together."

Helen (off camera): "Larkin hasn't even had his coffee yet." A lucky thing that was. Helen served Nature's Broom Decaffeinated, a purgative blend that had kept me in the bathroom most of the night.

Ray: "I'm sure Larkin doesn't mind my holiday routine." I

nodded, having been taught always to be polite to parents no matter how ridiculous they were.

Laura (barely audible): "Compulsion, more like it." We climbed the carpeted stairs and rushed down them again, hands raised like surrendering infantry.

Ray: "Look like you're happy."

I pressed fast forward and watched four speed freaks ripping open presents and kissing each other like woodpeckers. I ejected the tape and tossed it in a cardboard box of cassettes for recording client presentations. Back in my office, I put a yellow post-um on my door that said: "Busy. Do not enter without knocking. Do not knock without a reason." Ellen was right. Slowly but surely, I was becoming a jerk.

I stopped again at about five and read the pages I had written, dizzy and disgusted from so much lying and from the greasy Chinese lunch special I had eaten at my desk. I printed out the pages and read the glib, confident predictions that Davy wanted. But I still needed more quotes. I pulled the rice-splattered *Times* from the trash and found a couple of businessmen in the obits. I wrote some great quotes backing up my major points and attributed them to these stiffs. Dead people had such a way with words. I typed on.

Out in the main office, the tempo slowed and volume lowered as business ground to a halt. When Friday-afternoon cocktail hour ended at around six, the Crockett Company began to drift home for the weekend. My back hurt from leaning over the computer, which sent out a hot breeze that smelled like a lamp left on too long. A half-pack of cigarettes, three cups of coffee, and a Pepsi had worked me into a frenzy. The top of my head tingled and my mind raced. My eyes were glassy as marbles and veined with red. I couldn't sit still. I crouched as I typed. I flipped through notebooks and legal pads, looking for more information, more facts to feed the little monster, my book.

When little specks started floating in front of my eyes, I decided to take a quick break with one of my favorite after-hours pastimes. I opened my office door to make sure that everyone was gone, then walked down the row of empty offices. The contents of a desk can provide insights on the soul of its occupants. Ellen's was perfectly arranged and contained nothing out of the ordinary. Her paper clips were organized by size in little tins that had once held expensive breath mints. Across the bullpen, Davy's desk drawers were filled with cigars, old invoices, some news clippings about himself, a couple of autographed baseballs, and a recent issue of *Playboy* featuring a centerfold who was born when I was in high school—a fact that squelched any desire her airbrushed breasts had stirred. I put the magazine back in its place and walked on.

Lillivale's neatly labeled folders were arranged alphabetically in his desk. But when I opened them, all I found were lunch receipts, a few pages of notes, and some photocopied articles. One of the folders held a thick stack of résumés and copies of letters he had written to other consulting firms looking for "new employment opportunities for an aggressive self-starter, a proven rainmaker in management consulting." Guys like Lillivale always kept their feelers out for a higher bidder.

Back in my office, I picked up the phone and pressed a pre-programmed button that dialed Laura's work number.

"DataTech."

"Laura Stride, please." The receptionist buzzed her, but no one answered. Then I remembered that she was planning to go out for a celebratory dinner with some people from work. After weeks of confusing signals from DataTech, Laura had finally been promoted to vice-president of operations; the news had made her more worried than happy. I hung up and called our home number.

"Laura. Hi. It's Larkin," I said after our message ended, never convinced that she would recognize my voice. "Hope you had a nice dinner. I'm going to work pretty late, so don't wait up. Love you. See you later. Bye."

156

I hung up and pressed another button. Mariah answered after about a dozen rings.

"Took you long enough. Were you in bed with another man?" I said.

"You must have the wrong number. I'm not that kind of girl."

"Hmm."

"Maybe if I got the right offer," Mariah said. I heard the clink of her Zippo.

"Meet me for coffee at Park's. I'll buy."

"I'm impressed."

"How about a romantic drive in the country?"

"It's dark and there's a foot of snow on the ground."

"We'll pretend," I said.

"I've got to finish up some stuff in the darkroom first."

"Eight?"

"Okay. I missed you today. Why didn't you call?"

"I've been in my lunar module writing fairy tales for corporate illiterati," I said.

"Did you just think of that?"

"No, I made it up a few weeks ago."

"Just checking. I thought you might be getting witty on me."

"Don't worry."

"How will I know it's you? I haven't seen you since Wednesday."

"I'll be the one with road maps for eyes," I said. "See you soon."

"Ciao," Mariah said, followed by the click of the receiver.

I worked on a brief conclusion. "To make your business grow, you may have to destroy it," I wrote, laughing out loud. What that meant was anyone's guess, but it had a certain ring to it, a doomy credibility. I hunched over the keyboard like a true desk jockey. "The world changes too fast to hold on to the old concepts of loyalty and honesty." I wondered what Davy would say when he got to this part. If he wanted some serious stuff, he had it.

After about an hour, I leaned back and rubbed my eyes. I still had some editing to do before I gave Davy the draft, but it could wait. I switched off my computer, put on my coat, and walked through the deserted office, turning off the coffee machine and the lights on the way out.

The square was crowded. Despite the bitter cold, people stopped to talk, to read posters, to listen to two blissed-out hippies play electric flutes in front of the Coop. I shoved my hands into my coat pockets and wrapped my scarf around my face as I walked on snow the color of ashtray sand. A line stretched into the street at Crème du Jour, expensive ice cream having replaced dope as Cambridge's most popular sin.

I saw a couple waiting patiently in line, the husband carrying a small child in a backpack harness that kept the kid's head high above his own. The child wore a bright red jumpsuit and stared right at me. I didn't recognize the father, a bearded man in a down jacket and woolen mittens. But when his wife turned toward him, I slid to a halt. Even beneath the dim streetlights, I could see it was Patina, older, but with the same half-smile I remembered from more than a decade before. I wondered what she was doing back here, but nothing surprised me anymore. In Cambridge, old acquaintances could never be forgotten, since they never seemed to leave. The line moved forward and I lost sight of Patina, but her child kept staring at me. If things had sorted out a little differently, this could have been my son, and it could have been me waiting for ice cream. I hurried on through the square.

I looked through the steamy glass window at Park's. Mariah sat at an orange plastic table, a coffee in front of her. She waved me inside.

"Hey. You got here fast," I said, sitting down. I put my hand on top of hers.

"I took the bus."

"Meet anyone?"

"No. Your hands are freezing," Mariah said. "Don't you have any gloves?"

"I don't like gloves. They make my fingers itch." I took a drink of Mariah's coffee. Cream and extra sugar.

"Well, you can't complain about being cold, then."

"It gives me something to talk about all winter." I stood up and took Mariah's heavy shearling coat down from a peg. "Come on. We're going for a drive, remember?"

"I thought you were kidding."

"No. I really want to get out of here for a little bit. Get some air."

"You okay?" Mariah watched me with a variation of the worried look Ellen had given me earlier in the office.

"Don't I look okay?" Why was everyone so concerned about me?

"You look a little crazed." Mariah stood up and took one last sip of coffee, then put her coat on. "But I like that in a man."

We left Park's and walked through the square toward the Crockett Company parking lot. Mariah reached over and tugged on my uncombed hair. "Looks like you got hit by lightning."

"It's been a long day." She slipped her hand into my overcoat pocket and gave my icy fingers a squeeze. I tried to push Patina out of my mind, but I kept seeing that kid's head peeking up over his father's shoulder like a periscope.

We drove along the river and turned at the Fresh Pond rotary, a traffic nightmare that reminded me of amateur night at the Pine Bluff Speedway. A Honda slid in front of me without signaling, as usual, since Boston drivers thought using the turn signal cost extra.

"Dickhead!" I hit the horn and edged around the Honda, then spun off at the exit to Lincoln.

Mariah shook her head. "We need to get you to relax. Have you considered having sex more often?"

"I thought you might recommend that, Dr. Callahan." I looked over and Mariah stuck her tongue out at me.

We raced down the salt-dusted road in silence, our faces lit by the glow of the dashboard. The trees on both sides were bare, their branches pale in the headlights. A few stars gave out a dim light as if they were farther away tonight. Looking at the frozen landscape, I recognized some familiar sights—an abandoned fruit stand, a farmhouse, a tilted barn. In college, I had driven the Chevelle down this road many nights when I needed to get away from Harvard. I downshifted into fourth gear and hit the gas, the Volvo lunging forward obediently.

"So what's bothering you?" Mariah took a cigarette from her purse and pushed in the dashboard lighter.

"I don't think I should tell you."

"I'm your friend. You have to tell me."

"Promise not to take it wrong?"

"Okay."

"I saw an old girlfriend in the Square," I said.

"Which one?"

"Patina."

"You told me about her. Wasn't she the one who read Anaïs Nin out loud to you?" The lighter popped out and Mariah lit her cigarette.

"Right. That one."

"I don't know why you thought I'd be upset by your old loves. I don't have any right to be jealous."

"I know. I know," I said. Lately, Mariah kept making it clear that we had no responsibilities to each other, that we were just friends who made love a lot. "It's just that it always throws me for a loop when I run into old girlfriends."

"I'll say. Did you talk to her?"

"No. She was with her husband and kid."

"Surprised?"

"I guess."

"Praying mantises eat their lovers when they're done screwing," Mariah said, always ready with a nature fact. "Know why?"

"Do tell."

"So they never have to run into them years later at a cocktail party."

We came to a section of road where the trees intertwined above us in a gray tunnel. A low hump of plowed snow stretched along both sides of the road. Then the woods gave way to ice-crusted fields broken by low stone fences, farms that reminded me of Arkansas. We passed the neon Schlitz sign in the window of the Willow Pond Kitchen, a roadhouse where Patina and I used to get boiled lobsters for three dollars, beers in frosted mugs for a quarter. I hadn't been there in years.

"Patina and I drove out this way sometimes."

"Is that why you wanted to come here?"

"I guess so."

"Tell me more about Patina."

"When I first met her I thought she was a chair."

"What?"

"It was dark and she was kind of . . ."

"Upholstered?"

"Voluptuous. We were together for most of my freshman year. She left me for her painting instructor."

"That's an old story," Mariah said. "I used to sleep with the guy who taught my photography workshop. I guess teaching is a good way for arty guys to get laid."

"Patina was the first woman I ever slept with."

"Anything special about it?"

"She liked to do it outside."

"Like in public?"

"No. Just outside," I said. We drove past a park with open fields where colonial troops had marched. In one, I saw another familiar landmark, a large beech tree that stood alone in the middle of a pasture, its branches bent all the way to the ground.

"As a matter of fact, we did it in that field once. There. Under that tree." I pointed. The spring night had smelled of honey-suckle and worms. Patina was naked, her arms around the tree trunk. I stood behind her and held on tight. Her skin looked pale as paper in the moonlight, we were hidden from the road by the thick wall of leaves. A swelling chorus of crickets accom-panied us as we slapped together like two hands in the dark.

Mariah grabbed the wheel. "Pull over." We swerved into an unplowed parking lot. I hit the brakes and the Volvo fishtailed a little.

"Are you nuts?"

"Now turn around."

"What?"

"Turn around," Mariah insisted.

I put the Volvo in reverse and did a sloppy three-point turn.

"Where was that tree you were talking about?"

"Back a little bit."

"Pull down here," she said. I turned on a narrow road that bisected the field. Past a barbed-wire fence and about twenty yards of unbroken snow, I could see the beech lit up like a billboard in the Volvo's headlights. I parked to the side of the snowy lane.

"You think too much about this Patina," Mariah said. She took off her coat and threw it in the backseat, then pulled off her shoes, socks, pants, and underwear in quick succession, leav-ing only a sweater. "I'm going to get her out of your system."

"Wait a minute," I said. "People drive down this road a lot." I looked in the rearview mirror.

"Then we'll have to hurry." Mariah slipped her hands beneath my jacket and unfastened my belt in one deft motion. I lifted up and she pulled off my pants and shorts. She backed against the passenger door and kicked her legs out in front, knees pointing to the roof.

"Go on. Pretend I'm Patina."

I climbed forward awkwardly. Making love in the backseat of a car had always been a challenge, but the front seat required the grace of an Olympic gymnast. When I lay heavily on top of Mariah I nearly impaled my thigh on the gear shift. The Volvo's clever Swedish engineers hadn't considered this particular driving situation.

Mariah took my hand and moved it between her legs, where I felt her on my fingers like warm lake water. I pulled her close, kissed her, then slid inside her.

"You've got to look over there," she said, squirming beneath me.

"What?"

"Watch the tree." She turned my head to the side with her hand and I looked out the windshield at the tree, the gray branches that had been covered with leaves on a spring evening years earlier. Then I thought about the Patina I had seen tonight, how happy she looked as she stood in line for ice cream with her family. I began to turn soft.

"Oh no you don't," Mariah said. "Think about screwing her. Did she like it?"

"Yes," I said. I shuddered a little as Mariah pushed against me in a rhythm echoed by the squeaking seat. Her skin clung to the cool leather.

"Think about the first time you ever had her, about how good it felt to be inside a woman."

"Yes. I remember." I saw Patina's room, lit only by a candle on an orange crate. We had grappled on the futon for hours, inept and fearless.

"Remember how soft she felt, about how much you loved to touch her," Mariah said, slipping my hand beneath her sweater. She gasped as I touched her nipple. The vent blew hot air in my face.

"Tell Patina you love her," Mariah said between clenched teeth.

"I love you, Mariah," I said, pushing deep inside her. She gave a small cry and spread her legs further, one foot up on the dashboard.

"No. Say it. Say her name." Mariah's voice turned insistent and her accent disappeared.

"Patina."

"Say it again."

"Patina."

"Again."

"Patina," I said, and Mariah shook hard and bit my chest. I put both hands beneath her, pulled her close, and thought of Patina. Mariah screamed and her foot slipped onto the steering wheel. The horn blared out into the quiet field, then stopped.

For a long time, we lay sprawled across the front seat as if in a scene from a driver's ed film. When I opened my eyes, headlights beamed through the steamy back window. A car had stopped about ten yards behind us and trained a light on the Volvo, shining on the license plate, then roving through the back window, fortunately opaque from our breathing. I slipped out of Mariah and scrambled into the driver's seat, feeling around for my pants.

"Mariah," I said, giving her a shake. "We better get going." She woke as I turned the key in the ignition.

"Are we home yet?"

"Not quite. Here's your pants." I reached down and tossed them into her lap.

"What's wrong?"

"There's a cop behind us."

"We haven't done anything."

"We should probably get going. I'm sure there's some kind of law against this in Lincoln," I said, shifting into first. I pulled back onto the road as Mariah put on her clothes.

"You sure knocked me out. You must have had it bad for her."

"I made love to you, not her," I said. As I picked up speed on the narrow lane, the police car followed close behind us, its headlights haloed in the cold air.

164

"It's okay. I wanted you to do it to her. Now you've gotten rid of her for good."

"I guess so."

"Every time you see that field, you can think about me instead."

"That's for sure," I said.

I looked in the mirror and watched the police car turn onto a side road. Mariah leaned over and kissed me on the neck.

"Sorry I bit you," she said.

"I didn't mind."

"Any other landmarks along memory lane you want to tell me about?"

"No, I think that's about all the sightseeing I can handle."

"Then take me home. My legs are sore and I have to pee." Mariah shivered, then reached over and turned up the heat.

"Home it is," I said.

12

CAPE COD

I REACHED into the backseat of the Volvo and pawed around in the grocery bags. The champagne would be warm but I decided to open it anyway. We were stuck in traffic on the Southeast Expressway, the two-lane stretch of rusting infrastructure that led down to Cape Cod. In the passenger's seat, Laura stared out the window at the sea of taillights ahead of us. She jumped a little when I popped the cork from a bottle that my wine advisor had described as light and playful. It would be nice if this weekend could be light and playful too.

"Why're you opening that now?"

"To celebrate."

"Celebrate what?" Laura said.

"Your promotion. Me finishing my book."

"I don't feel like celebrating. But you go ahead."

I tried another approach. "To the weekend." I poured two plastic cups full of champagne.

"No, thanks."

"Come on." Laura took her glass and I drank a deep swallow from mine.

"You're being silly. You could get arrested for drinking and driving."

"We've been stuck here for an hour. They can't arrest you for drinking and parking."

"I still think you should wait."

"Lighten up a little."

Laura said nothing. She hated being told to relax; it made her more nervous. The only thing that made Laura relax was a hot bath, and we were miles from one of those. I finished my glass while she was still sipping at hers.

"What's the matter?" I said. "I thought things were going better at work."

"Robert quit today," she said, quietly. I couldn't imagine that this made any difference now that Laura had beat him out for the promotion.

"That's a surprise."

"A disaster's more like it." Laura had a way of finding clouds in every silver lining.

"Wait a minute. I thought you didn't like him."

"I don't. It's just that he left without giving any notice."

"I'm sure you can find someone else for the job. Hank told me the guy was a real lightweight."

"Robert joined *Informatics*." Laura pronounced the name of her company's biggest competitor like an infectious disease. "He took a copy of our customer database with him." I looked over and realized that Laura's glass shook a little in her hand.

"That sounds bad. Can't you sue him or something?"

"It would take years to settle, and by then it'll be too late."

"I'm sorry, honey."

"I know you don't like it when I talk about work, but I'm really upset. It's hard to act cheerful when I know Robert's taking all our customers to New York."

"I'm sure it'll turn out okay." One glass of warm champagne and I almost giggled when I imagined thousands of tiny businesspeople screaming inside Robert's briefcase as he boarded the shuttle.

"Maybe," she said, not so sure. The traffic budged a little and we crept forward past three mammoth smokestacks that sent dirty clouds billowing into the sky.

Given Laura's gloomy mood, I didn't bother to mention my piece of good news. After our morning planning meeting, Davy had slid an envelope slowly across the conference table as if it might crawl away. Inside was a check for twenty thousand dollars, my share of the advance from Briefcase Press. Its Japanese subsidiary was interested in a translation, and there was even talk of a video series featuring interviews with top executives.

Laura shifted restlessly in her seat, the site of Mariah's sexual Olympics the week before. I could hardly look at the seat without pornographic flashbacks of Mariah's legs wrapped around my back as she ground away any memories of Patina. I hadn't heard from Mariah all week and hadn't called her either, ashamed, I guess, of what we had done on the snowy back road.

The traffic started moving again and we drove south. Hank had loaned us his summer house in Orleans for the weekend, a nice place near Nauset Beach with a view of the ocean. I never liked the Cape during the summer, when tourists in tan shorts crawled over it like ants on a doughnut. In winter, the good restaurants closed down and the tourists went only as far as Boston. Only the sullen natives remained, with their pickup trucks and drinking problems, not all that different from my relatives back in Pine Bluff except for the hard-edged Yankee names—Caleb, Freeman, Queequeg.

When we crossed the Bourne Bridge, traffic began to thin out a little. I drank another glass of warm champagne. Laura said nothing. I had to find some way to break her out of her funk, so I turned on the radio. Hyperactive Portuguese pop songs didn't succeed in amusing her, nor did an all-talk AM program about how the government controlled people with radio waves. Finally I turned on a classic hits station and sang along to a hippie anthem by the Youngbloods.

"Come on, people now, smile on your brother . . ." I sang off key, without enthusiasm. During the Summer of Love, I was growing up in Arkansas, my hair in a crew cut. We had only one group of counterculture types in Pine Bluff, three longhairs who lived with their tuber-breasted wives on a grubby commune that everyone called the Funny Farm.

"Everybody get together, try and love one another right now . . ." Laura started to smile. She even hummed along on a verse. I held out hope for the weekend.

After a half hour, Laura got tired and curled up in her seat, leaning against the window. Soon she was sound asleep. When I reached over to lock her door, I touched her face, my finger gently tracing the curve of her cheekbone, the soft hollow of her cheek, the hard line of her jaw as she ground her teeth slowly in her sleep. I moved my hand back to the steering wheel and piloted us down the dark highway.

The Cape in winter was a lonely place. The Volvo rushed past power lines and underbrush dusted with blowing sand that made the landscape lunar. Primeval birds' nests the size of small dog houses topped every electric pole. A sixteen-wheeler emerged from a silvery cloud of fog ahead and then raced by like a phantom vehicle in a trucker song.

My worries started acting up, set loose by the eerie road. Why hadn't I heard from Mariah all week? I hadn't called her either, but what of it? Would our accidental meeting on a bus end with a vigorous screwing in a car? I liked our time together, what we said and did together. It was a relief to be away from the Crockett Company, to put some miles between me and the unbearable whiteness of Cambridge. But I didn't want to be away from Mariah, not even for a weekend, and certainly not for good.

I took the turnoff to Orleans and immediately got lost. All the roads looked the same, and locals must have bent most of the street signs around to amuse themselves. Finally I drove past a landmark I remembered, a bar called the Foredeck that looked like a pirate ship with colored lights shining from every porthole. I thought about waking Laura to see if she wanted to stop for something to eat, but the wind had picked up. When I opened the window a crack the air felt like snow. From our other visits,

I knew that Hank's house was in the middle of nowhere, and I wanted to get there before a storm hit. I turned and drove down a winding road, through low patches of fog that rose like steam.

I tried not to think about escaped convicts, drunken locals, and all manner of psychopaths who might be lurking by the side of the road. I had driven down enough lonely stretches at night to recognize the telltale tingling on my forearms that meant I was spooked by the wind and the rabbits that darted off into the underbrush.

I reached over and shook Laura but she slumped away from me. Usually she couldn't sleep in the car, but she had been out for at least an hour. I shook her harder. She didn't move. Her shoulder felt cold through her blouse and I couldn't tell whether she was breathing. I thought of brain clots. Or an overdose of the Valium she took sometimes to relax. I slammed on the brakes and the Volvo skidded to a halt.

"Laura!" I shouted. No response.

"Wake up!" I screamed, inches from her ear.

Her arm moved beneath my hand.

"Larkin? What time is it?" she said at half speed, then sat up and rubbed her eyes. "Are we there yet?"

"No, we're about half a mile from Hank's place. Are you okay? You were really out of it."

"Yeah, I'm fine. Just sleepy, I guess."

"Are you sure?"

"I'm fine. I shouldn't have had that champagne," she said. "You know how I get."

"You had me worried." I put the car in gear and sprayed gravel behind us. "It was dark and you hadn't said anything in almost an hour. I couldn't tell what was . . ."

"It's okay, Larkin," she said, awake now. "I'm fine. You don't need to get all worked up. I can take care of myself."

"I know that."

"Then don't make me feel bad. I just fell asleep in the car."

"It's not a big deal." I spoke a little too quickly. "I was just worried about you." I looked over at the passenger seat and saw Mariah pushing against me, her eyes closed, her teeth clenched.

Laura didn't say anything, just stared out the window. When I worried about her, she got angry, as if my concern made her weaker.

"You know I can't drink like you can," she said when I took the final turn toward the house. According to the dashboard clock, it was a little after ten. The drive had taken us about twice as long as it should have.

"I know," I said. "I was just worried, okay? Anyway, we're here now."

We pulled into Hank's driveway and the headlights lit up a pile of lawn furniture covered with a plastic tarp. The wind rolled a couple of green garbage cans around on the dead lawn. Behind a thin row of trees, I could see the dark house, windows splattered with rain.

"Hank said he left a set of keys in the shed where he keeps the trashcans," Laura said. I wondered how the cans had ended up on the lawn.

"You wait here and I'll go check for the keys," I said.

"I'll come with you."

"No. I need you to stay here and keep the car running. I forgot to bring a flashlight."

"Why're you being so strange?"

"I'm not. I just want to make sure we can get in."

"You don't need to be afraid," Laura said. "There's nothing out there."

"I know that," I said. "Just let me get the keys."

I walked toward the house as the wind whistled across the lawn and blew salty rain in my face. The ocean was churned up by the storm and I could hear waves slapping on the rocky shore. The Volvo's headlights projected a gigantic version of me on the side of the house and my shadow grew smaller with every step. It was a contemporary place with lots of angles, a steep roof, and a wall of glass facing the water. I noticed that the screen had blown off one of the upstairs windows. Maybe someone had broken in and was living there now, thinking that no summer people would be back for months.

I lifted the hinged lid of the garbage shed and reached inside, wishing for a flashlight. I ran my fingertips along the back of the shed and groped for the keys. The nail was bare; the keys must have fallen off. I bent into the shed the way Harvard Square bums leaned into dumpsters. Halfway inside now, I smelled the faint musk of last summer's lobsters, oyster shells, and beer bottles. I thought I heard footsteps, someone creeping out of the woods. Laura would honk if she saw anything strange.

I stood up quickly and scraped my head on the lid. A few yards off, one of the trashcans banged against a tree, over and over.

It's not the woods you need to be afraid of.

"I know that," I snapped, rubbing my head. On a night like this, I didn't need an ancestor chiming in with advice. The Cape had me nervous enough. I had become rarefied as a hothouse flower, a city boy no pioneer would claim as kin.

Laura rolled down her window. "Larkin. What is it?"

"What?" I yelled at the headlights.

"What did you say?"

"I can't find the keys. I hit my head." I touched the spot with two fingers. It hurt but didn't seem to be bleeding.

"Hank said the keys were on a nail," she shouted over the car. "Just . . . look . . . for . . . the nail!"

I turned and leaned into the shed again.

"Fuck this," I whispered softly to myself, feeling around in the dirt. I had just about given up when my fingers brushed against the cold metal key ring, which I pulled out of the dirt like a clam. Thanks a million, Hank. Next time just bury the keys on the beach somewhere.

I held the rusted key ring overhead and took a victory bow. There was no applause, just silence as Laura shut off the Volvo.

Inside the house, I turned on every switch, until the lights blazed in the kitchen, from under the eaves, on poles in the backyard. Laura banged through the door with her suitcase and two bags of groceries.

"I'll get the rest," I said. Halfway to the car, I stopped and wondered what would happen if I started up the Volvo and drove back to Watertown, to Mariah. Maybe Laura knew I was seeing someone else. That might explain a lot.

In the kitchen, Laura was already hiding the groceries. She opened cabinets, slammed drawers, folded the paper bags and shoved them under the sink.

"Why don't you leave everything alone?" she said. "Just let me do it." The irritation in her voice reminded me of all the other couples I had seen in Harvard Square over the years. They argued in the aisles of kitchen supplies at Crate & Barrel. Huddled red-eyed and sniffling in line at the Brattle Theater, they tried to sort things out, as if emotions were socks.

"It's cold in here," I said. "I'll get the heat going." I picked up our suitcases and climbed the wide staircase at the center of the house. An angry Laura was like a washing machine; she had to run through several cycles before everything came clean. Right now, she was still agitated, and I knew the best thing for me to do was to stay far away from her, which wasn't easy in Hank's house. It was built in the sixties, when houses were supposed to be as open and free as the people who lived in them. The upstairs rooms faced the empty middle of the house, where the staircase rose in a slow spiral.

The corner study gave some semblance of privacy. Hank had traveled a lot, and the rooms upstairs were decorated with carved masks from Mexico, drums and ceremonial spears from Africa. With each gust of wind, cold air slipped past the uninsulated windowsills. I turned the thermostat up to eighty and heard a distant whoosh as the gas furnace kicked in. It would take hours for the house to warm up on this cold night.

I leaned against the railing on the landing and watched Laura in the kitchen. She made sure our weekend supplies were stored away, checked the closets. When we first met, I admired how organized she was. I had craved order then. Now I just wanted to have a quiet, relaxing weekend without a lot of arguing. I wanted to drink a few beers and read magazines, maybe go someplace nice for dinner the next night.

I carried our suitcases into one of the bedrooms and turned on the nightstand lamps. Hank was a reader; books were stacked everywhere. I hadn't read a real novel in years. I looked around for a paperback, then chose one with its pages splayed and faded from long afternoons on the beach. It looked kind of interesting. I walked back into the study and pulled away the metal screen of the fireplace, then reached up and opened the flue.

I stacked three pieces of firewood over some kindling, tore out a few pages of the book, wadded them up, and stuffed them underneath. I lit a match and touched it to the dry pages, then tossed the rest of the book on top. The wood smoldered for a minute, then caught and sent a pale orange light over the study. I lay down on an old Oriental rug next to the fireplace and watched the fire grow into a crackling blaze. I closed my eyes and basked in the roasting words as the paperback turned to ashes.

A few minutes later, Laura clicked off the kitchen lights. I heard her walk upstairs, the space between her steps so familiar I could pick her walk out of a thousand. She came into the study and sat down on the hearth.

"It looks like you've made yourself right at home," she said.

"I thought a fire might be nice."

"It is. Thanks for making it."

"Thanks for putting the groceries away." At this rate, we'd be sending each other memos soon.

She tugged the mesh fireplace screen closed. "It was easy."

"I know you're tired," I said, "but I want to apologize for whatever I did in the car."

"You didn't do anything. I just have a lot on my mind, that's all. I'm sorry," she said. Now we both felt thankful and sorry. I reached over and touched the warm, smooth skin of her ankle. Maybe we would make love tonight.

"Got any plans for tomorrow?"

"I want to get up early and walk on the beach," Laura said.

I wondered whether she wanted me to come along. "It's supposed to be a good day."

"Coming to bed soon?" she asked.

"I'm going to stay here for a little bit and read."

"That's fine. I'm going to take a bath first."

"Good night," I said. So much for making love.

She leaned over to kiss me on the forehead, then backed away and stared at me hard for a moment. I wondered what I looked like to her, whether I matched the man she thought she had married. Laura walked down the hall to the bathroom. I lay back on the rug and listened to her running water in the tub, pictured her swirling a washcloth between her legs. The water made a soothing, distant roar that lulled me to sleep.

I woke on the floor hours later, the house dark and the fire out. My mind was dull and I wasn't sure exactly how long I had been asleep or even where I was. Outside, someone pounded a fist against the side of the house. Who would be out this late on a rainy night, miles from the main road? Rain splashed against the windows and the wind howled in the chimney. The pounding started again—much louder now. It could have been someone who needed help. But then again, it could have been anyone.

Whoever was banging on the house wanted in right now. I felt along the ground for a weapon, maybe a piece of wood or a fireplace poker, but I couldn't find one. I stood and took down an African spear, one of Hank's souvenirs. It was about five feet long, and its heavy wooden shaft ended with a sharpened triangle of steel that gleamed in the gray light.

I walked toward the door with the spear over my shoulder, when the pounding started again. I turned the door handle slowly but the wind hurled the door open. Rain blew in.

"Whoever you are, get the fuck away from here. Now!" I tried to sound threatening, but my voice cracked and my heart beat a galloping rhythm that made me dizzy. I couldn't take things like this anymore.

The pounding started again. Someone stood just outside the front door, slapping a hand against the house. And whoever it was wasn't going away.

"Get out of here!" I screamed. No answer.

The hallway light went on and I turned, spear in hand.

"Larkin!" Laura stood in the hallway, her bathrobe open.

"Get back in the bedroom! There's someone out there."

"Who?"

"I don't know. Someone. A robber. I don't know. Just get back."

Instead, Laura walked past me into the study. Christ. I thought of all the terrible stories I had read in the newspaper— husbands forced to watch while convicts raped their wives for hours, heavy-metal cults that made human sacrifices to Satan.

Laura flipped a wall switch, and floodlights lit the front yard. I couldn't see anything but rain and a couple of evergreens. I wondered who hid behind the trees, waiting for us to go to sleep again. The wind began to blow harder, and the trees rippled and thrashed.

"Wait!" I pointed my spear at the door, ready to strike, to protect my wife like a true son of the pioneers.

A broken shutter swung on one hinge and banged against the side of the house.

"Is that what you heard?"

I stared outside and let my spear dip slowly to the ground.

"Come to bed. It's late," Laura said. "You can fix the shutter for Hank in the morning."

"I'll be there in a bit," I said. She was being nice and not making a big fuss, but I knew that my ridiculous spear-toting helped convince her that men were less evolved than women. She was probably right.

Laura turned and walked down the hall to the bedroom. I closed the door and put the spear back on the study wall, where it became a decoration again. With the lights off, I stretched out on the floor. The shutter slapped against the wall, triumphant, loud as a rifle shot, as I lay on the faded rug, wide awake.

13
SORTING THINGS OUT

I WAS READY to go out Saturday night even if it meant driving all the way to Provincetown to find a restaurant. In the bedroom, I put on the new shirt Laura had given me for Christmas, and a tie, a ridiculous formality on the Cape, where everyone wore lumberjack clothes. Seven-thirty found me dressed, staring out the window at the rain. I looked at my watch again. Most restaurants closed at nine during the off-season. Laura walked in and sat down on the bed, her face still flushed from a hot bath. Her wet hair left dark patches on the shoulders of her bathrobe.

"I don't want to go out," she said. I tried to find some explanation on her face but she was inscrutable.

"I guess we could make dinner here if you want," I said. "Do you feel okay?"

"I feel fine. I just don't want to go out, that's all."

"Then we won't."

Laura had been quiet since we got to Hank's. We had been sending signals back and forth all day like the semaphore flashes of ships lost in a fog. She spent most of the afternoon walking on the beach by herself. I decided not to argue about dinner, even though I thought getting out of the house might do us good. I wanted to have a nice dinner with a bottle of wine, to try to salvage what was left of the weekend.

"Don't act hurt, Larkin. It's not the end of the world if we don't go out tonight."

I took off my good shirt and put on the frayed button-down I'd been wearing all day. "What do you mean? I'm just changing clothes."

"That's just it. You never say anything. Why don't you just come right out and tell me what's on your mind?"

"Nothing," I said. "There's nothing on my mind. You're the one who's been acting strange."

"We've got something to talk about. It's time we started being honest with each other." The floor sank beneath me for a split second. I stopped buttoning.

"What do you mean?" I sat on a wooden chair facing the bed and took a deep breath, waiting for Laura to tell me she knew about Mariah.

"I'm going to New York," she said.

"To get Robert? Don't you think you'd better let a lawyer or the police handle something like that?"

"Not because of Robert. DataTech's moving the operations group to the New York office next month."

"You mean you're going to take the shuttle every day? If they make you do that, they better pay you more."

"No, you don't understand. I'm going to live there."

I walked to the other side of the bedroom and looked back at Laura. "That means you're leaving Boston?"

"Right."

"That means you're leaving me?"

"Not necessarily."

My mind raced as I tried to figure out what Laura meant. "Not necessarily? We're married, remember. We live in Watertown. If you leave and go to New York by yourself, we won't be together, and we won't be married. As far as I can tell."

Laura raised one hand, then lowered it to her lap again. "I knew you'd take this and turn it into something else."

"Then explain." I circled slowly around the edge of the bedroom, pausing in the corner.

Laura looked right at me. "Every night is just like this. We just go to restaurants. We never talk about anything."

"I don't know what you mean," I said, although I had a pretty good idea. I hadn't been quite as clever about sneaking out to see Mariah as I thought. Laura would drop the bomb any minute.

"I need to think some things through without you around. To figure things out. I think I deserve that."

"You do. But we hardly see each other anyway. Maybe a couple hours a day. I don't think living in different states is going to bring us closer." I opened and closed my fists, squeezing invisible rubber balls to keep calm. I was glad I hadn't had a drink.

"I have to report for work in New York next month. I've decided that I'm going, and there's nothing you can do to change my mind. I think I'll be happier."

"How can you just sit there and tell me that you're leaving without even trying to work things out? It doesn't make sense!"

Laura closed her eyes. "Don't scream at me, Larkin. Besides, you tell me: Do you really want to work things out? You don't have to answer now, just think about it."

"Of course I do, I'm your husband. . . ."

"That's no reason to stay together."

"Really? I think being married is a pretty damn good reason why two people should stay together. We had this talk a long time ago, remember? The counseling sessions with the minister, the guy with the funny collar who kept trying to look down your dress?"

Laura turned away. "You're so insulting to me."

I looked out the window at the ocean, the water and sky merging into a dark blue wall with a few dim stars attached. I took a deep breath. "When we get home maybe we should go

see someone. A therapist or something." This sounded like the
right thing to say, even though I never liked talking to strangers,
particularly if I had to pay them a lot of money to listen.

"I'm not going home with you tomorrow," she said.

"Wait a minute. Don't you have to get back for work on
Monday?"

"I called Kendra this morning. She's going to pick me up
tomorrow afternoon. I'm moving back into their place in Cambridge until I go to New York." She said this last part as if she
were telling me she had signed up for a pottery class.

I slapped my hand against the wall. "You've got to be kidding.
You can't just make a decision like that without talking about
it. It's not right. Not right!"

Laura rolled her eyes. "You're getting angry," she said. "I
knew you would, but you don't have anything to be mad about.
I just need some time away from you. I feel like I can't breathe
when you're around."

"If you loved me you wouldn't be doing this."

"I don't have much of a choice."

"Of course you do. Everyone has choices. It's making them
that's the hard part."

"I've made mine. I think it's time for us to take a look at how
we're really living."

"That's complete bullshit." I stood up and clomped around
the room in my boots, playing the part of angry husband to the
hilt. "We're married. We can't just run away from each other.
We either work it out or get divorced. Do you want a divorce?
Is that what you're saying?"

"I don't know. It's not fair to ask me that now. Maybe we'll
get back together and be closer. Maybe we won't. I don't know."

I sat down on the bed next to Laura and put my hand on her
shoulder. "Things have been bad lately. And I'm sorry."

She pulled away. "Don't touch me now. You're all worked
up. Kendra told me I should have waited until tomorrow to tell
you."

"So she could enjoy this little scene too?" I pictured Kendra's self-righteous smile as I confirmed her theories about the impossibility of marriage.

"No, just in case you lost your temper."

"I'm not going to hit you. I haven't ever hit you." I knew that it wasn't out of the question, though. My mind raced and my voice shook a little as I stumbled through the narrow corridors of our argument, looking for some way out. "You just caught me by surprise. Didn't you think I might be a little upset by your *plans*? What the fuck is wrong with you!"

Laura backed away as if I had pointed a gun at her. "If you don't stop yelling I'm going to call the police."

"Fine. Fine. Call the police. Call your friends. Call the *Globe*."

"You're being ridiculous. You're the one who's turning this bad instead of trying to change things for the better, to move ahead," Laura said.

"To move to New York, you mean. You know I hate New York."

"You don't like Boston much either."

"That's not true." In fact, it was true. But mostly I hated fights like this one, freighted with too much emotional algebra.

"All I want is a chance to grow, and you're acting like I'm doing something wrong. Like seeing someone else or something."

"Well. Are you?" I looked at her eyes, which told me nothing.

"No."

"Then why do you want to get away from me so badly? Tell me." I stood in front of her as she sat at the end of the bed, her bathrobe falling open to reveal a white breast shuddering gently. The room started to close in, and Hank's collection of tribal masks stared down from the walls like the cast of *Zulu*. If Laura knew about Mariah, then she was holding it back like a trump card.

"I told you already," she said. "I'm not happy. I don't like the way we are together anymore. I'm just staying the same with you now. It's like we're in suspended animation. This promotion's important to me."

"It's been a tough few months." Now that yelling hadn't worked, I tried another approach, squatting on the floor in what I thought was a nonthreatening posture. But I wasn't a Gandhi, I was a Stride.

"You can't talk me out of this."

"I'm not trying to," I said. "You're right. I think we both have some choices to make, but we need to make them together. Let me tell you something, then I'll leave you alone."

Laura nodded and tightened the robe around her.

I stood up and started talking, not knowing what I would say. "I was at the bus stop a few months ago. It was a normal day. Fall. Nice sunset. And then something strange happened that made me realize the world wasn't as simple as it seemed." I stopped for a moment, wondering if I should go on and confess about Mariah.

"I have no idea what you're saying." Laura liked stories that cut to the chase.

"I'm not saying anything," I said. "I'm just telling you a story about being at the bus stop. It would have been easy to take another bus and not come home. I could have ended up in Belmont. In Allston. In Kenmore Square. But I didn't. I got on the bus and came home to you."

Laura laughed and shook her wet hair. "I'm glad you know your public transportation so well."

"You don't get it, do you?"

"Get what? Your story about the bus? No. I don't get it."

"What I'm saying is that sometimes I don't want to get on the right bus."

"Oh, *now* I get it." Laura said. "Honestly, you have the most complicated way of saying absolutely nothing."

"What I mean is, there are any number of ways we could decide to leave each other. I could move back to Arkansas. You could move to New York. We could go anywhere and not even look back." Now that I had decided not to say anything about Mariah, I rallied behind my confusing homily.

"I'm not sure I want to, Larkin. And I'm not convinced you do either. I don't know if people should stay together forever. We'll just have to see."

She had a point there. I got up from the floor and opened my suitcase, throwing in a shirt, a magazine, the few things I had taken out during the day. I looked around the room. Laura faced the window and fiddled with the belt of her robe.

"We have more to talk about," I said, "but I don't feel like doing it now. Not here. I can't believe you didn't tell me about moving to New York earlier. You must have known for weeks."

"Don't start feeling sorry for yourself."

"We're supposed to be able to put up with bad times, with the rough spots. For better or for worse, remember? I know I'm not the easiest person to get along with. I made a lot of mistakes. I admit it." I tossed in a pair of shoes and closed the suitcase, then realized all I had left to do was leave. So I kept talking.

"I love you, Laura. I know I do," I said, the words hollow. What I really knew was that I didn't want to be alone again like back in Kansas City. "We've got some problems to work out. I'm willing to try, but I don't think we can if you move in with Kendra and Tammy. They told you not to marry me in the first place, remember?"

"I can make up my own mind," she said, "and don't say anything about my friends. At least they're supportive."

Taking the first step toward the door seemed impossible. I could have stayed the night and waited for Kendra to come pick Laura up, but I couldn't imagine anything more pathetic than waiting around for radical lesbians to repossess my wife. I looked out the window and watched the flickering lights from a fishing boat off in the distance. I thought of a cabin below the waterline. There would be a bunk, a table, a hotplate. The smell of coffee, bacon, and cold salt air.

"It's just not right to run off," I said, still hoping I could convince her to change her mind. The idea of her actually leaving scared me. It scared me a lot. "Rabbits, dogs, cattle—they go off in the bushes when they're hurt," I said. "But people are supposed to stick together. Maybe if we both took time off from work . . ."

"I'm still behind from the holidays. I can't afford to take any more time off."

"Why not? We can do whatever we want. We've got money. We're smart and we're still young. We can quit our jobs and do something else. Make some changes."

"I think there are some things about you that aren't going to change much," she said.

"Maybe. Maybe not. But you're not going to find out by running away." Anger crept up the back of my throat again. "I'm sick of DataTech, of the Crockett Company, of . . . of dry cleaning. We never used to be like this."

"Shut up, Larkin. You don't know what you're talking about. I'm just doing what I have to. You have to respect that."

"Fine, then. Be alone. Get in touch with your feelings. Pretty soon you'll be getting in touch with your lawyer. Then you can find another man and you can both get in touch with each other. Except you don't like to be touched."

"Don't start. You have no right to . . ."

"To what?" I picked up my suitcase from the bed and slammed it down on the floor. "To not go along with your little plan? Everything is always on your terms. You don't feel affectionate, so we don't make love much. You can't relax, so we never do normal things together. Like go bowling. Or drive out to the country on Sundays."

"Do you honestly think more bowling would help our marriage?"

"That's not what I mean."

"Then what do you mean, Larkin?"

"Nothing. All I know is that in my heart I don't think this is right." I put on my overcoat and picked up my suitcase.

"I don't think you're in any position to tell me what's right and what's wrong," Laura said softly. It was true, and as she looked up at me I checked her eyes for any sign that she knew about Mariah, but found none.

I paused for a minute, wondering whether I should reconsider and tell her. It had a simple, slash-and-burn appeal. "I guess I'll see you before you go," I said, not sure that this was really happening. I walked slowly across the room and waited for her to say something to stop me.

I put my hand on the door. "Well. Good-bye."

"Good-bye," Laura said, turning toward me. I wished that just once she would let down her guard. But I could see that she wasn't about to cry, to yell. She was just waiting for me to leave.

I walked out to the hallway and past the study, where the shameful spear hung over the fireplace. The night before may have been the last straw, but I knew there was more to it than that. If Laura had decided to go to New York, it was after careful deliberation—at work, at home on late evenings when I was with Mariah, in the bathtub on Saturday afternoons while I was supposed to be at the office.

Downstairs, I walked through the kitchen to the back door. I took Hank's keys out of my pocket and shoved them down into the garbage disposal. I slammed the door on my way out.

Top Shelf had tried to strangle my father one night as they watched TV, sneaking up behind him with a length of knitting yarn for a garrote. My father had asked her to bring him a beer. He managed to break loose, but for weeks an angry purple bruise circled his neck. Top Shelf offered no explanation other than that he had pissed her off. They still loved each other after the attack, maybe even more than before.

I drove down the dark road, leaving the Cape. With every mile I became more convinced that Laura was seeing another man. It made perfect sense. She knew I was cheating on her, and while I was off screwing Mariah, Laura had been with someone else, probably some creep from work. Horny telemarketers were always putting the moves on her. At company gatherings they sidled up to Laura, their buxom boss. I pictured her straddling Jerry Klepner, the bearded jazz casualty I had talked to at Robert's party. Jerry's hands reached up, eager to cup her full breasts. His goatee twitched slightly, as if he were about to bite into a ripe peach. He took her hand, licked it, stopped to run his tongue around her wedding band. Then they both laughed.

"God damn it!" I slapped my hand against the dashboard, and the Volvo swerved a little, then straightened out. But my suspicions were unfounded; Laura was too honest to sleep with anyone else.

I drove through the deserted center of Orleans and turned onto the empty highway back to Boston. Then I had another idea. Maybe it wasn't a man. Even though she told me she had roomed with Tammy and Kendra just out of convenience—the apartment was cheap, an easy commute to downtown—I always wondered if they had managed to tempt her into bed. I pictured Tammy, the scrawny socialist, naked but for her steel-toed workboots. She knelt in front of Laura, smiled up at her, stroked her with greasy cab-driver fingers. Hungry, she kissed Laura's thighs and moved farther and farther up her pale, soft legs. . . .

"Stop it!" I pulled off the road and skidded to a halt in front of the Windjammer, a motel with peeling paint, closed for the season. A phone booth at the end of the gravel parking lot glowed as if it had just landed from another planet. The Volvo's tires spun. I put on the brakes a little late and skidded to the left, smashing into the phone booth so hard I almost knocked it over. I backed away, shut off the engine, and got out. When I ran my hand along the fender I felt a small dent.

"Shit." Another bill from the auto body place.

I stepped inside the wobbly phone booth and my feet crunched on shattered glass. When I called Hank's number, the operator came on to tell me that three minutes cost a dollar-fifty. I emptied all the change from my pockets and fed it to the phone. After a dozen or so rings, Laura answered with a slurred hello. How could she sleep on a night like this?

"It's me, Larkin," I said. "I just have one question. Are you seeing someone else? Because if you are, I think you should tell me now instead of hiding it. I don't want to know their name. Just tell me if it's a man or a woman."

"You haven't been gone long enough to get drunk, so I have to assume you're insane."

"Never mind that. Just answer me."

"No. I'm not sleeping with anyone. Not a man. Not a woman. Not you!"

"Okay. Fine. Settle down. I didn't mean to wake you up. It's only nine."

"You didn't wake me up. You just . . ."

At this point the phone began to buzz like an angry wasp. I held it a few inches away from my ear as Laura told me that I was ridiculous, that I had no right to call her, and that if I had anything important to say I could reach her at Tammy and Kendra's on Monday. If I kept harassing her she would call the police.

The wasp quit buzzing, and then I heard a loud click.

I looked through the broken glass of the booth. The parking lot faced the boarded-up windows of the one-story motel, not all that different from the one where Mariah and I began whatever it was we were having—an affair, a friendship, a hormonal convergence. I stood for a minute in the raw mist before I started to drift toward Boston like a bottle without a message. I knew one thing, though. Laura wasn't leaving because of her job, or because of Mariah or anyone else. She was leaving because of me.

14

GOOD BREEDING STOCK

MARIAH LEANED across the kitchen table and lit my cigarette with her Zippo. I was weightless from whiskey, untethered now from Laura, who slept alone back on the Cape. Still breathing, I sat stunned but alive, like a squirrel that had ricocheted beneath a passing car.

"Want some more tea?" Mariah said. "I think I'm going to have some." I nodded. More tea would be nice. She got up from the kitchen table. I liked being in her warm kitchen tonight. Cigarettes, whiskey, and a wild woman—I had all the elements of happiness, or at least of a country-western song.

A small antique lamp, black with an amber shade, turned the kitchen to honey. Mariah wore a dark sweater over her gray dress, its pockets weighted with her cigarettes and lighter. She turned on the gas beneath the kettle, then leaned against the doorway and looked back at me, her eyes glassy, as if she had been reading too long. I wanted to kiss her, to pull her down on the kitchen floor again.

"So did you tell her about me?" she said.

"Yes." I thought it was the right thing to say, that it made everything so much simpler. Mariah gave me a look that told me she wasn't so sure.

"Well, this certainly is a new development."

"She's seeing someone else. Some guy in New York. That's why she's moving there. To be with him." Another simplifying lie.

"Were you surprised?" Mariah brought me a cup of tea and sat down across the table from me. She poured more whiskey into my shot glass, old and opaque, with embedded bubbles of air.

"Thanks. A little. But I always thought Laura might be happier with someone else. Maybe this other guy's nicer. I don't know. We talked it out, and we both agreed it would be a good idea to split up for a while, maybe for good."

"Just like that? One minute you're married and the next minute you're not? I don't know, Larkin. You weren't roommates or something."

"I know, but we realized that we shouldn't be together anymore."

"Did you shake hands before you walked off into the sunset?" Mariah said, drinking from a delicate blue teacup. She seemed almost angry that Laura and I were apart, and I didn't quite understand her reaction, although nothing would have surprised me tonight.

"What are you so upset about? I didn't realize you had such a soft spot for Laura. You certainly didn't think about her much before."

"I don't care either way about her. It doesn't sound right to just be able to break up just like that." She snapped her fingers. "It's too easy. How can I be sure you won't do the same thing to me?"

"I won't. All I want is to stay put for a while and get things together again."

"And once they are, you'll be gone again. Don't tell me any different. I know about how men are. They want security, then when they find it they throw it away. You're living, breathing proof of that."

"Whoa. Hold on. That's not fair," I said, my voice strange,

a little too loud. Everything I said tonight sounded as false and automatic as the Pledge of Allegiance. "I'm not the one who's throwing anything away. It's not my fault Laura doesn't want to be married to me anymore."

"Well, I can't blame her," Mariah said. "You don't exactly inspire trust in a woman, Larkin."

I leaned down and put my head on the table, dizzy. I wished I were home in bed, even if it meant being alone.

"I'm sorry," she said. "I don't mean to be so hard on you. I know what you're doing isn't easy. But I don't think it should be easy. And I'm not sure I'm going to make it any easier."

I sat up slowly. "I appreciate your lack of sympathy."

"Come off it," she said. "You expect me to be sympathetic? We have no commitments, remember. I made sure of that. And now, here you are, wanting me to take you in out of the cold. I just don't know if I like being a port in a storm."

"I know that I love you." I had said these words hundreds of times over the years, and they weakened each time they passed my lips, devalued now to the point that I could say them to two women in an evening.

"Oh, stop it. I don't want to hear that now."

"Why not?"

"Because you don't mean it. You can't mean it. I'm someone you met at the bus stop. If Laura had thrown her arms around you tonight and said she wanted everything to work out, would you be here now?"

"Yes. I'd still have left."

"You don't know that for sure."

"I do." I started to get angry at Mariah, or maybe it was just some of my being angry at Laura spilling over. I couldn't tell.

Mariah looked down into the spiral pattern at the bottom of her teacup. "I didn't call you all week. Maybe I didn't want to see you again. Did you even think of that? Couldn't you have found someone else's kitchen table to sit at?"

"I don't know anyone else anymore. Look, why are you asking me all these questions? I can't guess why things happen the way they do. It's not in my hands. That's fate, or whatever you want to call it. All I know is that I'm here now and I'm glad I am." I poured myself another whiskey.

Mariah shook her head quickly. "That's just what I mean. I don't want things to be up in the air anymore."

"That's asking a lot," I said. "I mean, I could act like I knew what was going to happen tomorrow. But I can't pretend that everything's all figured out, all part of some plan."

"Then you'll like this part," Mariah said. "I have something to tell you. I know this isn't a good time for you, but in a way it's the best time for me. When I like you the least."

"What're you getting at?"

"I know this isn't going to be easy, but I'm just going to say it." Mariah paused for a second, drew a deep breath, and looked me right in the eye. "I'm pregnant."

I sneezed half a glass of whiskey onto the kitchen table and into my eyes, where it burned like salt water.

"It's my child," she said, "not yours or ours. I've thought a lot about this."

For a minute I thought Mariah had to be joking. But then I looked at her face, drawn and tired. A muscle in her jaw twitched.

"Larkin. Are you okay? Say something."

I wiped my face with my sleeve, then leaned down and put my head back on the table. I wished I could shut my ears like I could shut my eyes, but Mariah kept talking.

"I'm thirty-five and I'm still living like I did ten years ago. If I don't have a child in a year or two I can forget it. Then what would I have to show for my life? Some photos. Some clients. A little money in the bank. An overpriced apartment in a grubby town. The occasional visit from a lover who's married to someone else. I had to do something."

She walked over and leaned with her hands on the yellow

tablecloth. I noticed the ends of her fingers, chapped and red from darkroom chemicals. The skin looked tight, as if she were wearing gloves one size too small, and I could see each bone beneath it. When I had first met her at the bus stop, I hadn't noticed her hands. I hadn't realized how strong they were.

"If you're pregnant, then that's the way it was meant to be." The room kept rotating counterclockwise. I was too drunk to be having a serious conversation.

"The way it was meant to be?" she said. "God's will? You sound like my grandfather back in Charleston. Things don't just happen. You have to make them happen."

"Well, you've sure done that," I said. "How pregnant are you?"

"Almost three months."

"And you're sure it's my child?"

"Yes."

"You had this all figured out from the start, didn't you?" Suspicion mushroomed in my sodden mind.

"That's not true."

"You had your eye out for a healthy, heterosexual man with good genes. Is that it? You tricked me. It's immoral." This wasn't what my family meant about Strides being good breeding stock.

"Don't talk to me about morality. You're the one who committed adultery."

"At least I never lied to you. You knew from the start that I was married. I didn't know all you were after was my sperm."

"I wasn't. I've been off the pill for a year," she said, walking back over to the sink. She leaned down and put her face under the tap, sucked in a mouthful of water and then spat it out. She wiped her lips with a dishtowel and then turned toward me, water dripping from her chin. "I'm not asking you for anything. You have no obligation to me, and you don't even have to tell anyone he's yours."

"It's definitely a boy?"

"I'm just guessing. I want a boy."

"So do I," I said, surprising myself. "I just don't think this is the right way to go about it. I mean, maybe if Laura and I got a divorce, we could talk about getting married. And after that, we could talk about having kids. But that's a long time from now and there's a lot of things that could . . ."

"Hey. Hold on. Why would I marry a man who cheats on his wife? You've got to be kidding."

"Why not? Didn't you like me even a little? Or was all that screwing just biology in action, like a bee gathering pollen. Tell me."

"Of course I liked you. I'll always like you. But I know enough not to fall in love with you."

"That's great, really great," I said. I wanted to leave now, but I couldn't get up from the table. The air in the kitchen grew thick and the room took another gyroscopic plunge. "You like me enough to have my child but not enough to fall in love with me. That's a real piece of work."

"It's true," she said.

"If you wanted a kid so much, why didn't you just adopt one?"

"A woman? A free-lance photographer? Forget it."

"It's just not right, Mariah. If you want seeds, go to a gardening store. If you want a child, you've got to have love. You have to be married."

"You're married. Are you in love?"

"For a while I was. I don't know now."

"I'm going to love my child forever. That's the kind of love I want. The kind that doesn't run out."

I found myself in what salesmen described as a "no-win situation." Mariah was right and I was wrong, on all counts. The best thing to do now would be to cut my losses and go home. I poured another glass of whiskey and offered some to Mariah, who shook her head.

"No, thanks. I shouldn't drink, on account of the baby. The fetus is . . ."

"Fetus!" I raised my glass and missed my mouth, the whiskey dribbling down my chin. "Jesus Christ! Don't say things like that!"

"Like 'fetus'? Get used to it. Fetus. Fetus. *Fetus!*" Mariah's face turned red and splotched as she yelled.

"You're crazy. You're aware of that, aren't you?"

"No, I'm not," she said. "I'm not asking you for anything, especially your opinions. I knew you wouldn't be able to deal with this." She stalked to the other side of the kitchen, arms crossed. "Having a child is a serious commitment. You can't even talk about it without getting upset. Imagine how much worse you'd be if you actually had to take care of it, wipe up its crap, let it puke on you."

"If I decided that's what I wanted, then I'd do anything I had to do," I said. Mariah was right. I would be a bad father. I had enough trouble taking care of myself.

"Well, I know that I want a child of my own. Someone to love and to love me back. Just the two of us."

"I still don't think it's right. I never will." I shook my head slowly and stared at the crumbs on the tablecloth in front of me. I picked one up and put it in my mouth.

"You don't have to feel bad," she said. "Or feel anything. You can just forget the whole thing. Forget you ever met me. That you ever made love to me."

"I'm not that good at forgetting things," I said.

"Maybe now's a good time to start."

"Maybe so," I said. I watched the kitchen wall shimmer like hot pavement. My son grew in Mariah's womb, turning slowly in his fluid, staring with huge eyes. He was a little frog, like the tadpoles I used to find along the riverbank when I was a kid. I had to think of him as a little frog. Anything other than my son. I stood up and the floor shifted under my feet. The kitchen was a funhouse with huge furniture and warped walls. I put my hand back on the table to stop it, but the room kept spinning around me like a revolving door. Mariah. The kitchen table. The lamp. Laura in her bathtub. Tadpoles in the river. The fetus in its womb. Green clouds blew into the corners of my eyes and a telephone rang in the distance as I spiraled toward the kitchen floor. Someone really should get that telephone, I thought. It might be important.

15

HOME ECONOMICS

I STOOD in front of a flip chart and pitched the Crockett Company's method of achieving higher performance to a group of prospective clients from an innovative but insolvent software developer.

"So, as you can see, the connection between Individual Competency Assessment and the bottom line is clear," I said, setting the hook. I flipped the next page over and revealed a chain diagram. "We increase productivity, which increases sales, which raises overall corporate profitability. The Crockett Company can help you find the key leverage points that let you make breakthroughs in performance." I pointed at the links in the chain as I had so many times before. "Because if you want a breakthrough in performance, you need to start with a breakthrough in thinking."

Ellen came to the conference room door and signaled to me through the glass by raising an invisible telephone to her ear.

"Excuse me. I'll be right back." I left the head of the table and walked into the hall.

"Sorry to bother you," she whispered.

"This better be good. I've just about got them in the bag."

"Somebody from your family is on the phone. They say it's important."

I walked quickly to my office, worried that something was wrong with Top Shelf or my father.

"Hello?"

"It's Mariah. Sorry to call you at work, but you're never home lately. I just wanted to tell you that I got your check and I'm sending it back today. Thanks but no thanks for the handout." I had signed over my advance from Briefcase Press to Mariah the week before and mailed it to her with a note that told her she could have the twenty thousand dollars, no strings attached.

"Look. I know you didn't ask for anything from me, but I'm just doing what I think is right," I said. "I'm not going to bother you. I won't even call if you don't want me to. But just listen for a minute."

"Fine."

"How much money do you have in the bank?"

"That's none of your business."

"Just tell me. Come on."

"About five thousand in a savings account, about three thousand in an IRA."

"Well, forget about the IRA. You can't touch that. I'm telling you this straight, like a friend. Your savings aren't going to cover what it costs to have a child."

"Why don't we just stop here before you start telling me how to run my life. I don't need your help and I don't want your money," she said. I took notes on a yellow legal pad and pretended this was a business call instead of a personal one. Getting angry wasn't professional. I drew a dollar sign, circled it, then wrote "doesn't want" next to it.

"I don't doubt it. I know you've got this all figured out. I just think you should let me help out with the one thing that's going to be a problem."

"I already told you I don't expect anything from you."

"You can't feed a baby lentils and coffee. You can't take off

197

and travel on assignment for a week and leave it crawling around your apartment. You're going to have medical bills, food bills, not to mention day care. I'm not trying to lecture you, I just want things to go right."

"Thanks for your concern," she said, as if I were a dentist telling her she really ought to floss.

"It's not concern I'm trying to give you. You won't let me do that. I'm trying to give you some money. Right now I happen to have some, so take it and spend it on whatever you want. If it makes you feel any better you can pretend you found it on the street." If Mariah wasn't going to let me be a real father, at least I could be a hidden one. "Pretend you found it at a bus stop."

"That's not fair."

"You think it's fair to have my child against my will? Is it fair to raise it like you're squatting in a rice paddy somewhere?" My voice rose as I paced away from my desk, pulling the phone console to the floor. So much for not getting angry. "In case you didn't notice, it's not a fair world. One of the only things that can help is money."

"I don't believe that, and I don't think you do either."

"Right now I do," I said. "And at least until the kid is raised you'd probably better believe it too. You don't know what's going to happen. For now, deposit the check."

I could hear Mariah breathing. "I didn't ask for this," she finally said. "I want you to remember that I didn't ask for this."

"And I didn't ask you to have my child either. So we're even." I drew an equals sign on my legal pad and underlined it so hard I ripped the paper. Through the glass partition of my office, I could see Davy following my prospective clients to the front door. "I've got to go. Things have been kind of strange here lately. Call me at home if you want to. I'm there late and on Sundays."

"Don't be mad at me. I appreciate the money. It's very generous."

"If you think I'm such a swell guy, maybe you'll think again about us getting back together."

"You know how I feel about that."

"There isn't an hour that goes by when I don't think about you."

"Don't say those things."

"It's true," I said, thinking that it was. Actually, I thought more about our child growing inside her, and my thoughts about the two—mother and child—fused until I began to think of Mariah as my helpless child.

"I'll talk to you in a few weeks." She hung up. I took a handful of hair in each hand and pulled hard—one of the stress-reduction tips for businessmen I had read in an in-flight magazine a few weeks earlier. I noticed that a lot of hairs fell out, and I didn't find that development particularly stress-relieving. I opened my top desk drawer and rummaged through the candy, then poured out a handful of Fruitsters—yellow bananas, pink strawberries, blue grapes—and put them in my mouth with a furtive toss.

I closed the desk drawer and looked out my window at Harvard Square as I chewed my way to sugar-induced happiness. Beneath a tourmaline sky, people walked hunched into their overcoats, staring at the sidewalk in front of them. A strong wind shook the traffic signs. Rain was predicted.

Back in the conference room, Davy gave me a hard look that told me I wasn't being a model of high performance.

"You fumbled that presentation big-time," he said. "We were hoping to get them signed on for an R-and-D Report Card, or at least an Excellence Checkup. I don't have to tell you that this could really hurt our monthly billings."

"I'll call them back and get them in again later this week."

"Don't bother. They're pissed. They rescheduled for July," Davy said. "Come on, Larkin. Get with the program. We've been trying to crack MicroComm for almost a year."

"I'm sorry. It was an emergency."

"I had chest pains during a presentation last spring, and I didn't go to the hospital until I closed the deal *and* got a referral," Davy said. He looked to me for a compliment. I said nothing.

Davy's heroic tales of business were beginning to seem ridiculous.

"You're going to get back on track quick." Davy stared at a point directly between my eyes—this old negotiating trick always made me feel invisible. "Am I right or am I right?"

"You're right," I said. "Right as rain."

I got home late after wasting hours at my desk until Davy left. Overtime would help convince him that I was still committed to the company. The house was dark, since it was past nine, the Thompsons' bedtime. At the landing, I opened the door with my key, then walked into our apartment.

Someone had been there. I could sense it even before I flicked on the lights. My arms tingled as I looked at the rearranged furniture, the empty places in the rooms. Burglars.

"Get out of here!"

I listened for any scrambling around, but heard only my voice bouncing around the apartment. I peered into each room and took inventory. In the living room, they had taken the big Chinese rug but not the smaller dhurrie. The VCR was still on its stand but the television was gone and the speaker stands were emptied of the JBLs. The armoire was there but the dining room table wasn't. I threw open the cabinets in the kitchen and found that the dishes were gone, and even stuff from the pantry—sun-dried tomatoes, jars of Mexican peppers, Thai curry pastes. The table was missing from the breakfast nook but two of the chairs were stacked in the corner. They had taken the microwave but the toaster oven and the coffeemaker were still there. The Calphalon cookware we had gotten as a wedding present still hung from its hooks above the stove.

Down the hall, I saw that the bathroom was intact, maybe because the bathtub weighed too much to move. The Interplak machine was gone, along with Laura's collection of all-natural hair-care products. They had taken the lamp and a nightstand from the bedroom, and the closet was half empty. This break-in was too orderly for burglars but not for Laura. The apartment hadn't been robbed, really, just divided.

I knew I should start putting things back in place or maybe call Tucker for legal advice. But I didn't do either. I stood in the bedroom like a disaster victim whose house has been swallowed up by a tornado, too confused to do anything but stare at the place that used to be home. The red light on the answering machine blinked and I rewound the tape, the voices screeching like cartoon mice. I heard Laura's voice, calm and even, as if she were talking to a child.

> Hi, Larkin. I know you're probably angry now, but I want you to know that I think this is the best way to resolve things. It's been a month now, and I've had a chance to sort things out. I really think it would be better if we didn't get back together. I'm in New York now. Kendra and Tammy helped me move my things in their truck. I would have called to tell you they were coming, but I didn't want to upset you. I've rented a nice place on the Upper East Side. Prices have really dropped! I know that you're angry now, but I'm happier here already and I think that in a little bit you'll be happier too. We really need different things and I don't . . .

I yanked the answering machine's cord from the wall, slid open the bedroom window, and tossed the machine into the darkness. It clattered down the roof, paused as it fell from the eaves, then hit the pavement with a smash.

I stuck my head out the window and screamed long and loud into our tiny backyard, the sound roaring through the cold air. I pictured Mariah looking up from her dinner for a second at the sound, then going back to reading her photography magazine. I wondered whether my shout reverberated in her belly and disturbed the waters that held our child, squirming and kicking at the distant sound of his father's voice.

Did Laura really think she could get divorced on an answering machine? I couldn't think of anything crueler, although I knew she didn't mean to hurt me; she was just being efficient. I thought of her mother and father in their frozen little house in Maine, every little knickknack in place. The apple hadn't fallen far from the tree.

I knelt on the floor on my hands and knees, forehead down as if bowing to Mecca. I pounded my fist into the rug as hard as I could until the skin on my knuckles was raw. When I rolled over on my back, I noticed that one of the ceiling fixtures had burned out, or maybe Laura's friends had taken half of the bulbs. I thought of a necklace I had given Laura the past Christmas, a string of amber beads that smelled like a pine forest when you rubbed them together. Where was that necklace now? Would I ever see it around her neck again? Ever see her smile the way she had when I gave it to her?

After my mother died, my father had packed her things in boxes, which he sealed with duct tape and labeled with Magic Marker. When I felt lonely, I used to sit in the attic among the boxes and read comic books with a flashlight. Now there was no place to hide, to seek comfort. Laura and her things had flown south, leaving behind an echoing, empty space.

A loud ringing startled me and I fumbled for the phone on the floor where the nightstand used to be. Laura was calling to tell me that she had made a mistake, that she had changed her mind.

"Laura? Is that you?"

"No, it's your father. Haven't heard from you lately so I figured I'd call. How's things in Beantown?" I listened to the connection hiss, the sound of all the miles between Pine Bluff and Watertown.

"Dad. I don't know how to tell you this, but I guess I should. Laura's gone. She took her things and moved to New York. She wants a divorce."

I heard a low whistle.

"Well. Jesus. I'm sorry to hear it."

"I am too," I said.

"I don't know that I should say this, but Top Shelf had a bad feeling."

"Oh yeah?"

"She figured Laura was about to take off. Something about the way she looked at you at New Year's. Top Shelf's funny that way," he said. A television blared in the background, and I heard shouting.

"Dad, are you at a pay phone or something?"

"No. Top Shelf's watching the sports channel with some of her friends. So far she's got me for fifty bucks. Wait a second . . ." My father put his hand over the receiver and yelled at them to quiet down. "So what did she say?"

"Nothing. She left a message on the answering machine. Something about wanting to be happy."

"That's just bullshit. No one I know is happy. But that's no reason to take off."

"I guess she thought it was," I said.

"Your mother, God rest her soul, and I lived in a damn fishing shack when we first got married. We had a screaming little runt named you and hardly a pot to piss in. She didn't run off."

"Laura's different. She needs her own space."

"Space?"

"It's a thing that a lot of women around here have to have. I can't explain it."

"If she wants space, then she can rent a goddamn pasture. And if she don't appreciate you, then she can just sit in her goddamn *space* and stew."

"She's not the one who's stewing."

"You just find out?"

"Yeah."

"If it's any consolation, these things get better eventually, like anything else. After your mother died I didn't even want to get out of bed. But you know what I did?"

"No."

"Every day I dragged my sorry butt across the floor, put on my clothes, and went to work. And I stuck with it until things started to look a little better. I stayed out of the bars and did things just like I knew your mother would want me to, and pretty soon I remembered how to breathe." The hiss of the phone line filled the pause. "Then Top Shelf showed me how to fall in love again. You'll find someone else too, someone better."

"I may have already found someone. That's part of the problem."

"Well, that changes the picture a little, don't it?" Another pause. "Laura didn't catch you doing it with another woman, did she?" he whispered.

"Doing what?"

"You know. It."

"No. From what I can tell she doesn't know anything. Anyway, that's over now too." I couldn't bring myself to tell my father about Mariah's plan to raise my child—his grandson. He wouldn't have understood that at all.

"Then you got nothing to worry about."

"What do you mean?"

"I mean she can't stick it to you. You know. Take you to the cleaner's."

"I don't think she'll do that. She just wants out."

"Don't be too sure. Soon as she gets talking to some smarty-pants lawyer she may decide to make a little money on you. Hell, Top Shelf did it to her first husband. He pays her five hundred a month, and we've been married for years."

"She still takes the money?"

"Can't really blame her. Money's money, as long as you don't have to point a gun at someone to get it. We're saving it up to buy a new satellite dish. Anyway, to be on the safe side you'd better start socking away some cash where she can't find it. Give your friends money to buy short-term CDs in their names. Less than ten thousand dollars, so Uncle Sam won't know about it. Tell them you'll split the interest with them."

"Dad. Wait a minute. Where did you learn about all this stuff?" I was shocked to hear my father, an honest building contractor in Arkansas, give me the kind of financial advice usually offered by guys in shiny suits with spaghetti sauce on their ties.

"Around. And from Top Shelf. She's a smart one. Oh yeah, another thing you could do is send me down a cashier's check, and I'll put in in the Pine Bluff Savings and Loan. You remember Dwight Cummings from high school?"

"Yeah."

"Well, he's president of our bank now. With all the business I've given him and his daddy over the years, I'm sure he could find a safe place to deposit it."

"You mean *Do-right* Cummings? I can't believe that guy's running a bank." Last time I saw him, Dwight had been a thick-skulled linebacker for the Pine Bluff Pinemen.

"Don't take too much smarts to run a bank, just to rob one," my father said. "Speaking of same, I read about your friend Dan Holsapple in the paper the other day. Seems they think he held up a convenience store in Little Rock."

I switched the receiver to my other ear. "Wait a minute. I talked to him sometime in the fall and he sounded all right. He wrote me around Christmas. After his father died."

"Maybe that's what he told you, but I saw his father down at the Ranch O'Tel drinking coffee yesterday morning and he didn't look like no ghost to me. Zach Holsapple hasn't been in the hospital since the day he was born. Probably not even then. I think your friend Dan has a little explaining to do. Next time he calls, tell him the state police want to have a little talk with him."

"Wait a minute. He wouldn't make up a story like that."

"You'd be surprised. Don't matter if it's a friend, family, or your wife, if money's involved it's going to get bad, mark my words."

I couldn't think of anything to say. While I waited for my father to go on, I walked over to the dresser and lifted the lid of the small wooden box where I kept letters and things I found when I went for walks. The buckeyes, rocks, and coins were still there, but the stack of letters Laura had written me when we were first going out was gone. I had to say this for her Tammy and Kendra: They were thorough.

"You're old enough to know that people don't always do things the way you'd like them to. You just can't let it get to you. It's enough looking after your own little mess without worrying about someone else's."

"You got that right," I said. My mess grew larger by the day.

"One last thing. I'm going to tell Top Shelf and the rest of the family that you caught Laura fooling with someone and kicked her out. I know it's a little white lie, but it'll go over better than that bullshit about space. They wouldn't understand a woman leaving a man, particularly one of us."

"Okay." I heard screaming in the background.

"Christ. Someone must have scored. I'll tell you one last thing, something you need to know before you let Laura throw you for a loop. All women are crazy. We wouldn't love them if they weren't."

"I think I've heard that somewhere before," I said.

"I may not be original, but I know what I'm talking about. Give us a call if we can help. And stay out of the bars."

"I will."

I heard more yelling, and then my father hung up, finished giving advice. I got up and turned off the lights. I was in luck; Laura's friends had left the bed.

16

GODDESSES AND WARRIORS

As USUAL, my father's advice worked, most of the time. I got out of bed every morning, went to work, and waited for things to get better. The days weren't bad; I could get lost in the details—letters to write, client meetings, deadlines. But evenings were another story. Most men my age had a wife, kids, or at least a dog waiting for them. When I came home from work, only kitten-sized balls of dust swirled around my feet.

I hadn't bothered to clean up the place since Laura's friends had visited, so the apartment still had that just burglarized look popular among college students. The handful of bills I dropped on the hall table slid to the floor, joining a growing pyramid of unanswered mail. I threw my overcoat on a kitchen chair and opened the refrigerator. A stick of butter wore a leopard-skin coat of mold, the expensive honey mustard and mango chutney were crusted like dried-up house paint. Scabs of leftover pizza curled on a paper plate. The box of baking soda had given up long before, and a dank smell drifted up from the crisper, filled with gelatinous vegetables too scary to look at before dinner. I found a Coors and closed the door with the promise that I would clean out the fridge before cold fusion began. I sat down and dug into a carton of Thai fried rice I had picked up on the way home, since take-out was better than sitting alone at a restaurant table for two.

I moved the other chair in front of me to serve as a stand-in for the missing kitchen table and opened the past weekend's *Globe* magazine. A story touted Cuba as a bargain vacation spot for adventurous travelers who didn't mind rooming with lizards and palmetto bugs. The article told visitors to stay away from criminals, recognizable by their tattoos—a crimson knife on the hand of a slasher, blue tears dripping from the corner of a murderer's eye. Along with the shaky dice on my shoulder, I bore invisible tattoos—Laura etched on my back, tiny Mariahs on my fingertips, a crimson fetus on my stomach. At the thought of my child twisting inside Mariah's womb I tossed the carton toward the sink, splattering its contents on the wall, bits of rice sliding down like slugs.

My beer tasted fishy now, so I poured it over the dishes in the sink. Work was my excuse for ignoring everything else. Like my inflamed asteroids, clients were beginning to act up and make me miserable. One corporation was fending off a takeover bid, so it canceled a contract for a Total Quality Tune-up. Another announced its lowest quarterly earnings in a decade after we delivered our Profitability Pep Rally. Other clients told me their budgets couldn't handle our hefty day rate anymore.

Bert had called me "the man with the minus touch" during this morning's planning meeting, which set off choked laughter from Lillivale and Gillman. After the meeting, I had gone into the men's room and sat in a stall to wait for the inevitable colonic catharsis from three cups of coffee. I heard the bathroom door swing open, then voices.

"Davy asked me to take a look at this," Lillivale said. A heavy thunk followed as he dropped something on the counter.

"Stupid title. Think it's any good?" I recognized Gillman's voice above their splashing at the sinks.

"Far as I can tell, it's more of the same doom-and-gloom stuff

I've seen for the last couple of years. You know. Rearranging the deck chairs on the *Titanic*."

"Desk chairs?" Gillman asked, never up to speed on his business lingo.

"Just an expression. Anyway, Davy wants me to build a new marketing campaign around the book, but there are some problems."

"Like what?"

"Well, I don't think we're talking rocket science here, and there's . . ."

Someone hit the button on the hot-air hand dryer. I couldn't hear over the roar, and when it finally stopped, I was alone in the bathroom. The tube within me broke the silence with a rude tooting, a basso profundo song of the bowels.

Home from work now, I began to think that the company had turned against me. Davy had been mad at McCormick for a year after he blew a big contract. Lillivale had hated Gillman when he got an office with more windows. Lillivale and Gillman had both hated me when my first book came out. And Ellen had hated Davy after he reduced her to a whimpering mass on the Career Path one morning. That weasel Lillivale had a lot of nerve to criticize my book. Some team player he was. I slapped my hand down on the chair and sent an empty beer can clattering to the floor.

Down on the street, I saw Mrs. Pakarian walking through the small pools cast by the streetlights, a strange, hunched woman who gathered up the neighborhood's empty trashcans. She dragged two behind her like reluctant calves and put them on her porch. Laura had wanted to call the police the first time Mrs. Pakarian stole the green plastic cans stenciled with our address, but I just waited a few days and retrieved them. She was harmless, and besides, I liked her cluttered porch and yard full of rusting cars. They reminded me of home.

Home. A lightning bolt of fear struck me between the shoulders and pulled me away from the window. My hands shook and my heart pounded as panic sent me running down the hall. *The skull.* Where was the skull? I threw open the door to the hallway closet to look for its hidden reliquary, a shoe box under stacks of Laura's college books. But the closet was empty.

I ran to the bedroom and dialed Laura's number in New York. The recording said that Laura White wasn't in right now. I slammed down the phone. She never did like the idea of taking my last name. I kicked aside a pile of dirty clothes and sat down on the bedroom rug. That skull had been with me almost as long as my own. Now it was gone.

I called Tammy and Kendra's number.

"Yeah?" Kendra's voice had been coarsely sanded by years of yelling at community rallies.

"Kendra. This is Larkin Stride, I'm . . ."

"Laura's not here and I don't have her new number," she said.

"I already have her number. I just have to ask you a question." I stared at a cobweb hanging from the ceiling and tried to keep from getting angry.

"Ask away." After years behind the counter at the Red Star Bookstore, Kendra was used to stupid questions.

I took a deep breath. "When you and Tammy robbed my apartment, did you take a box of books from the hall closet?"

"Hey, just a second. I detect some heavy attitude."

"Just tell me if you took the box."

"We took what was Laura's. It wasn't stealing. Like they say, property is theft."

"I don't want dogma. All I want is for you to answer one simple question. Where's the box now?"

"The one with Laura's college books and stuff?"

"Yes."

"I don't know. Can't remember. Sorry."

"Wait! Don't hang up," I begged. "If you remember what's in the box you have to know where it is."

"Why's this box of books so important, anyway?" Kendra

said. "I mean, there's plenty of books in the world, believe me."

"I want to know where it is."

"Why don't you call Laura in New York?" Kendra said. She covered the phone and said something to someone else, probably Tammy, the feminist cab driver/social critic/heiress.

"She's not home," I said.

"Oh, yeah. She told me she's having dinner with some guy from her new office. Says he's nice." Kendra paused for a second and waited for me to get jealous the way breeders always did.

"If you know where the box is, just tell me. Please." I squeezed my right hand into a fist. Being polite was getting harder and harder.

"We took the books to the store. Laura gave them to us for helping out. She figured I could probably get a couple hundred bucks for them from college kids."

"That's all I wanted to know," I said.

"Tammy says she thinks we sold most of them already. Why don't you just go over to the Harvard Book Store. That's your kind of place."

"Why don't *you* go there," I said.

"No way. I wouldn't be caught dead in that place. They sell books written by men. But if you come by Red Star on Monday, I've got a book for you, *Man the Destroyer*. Have you heard of it? I think you'll like it a lot. There's a good chapter about . . . about spears." Kendra cackled and covered the receiver again.

I slammed down the phone. I wasn't in the mood for ridicule from the dyke diptych. I just wanted to get Catlett Stride's skull back before it was bartered off with a batch of Literature 101 paperbacks. As I pulled on my coat, various ignoble ends for a Confederate hero came to mind. A centerpiece for séances. A candle holder. Out in the stairway, I jumped two steps at a time, thuds loud enough to wake the Thompsons. The Volvo started on the first try and the wheels screeched as I headed toward Cambridge. The bookstore would be closed, but I drove there anyway. Maybe I could rescue his skull somehow, break into the store, anything. That is, if someone hadn't found it already.

I ran through a string of red lights in Little Armenia, the shops closed now, the produce carts roped together. As I turned onto the river road toward Cambridge, I nearly hit a scrawny jogger who leaped in front of the headlights like a crazed deer. I swerved and cut over into oncoming traffic to avoid clipping him with my fender.

"Come on, people now, get the fuck out of my way," I muttered through clenched teeth.

He shook his fist and yelled something in my wake that I couldn't hear over the heater. The jogger population needed thinning. I pictured this one strapped across the Volvo's hood, tongue flapping in the wind.

The drive down Cambridge Street to Inman Square was a time warp back to Cambridge's salad days, the hippie era. I passed Indian restaurants, health food co-ops, and a coffeehouse called the Magic Mushroom. A few doors down, the lights were on at the Red Star Bookstore. I parked in front of a fire hydrant and ran up to the door, marked with the universal sign for "woman"—or as Tammy and Kendra would have said, "womyn," always trying to keep men out of their language as well as their bookstore.

The front window displayed paperbacks on Central America, healthy grains, and the environment. Inside, I could see a circle of about a dozen people sitting cross-legged on the floor, their eyes closed. One of the largest womyn I had ever seen slapped a skin-covered drum with her mighty paw, which protruded from her woven poncho. On each hit of the drum her arm came down like a war club while her face showed a beatific peace, as if she felt extremely pleased with herself and her place—however spacious—on this earth. I knocked but no one could hear me.

The drumming became faster and louder, then stopped abruptly. Everyone remained seated, heads bowed during some kind of intermission. I knocked as loudly as I could. No response. When I started kicking the door, one normal-looking guy in a shiny blue running suit broke out of the collective trance. I caught his eye with a frantic wave. He walked to the door and opened it a crack.

"Sorry to bother you. It's an emergency," I whispered. I saw wire-rimmed glasses and gray eyes. A carefully cropped white beard. He looked like a lonely janitor.

"We're in the middle of a tribal drumming session. You're breaking the energy. Could you come back in an hour?"

"No. I need to find something. My wife donated some books and there's one that's really important. . . ."

"A book?"

"Yes, a book. It's been in the family for . . ."

"Sorry, we just rent the space from the Red Star people once a week for our class. We're from the Inner Fate Center. This is a Goddess Worship Workshop."

"That's a goddess?"

"She's the workshop facilitator. We visualize the goddess. The goddess within."

"Oh." I had flipped through the Inner Fate Center catalogue once when stranded in the laundromat with nothing to read. It offered half-baked educational programs that catered to the Cambridge self-help crowd, courses like "One-Hour Shamanizing" and "Laughing Towards Health with Aztec Healing Clowns."

"Can't you just let me in? I'll be gone in five minutes. I promise."

"We have strict instructions from the Red Star people not to let anyone into the store. You may be CIA or something. They sell banned books here. Some pretty heavy stuff."

"Look, I'm not from the CIA." I pulled out my wallet and flipped through it for proof of my neutrality, showing him my driver's license, my American Express Gold Card, my Crockett Company business card. "I'm friends with the owner. We go way back."

He scratched his beard as he read the cards I slipped to him through the slit in the door. Looking closer, I saw that his glasses were tinged with pink, and a gold chain twinkled at the V of his jogging outfit, unzipped to reveal a thatch of gray chest hair. I could picture him in a Holiday Inn lounge, drinking scotch and soda and doing the Latin hustle with secretaries. Maybe Inner Fate classes were just a politically correct way to get lucky.

"You're a warrior," he said, finally opening the door. "Did you know that?"

"Actually, I'm a management consultant."

"Exactly. Some men nurture the warrior within them. They go into business or other zones of conflict. Others look for the goddess and become healers, peacemakers, bearers of joy."

"Right now I'm just looking for something important that I lost."

"I know what you mean." He gave an empathetic nod. "Maybe our Refocusing Male Fierceness class could help you find what you're looking for. It's very powerful."

"I think what I'm looking for may be in the storeroom somewhere."

"Go through that side door," he said, nodding to the left, away from where the tribal drummers began to hum in unison like swarming bees. "Good luck."

I closed the door behind me and felt around on the wall for the light switch. The huge room was filled with hundreds of unopened boxes, each as anonymous and brown as the one from our closet. I took out my penknife and started with the boxes closest to the door, opening one with a fierce slash befitting a warrior. It didn't take long for me to find that the overeducated people of Cambridge all had about the same reading list—Henry James, *The Whole Earth Catalogue*, D. H. Lawrence, Freud, *Our Bodies, Our Selves*. I quit counting copies of *Ulysses* when I got to twenty. Box after identical box stretched off in the distance like cargo on parade.

After half an hour, my hands were raw and my clothes streaked with dust. I climbed higher and dug deeper, more frantic with each disappointing box. The drumming had started again, an unrelenting rhythm that seemed to come from everywhere at once. I leaned over and ripped into another carton, uncovering another copy of *The Bell Jar*. I almost tossed it aside, but then I noticed the inscription—"To Laura from Jill, may you always remember me and our haven in Haven House."

"Thank you, Jill. Thank you, Sylvia Plath." I kissed the cover before I tossed it over my shoulder, deep into the shadows. At the bottom of the heap, dented but still safe, lay the familiar shoe box that held the skull of Catlett Franklin Stride, its earthy tang filling the dusty air.

"Say amen, brothers and sisters." I peeked inside to make sure the blackened skull was safe.

Amen.

I tucked the shoe box under my coat and climbed down from Book Mountain, strip-mined now. Back in the store, the drumming had reached an incredible speed. Two lanky guys in T-shirts had joined in, their hands a blur as they slapped their tall drums. Between them, the goddess thrashed around, possessed, scattering sweat like the world's largest lawn sprinkler. Her poncho had fallen off her shoulder, and as she drummed the tops of her pendulous breasts flopped forward. On the upswing, a dark nipple rimmed by a reddish circle popped into sight, then disappeared like a winking eye.

While the others hummed and chanted in deep concentration, the guy who let me in stared at that winking eye, transfixed. His hands were shoved down the front of his running pants and he stroked himself like a zoo baboon. Sweat dripped from his nose. He smiled weakly at me and then concentrated on the work at hand. I didn't think this was the kind of enlightenment the Inner Fate Center had in mind, but to each his own. I stepped outside and left as quickly as I had arrived, the shoe box tucked under my arm.

17

IN TROUBLE

MORNING CREPT over the brown lawns, matted as un-washed hair. I squinted out the kitchen window at the street and rails of gray snow that had been there since Christmas. The houses were overexposed like a photograph taken at ground zero, shadows burned to the walls. The official first day of spring was only a week away, but winter still held on with a miser's grip.

In living rooms and kitchens up and down the street, people brushed their teeth, pulled the plastic bags off dry cleaning, stared blue-faced at *Good Morning America*. Out of a million ways to start the day, we were all doing the same things. No one stopped and decided today would be a good day to stay home and start learning how to play the piano, to walk through the woods and look for the first green talons of spring clawing up through the leaves. Instead, we rustled like mice in our warm cages, preparing to scurry out into the cold world.

A stranger broke this morning's tedious symmetry. I watched him down on the sidewalk, astride a mountain bike with knobby tires and straight handlebars, the kind of bicycle that could go anywhere. He looked too old to be a neighborhood kid but too young to be one of the gentrifiers who had laid claim to the best houses on the street. I guessed about nineteen, the age at which he belonged only to himself, and I envied him, unbound by mortgage, marriage, or career. His hair was long and stringy, like that of the heavy-metal kids who hung around Harvard Square, and the cold wind rippled it around his high cheekbones and a chin still unaffected by gravity. He reached into the pocket of his leather jacket and pulled out a small brown notebook. On the ground next to him, my empty trash barrels lay where they had been tossed by the garbagemen. It was too early for Mrs. Pakarian to come steal them, but not for this stranger, who read from his notebook, waiting for something. I put on my coat.

Downstairs, I picked up the newspaper from the front porch and tossed it on the pile next to the door, then walked down the sidewalk to where the Volvo sparkled in the cold sun. The stranger rolled slowly toward me.

"Larkin Stride?" he said, braking. Maybe he was a paper boy. It had been months since I had remembered to leave my payment taped to the front door the way I was supposed to.

"Sorry, I forgot to get cash," I said. "I'll have to write you a check."

"This is for you." He pulled a yellow envelope out from under his jacket and handed it to me the way the newspaper seller in Harvard Square did with my prefolded *Herald,* tucking it under my arm so gently I barely felt it.

"Thanks," I said, but the stranger was already riding away, curls trailing in the wind as he headed up the hill to Cambridge. I thought the envelope might be some vacation giveaway scam, or maybe *The Watchtower.* Two blue-suited Jehovah's Witnesses quoting from Corinthians had talked me into the subscription, a small price to make them leave. With the end of the world approaching, they probably didn't trust the regular mail.

My eyes watered in the cold as I fumbled with the envelope and pulled out a thick document joined at the top with a serious black clip. The cover said something about a proceeding in the Commonwealth of Massachusetts between Laura White Stride and Larkin Stride. I didn't need to read any more. I shoved the divorce papers back in the envelope, but they wouldn't go. Someone looking down at the street might see me and decipher what had just happened. I had been *served*, which never meant anything good except in restaurants.

I rolled up the whole mess and crammed it in my overcoat pocket, then walked to the Volvo, unlocked the door, and got in, mechanical as a wind-up toy. My briefcase waited in the passenger seat, its cold leather dividers full of work I had intended to finish the night before. I tossed the papers in, then slammed the case closed and clicked the little gold latches.

I smashed my palm into the steering wheel.

"Shit. Shit. Shit!" My breath steamed up the inside of the windshield. I might have been expecting Laura to file for divorce, but these serious-looking papers still blindsided me. I sat for a minute until my hands quit shaking, then took my keys from my overcoat pocket.

Already late for work, I jammed the key in the ignition and twisted it. The car made a grinding sound. All winter, the Volvo had started on the first try, faithful as a dog. Now my dog had turned on me. I stared at the steering column as though I could shame the engine into starting, and twisted the key harder and harder until the grinding noise faded. Something snapped and I held my keys up to the light.

"Shit! Shit! Shit!" I smashed the steering wheel again. The ignition key had broken off. Now I would have to get the car towed, except my AAA membership had expired a month earlier. I reached back and grabbed my briefcase, then got out and slammed the door. Without the ignition key, I couldn't lock up. Maybe some kids would steal the Volvo and go for a joyride in Chelsea. That would serve the thankless cur right, I thought. Then I remembered I hadn't paid my insurance either. I got out and walked away without looking back, still trying to act as if nothing were wrong.

My head buzzed with white noise, and sweat coursed beneath

my overcoat. I should have just walked to the Verona Lounge, ordered a double Jack Daniel's, and called in sick. But I had to go to work to try to salvage what was left of my reputation, to put out the smoldering fires Lillivale and Gillman were setting behind my back. As I walked, I thought about the divorce papers, about the car, about work. I couldn't say which made me more angry. They all jumbled together into one throbbing vein in my forehead that pounded in rhythm with my footsteps.

Tuxedo Junction's display window was a war zone of ravished brides and monopedal prom dates. All winter, cracked fingers had fallen from lace-covered wrists, dresses had yellowed in the sun, flaking chips of paint had pockmarked tanned mannequin faces. The brides stared at me with wide eyes as I walked past, locked in on the bus stop ahead.

As I crossed the street something whistled toward me and slammed into the back of my head. A bright blue flash. A numbing crack. I fell to the ground and lay still. The buzzing in my ears grew louder. My head pounded. My brain had hemorrhaged. I had been hit by a car. Someone had shot me. I opened my eyes and saw my papers waltz around the street in the morning breeze. I reached back to touch my head, fearing what I might find there—sticky shards of skull, spongy gray matter. But I felt only dampness and grit. I wiggled my fingers, stretched out my legs. Except for my throbbing head, I seemed to be all right. I looked up from the sidewalk and stared across the street at voices that came from the cemetery.

I heard laughter as I knelt on the sidewalk, my cashmere overcoat covered with wads of damp newspaper, winter sludge, and dog shit. I rose unsteadily to my feet and touched the back of my head again. What could be so funny. I squinted, my hand above my eyes. Three boys in red and white Watertown High jackets pointed at me. One bent over and held his knees as he laughed. There hadn't been a car wreck, any gunshots—only a ball of ice pressed together from the last remnants of winter snow and thrown by a high school kid. My arms started to tingle.

219

Across the street, two of the pranksters slapped the third on the back—the thrower, the marksman who had found his mark. These boys had declared open season on men in suits and I had been a perfect target. They sure had got me good. Now they could have a laugh in the locker room when they remembered me huddled on the sidewalk in the fetal position. When I was their age, I had done worse. I had set fire to outhouses, dumped sugar in gas tanks, driven through fields at night to hear the watermelons pop beneath my tires. Something made a boy want to hurt things.

I crossed the street through the fluttering papers and walked over to the boys, as if I were coming to scold them, maybe ask for an apology. They shifted nervously as hens, wishing I would just keep walking. A lecture wasn't in their game plan. They stood behind the low cast-iron fence around the cemetery and looked at their feet, confused about this strange man who hadn't gone away, who now stood before them filthy but smiling.

I walked into the cemetery. "Hi, guys." They said nothing.

"Who threw it?" I spoke quietly, as if I were asking for directions. I already knew the answer but just wanted to see what they said.

A larger boy pointed at a shorter one with a whiffle haircut and an unlit cigarette stuck in his mouth. His skin was dark and oily, its shiny varnish broken by ranges of whiteheads; his eyes were dark with black eyebrows one size too large. He took out the cigarette and flicked it behind a tombstone, practicing all his tough moves.

"What's it to you?" His voice was high-pitched and quavering, unaltered by the raging hormones that gave him pimples and false courage.

"I just wanted to tell you that was a hell of a shot. You ought to go out for the majors."

"Thanks." The boy looked at the horizon as if I were invisible. He turned to the other boys but they had backed off. Maybe they had dared him to throw the iceball, but now they acted as if they had never seen him, even though they all wore the same jackets, red felt with dirty white leather sleeves.

"There's just one more thing I want to say." I dropped the smile, and my fingers wrapped into a hard fist. "I'm going to mess you up, you little shit, and there's nothing you can do about it."

I threw the first punch and caught the boy deep in the stomach. His mouth opened in an O as he bent over my fist, all of the air inside him coming out in one long wheeze. His eyes went wild and his face turned pale. He fell to his knees, then managed to scramble a few steps after his friends, who were already out of the cemetery and running toward the high school.

He slipped on the icy ground every time he tried to get back on his feet.

"Come here, boy." I walked toward him. "I got some other things I want to tell you." He gulped air and tried to get his footing. I dove forward just as he started to run, and knocked his legs out from under him. His high-topped sneaker caught me in the mouth. The salty, metallic taste of my blood. He rolled onto his back and pushed away with his elbows the way we used to when we played crab soccer in gym class.

"I didn't . . . throw it," he said, then got another breath and spat out a few more words. "It. Was. Them. Not. Me." Another breath. "You're . . . you're crazy," he whispered, still crawling backward as I threw the second punch from a crouch, hitting his jaw with the crack of a baseball bat connecting.

He skidded backward from the punch, and I walked to where he lay like a broken doll, his head flopped to one side, blood running from his flattened nose. My arms hummed with electricity. Even if I wanted to I couldn't stop now.

"Let me tell you something, boy." I was out of breath, and blood sprayed from my split lip. "A lot of things in this world don't go like you planned. Being young and stupid ain't no excuse. You got to learn that the world don't make any sense."

"Leave me alone." He rolled onto his stomach and coughed

up a mouthful of glistening beige vomit. I couldn't blame him
for not listening to me. When I was sixteen I thought I could
get away with anything. I broke things that didn't belong to me.
I stole things. I lied to girls I didn't love. And I always thought
the future could save me, as if it were a quiet room where I could
hide from everything I had done wrong before.

"I mean it. You don't know how things are. You've got a lot
to learn and I'm going to help you." My words sounded harsh
as an AM radio. "You'll thank me someday. Maybe you ought
to thank me now. Why don't you just sit up and thank me, okay?
I'll leave you alone. Then you can go to school and tell your
buddies how tough you are." I stood over him and looked at his
broken nose, strings of bloody mucus that connected him to the
ground. "Thank me, you little shit," I said.

Then his lips moved. "Stop it. Please, mister," he whispered,
his chest heaving. He cried with his eyes closed, and tears dripped
down his cheeks.

"No, I won't. I'm here to tell you something important."

He nodded a little and sat up, crossing his arms over his
stomach, then lowered his head, praying for me to leave him
alone. From the road, we might have looked like two brothers
having a quiet moment at their father's grave. But we weren't
brothers, and as I watched the stupid boy cry, my head roared
with a jittery anger. Laura. Mariah. Lillivale. My car. Right
now, the boy was the only one in front of me. I grabbed the
longer hair on the back of his head and shoved his face down
hard to the ground, the grass moist with his sour-smelling fluids.

"The world." I pulled him back up. He sputtered and tried
to catch his breath.

"Is not." I shoved him back down hard. He heaved again but
nothing came up. Then he went limp and his eyes rolled back
in his head like a frightened dog's.

"A fair place." I pulled him up and smashed him one last
time into the frozen ground, where I let him stay. I stopped,
although part of me wanted to keep going until there was nothing

left but a bloody jacket. The boy lay motionless in front of me, a crumpled heap that moaned. I looked up at the oversized tombstones around us, the gray slate carved with lightbulb-shaped skulls. Skulls with wings. Willow trees and skulls. Among the tombstones, two policemen stood still as archers, their service revolvers pointed at me.

"Party's over," one of them said. "Hands over your head."

He looked like a nice red-faced Irish cop, the kind who might direct traffic down in Watertown Square. The other was small and wiry in a leather motorcycle jacket. The dark visor of his helmet made him look like a fly. I smiled and raised my arms over my head, then stood slowly.

"These kids attacked me. I caught this one." I wanted them to let me get on my bus. I was really late for work. My head throbbed.

"I said get your hands over your head," said the Irish cop. "Now!"

As I raised my arms I noticed that my gold Rolex, a gift from Davy, had come off during the scuffle. Some lucky kid would find it when the snow melted and have drug money for years. I stared at my wrist so long that the policemen started getting nervous. The boy pulled up on all fours with his head on the ground, mumbling as if he were dreaming. While the motorcycle cop went to help him, the Irish cop stepped slowly forward, his gun pointed at my chest.

"I don't know who you are, pal." He reached behind with his free hand for the shiny steel handcuffs that hung from his belt. "But you really got yourself in a lot of trouble."

"I know," I said. "I know that."

18

JAIL

I SHIVERED in the backseat of the squad car, separated from the front by a protective steel-mesh screen. My overcoat was in the cemetery and my shirt was soaked, but it wasn't the cold that made me shake. I was caged, scared. As the squad car pulled into a circular driveway, the Watertown police station looked stark and serious, a place where no good could possibly happen. I had walked past the station hundreds of times without ever really noticing it, a squat, two-story brick rectangle from the 1950s, topped by a radio antenna and a flagpole where a tattered Massachusetts flag dangled.

The policemen escorted me up the front stairs, one on either side, as if I could make a run for it with my legs shaky and my wrists handcuffed behind my back. They propelled me through the front doors by the elbows. We entered a small lobby with a linoleum floor and a low suspended ceiling where years of rain were recorded in yellow splotches ringed like a topographic map. Swinging doors took us into a large office with windows high on the walls. The morning light fell in visible columns through bluish air that smelled of coffee and cigarettes. Rows of steel desks, most empty, stretched down one main aisle. The room was quiet except for occasional berserk squawks from a police radio.

The cop who arrested me took off my handcuffs and pointed at a cluster of scuffed plastic chairs with holes in the back, the kind we sat on in junior high. In front of me, an officer bent over a desk, official police business spread out impressively before him. I sat up straight. I wanted him to think I was an honest man, a good citizen of Watertown. But he didn't look up.

Old copies of *Time* covered the small table in front of me, and to my right a glass case was crammed full of bowling and softball trophies. On the wall next to it hung a framed photo of the governor and the obligatory faded cardboard print of John Kennedy, patron saint of Massachusetts. A couple of officers gave me hard looks when they glanced up from their desks off in the distance. I could have done anything, for all they knew. My lip was swollen and crusted, and the cut had left a bloody lobster bib across the front of my white Christian Dior shirt.

I knew I had done something wrong, that I shouldn't beat up anyone, much less a kid. But I also knew that in the big scheme of things, it wasn't that bad. These things happened all the time. I would have to sign something, maybe get a ticket for disturbing the peace, assault, or whatever they called it, and then go home. Until then, I tried to look as innocent as I could with blood dribbling from my lip and dog shit in my hair.

When the booking officer looked up from reading my report, I stared at a spot on the floor in front of me, exploring the gummy crevices in the linoleum.

"Think you're tough? What the hell'd you think you were doing? You're twice that kid's size." The booking officer had a booming voice for a small man. Even the policemen in the back of the room could hear him. His hair was dark and his thick black moustache looked like a plastic comb from a bus station vending machine. Behind silver wire-rimmed glasses, his dark eyes scanned me efficiently and recorded the details. The officer seemed completely at home in the dim police station, as if he had been born in his crisp blue uniform with gold buttons.

"First things first. Name?" When he spoke, the smoking tip of his cigarette waved like a conductor's baton.

"Larkin Stride."

"Address?"

"One-oh-three Chestnut Avenue, Watertown." I noticed that he wasn't writing any of this down. The arresting officers had taken my wallet back at the cemetery and it had all the information anyone could want. He just wanted to make me say it out loud for punishment.

"Age?"

"Thirty-three."

"Occupation?"

"Management consultant."

"Employer?"

"The Crockett Company. In Cambridge."

"Prior criminal record?"

"None."

"Very good, my friend. So far you get an A," the officer said, then spun around in his chair and pointed a finger at the back of the room.

"Bobby. Come here, please."

A younger officer walked down the aisle carrying a battered Polaroid Swinger, the kind of camera we used to take on vacation when I was a kid. His chinless face was as red as canned ham and his uniform looked too small at the neck. He knelt down and took my picture with a flash that got everyone's attention again. Then he put an ink pad and a piece of paper on the officer's desk and grabbed my hand clumsily with his own fleshy mitt. I wondered if this was the first time he had taken fingerprints. As he inked my fingers and mashed them on the paper, I glanced at the clock on the other side of the room. Ten o'clock. They would be finishing up the morning planning meeting at work now. I pictured Davy, Ellen, McCormick, Lillivale, and

Gillman sitting around the conference table. I wanted to be there, bored, staring into my coffee. Bobby huffed back down the aisle to his desk. The officer waited until he was gone before he spoke again.

"I'm done with the booking," he said. "But I'm not done with you. Before Bobby takes you away, I want to have a talk, *mano a mano*."

I nodded. He read from a piece of paper in front of him.

"The kid's name is Nicky Badrosian. He's sixteen, five-foot-six, and weighs one hundred and ten pounds. He goes to Saint James's Armenian Church every Sunday. My wife and his mother are friends. His father runs a laundromat. He's filing charges against you right now." The officer tugged his head slightly upward at the end of each sentence to add special emphasis to these facts. I already knew the boy was small and from Watertown, but I didn't know he was Armenian. When I looked over at the brass name plate on the booking officer's desk, my stomach rolled over. SGT. GOSGARIAN. When he finished speaking, he rolled his cigarette carefully between his fingers and waited for me to apologize.

I said nothing. All I could think about was leaving. If I paid my fine now I could go home, change clothes, and be at work by noon.

"Nothing to say for yourself, huh? You got the right to remain silent. But I also got the right of free speech, and I'm not done talking yet. You come here and beat up on one of our kids. Why? Watertown is a quiet town. You see anyone else waiting around to be booked?" He glanced toward the empty chairs with a quick shift of his dark eyes. I looked over and met the unforgiving gaze of JFK.

"The last real problems we had were on New Year's Eve. We arrested a few drunks. Otherwise, it's stuff we can live with. Some shoplifting. Vandalism. Complaints about crazy landlords. The usual problems. Not aggravated assault. That's what you're charged with, you know. If we hadn't got there when we did,

227

STONA FITCH

you'd probably have killed the kid. Even so, he'll be in the hospital for a couple of days."

When I didn't say anything, Officer Gosgarian kept going.

"Like I said, why would a guy like you want to come here and beat up on our kids, make trouble for everyone?"

"I live here too," I said, softly.

"I know that, but how *long* have you lived here?"

"Long enough."

"No. You're from somewhere else. Somewhere where they beat up on innocent kids. My family's been here since 1920. They came over after the Turks killed my grandparents." His cigarette bobbed faster and faster, and ashes rained down on his green desk blotter. "You come here, spend your money on some real estate and think you own the town. But you don't really live here. If you did you would't beat up a boy half your age, half your size."

"I'd like to call my lawyer." This was what people said on television. Officer Gosgarian picked up a clipboard and slammed it down on his desk with a crack that echoed through the room.

"The whole fucking world wants to talk to its lawyer. Then they won't have to talk for themselves. You can call your lawyer soon enough, but I want you to know something. I could send you over to the courthouse this afternoon, but I'm going to hold your paperwork so you'll spend the night here waiting for tomorrow's arraignment. That way you'll have to do a little thinking before you get out on bail."

"I don't think that's right."

"I'm a policeman. Don't tell me what's right. Remember, this is a small town. News travels fast. I don't think anyone in Watertown is going to think what you did to Nicky Badrosian was right." Officer Gosgarian took out his cigarette when he finished his speech, and ground it into an ashtray. I wiped my leaking lip on the dangling French cuff of my shirt.

"Bobby. Take Mr. Stride to his home away from home." Finished with me, Officer Gosgarian swiveled his chair back to his paperwork. Bobby, the fat cop-in-training, pinched my shirt with two fingers and led me through a side door. Connected, we walked up a flight of stairs and down a long windowless hallway lit by fluorescent tubes. Gray doors lined the hall, each with a stenciled title—DEPARTMENT OF MOTOR VEHICLES, REGISTRY, LICENSING BUREAU, and at the end of the hall, a room called JAIL.

Bobby unlocked the door and it swung open to reveal a small room about twelve feet square, full of empty metal shelves, filing cabinets, and cardboard boxes.

"*Vwahla.*" Bobby bowed like a bellboy as I walked inside and looked around. He started to close the door.

"Wait a minute. Shouldn't you search me, take my belt or something?" If I was going to be locked up, I wanted it to be realistic.

"Why?"

"So I don't hang myself."

"Oh." Bobby looked surprised, wondering if he had forgotten some of his police training. "Are you going to hang yourself?"

"No."

"Then keep your belt. Don't try anything funny. I'll be checking on you." Bobby closed the door and locked it.

So far, being in jail was like being locked in the office supply closet at work. Only the metal frames over the windows reminded me where I was. No criminals had written their names, marked off the days, or drawn stations of the cross on the walls. No sex-crazed cellmate waited to forcibly make me his wife. In fact, I couldn't tell whether anyone had ever stayed here before. A child-sized bunk bed had been shoved in the far corner of the room almost as an afterthought and covered by a western-style blanket decorated with lassos, ponies, cactuses, and pistols—the same pattern as on a pair of pajamas I had when I was about seven.

I sat down on the bunk and waited for something to happen here in this office supply closet, my prison. I tried to muster up some guilt, but came up only with boredom. There wasn't much to do. I wondered if Thoreau's famous night in jail had started this way, although he never got arrested for aggravated assault.

After about an hour, I heard Bobby struggling with the key.

"You okay?" he said, expecting to find me dangling from a light fixture like a *piñata*.

"Fine. Can I make a phone call?"

"Yes. But just one. I think."

Bobby led me to a pay phone down the hallway, my filthy sleeve held tightly between his fingers. I stood for a minute and considered my options. I didn't have Laura's work number in New York. Mariah didn't want to hear from me. My father and Top Shelf would be worried.

I dialed the Crockett Company, and the secretary connected me to Ellen's office.

"Larkin. Where are you?"

"I'm running a little late."

"The phone's been ringing off the hook for you. Car trouble?"

"Yeah, I guess you could say that."

"Davy's been on the warpath and I need some help with a client presentation. I penciled you in for a meeting at three."

"I don't think I can make it, Ellen. I need to ask you to do me a little favor."

"Sure."

"Can you cover for me? Say someone in my family died or something. I won't be in until Monday. Cancel my appointments for today and tomorrow."

"Sure, but what happened?"

"You have to promise you won't tell anyone, particularly not Davy."

"I promise."

"I'm in jail." I listened to the miniature sounds of the Crockett Company.

Ellen hummed slightly as she weighed this information, decided what it meant. "Jail? What for?"

"Aggravated assault."

"That sounds serious."

"Some guys attacked me on the way to the bus stop," I said. "It was self-defense."

"Are you okay?"

"Yeah, just a little shook up."

"Did they have guns or something?"

"No. They hit me on the head and I beat one of them up."

"Hit you on the head! With what? With a club or something? That's awful. You could have been killed!"

"It wasn't that bad. They didn't have weapons or anything. They had . . . well, they had snowballs. I got hit in the head with a snowball, and I beat up the kid who threw it."

Ellen paused again and tried to tell where I was kidding. "I'm sure there's more to the story than that," she said. "You can explain on Monday. For now, I'll tell Davy something to calm him down."

"Thanks, Ellen. I really appreciate it." I promised that some-day I would pay her back for all the unrewarded kindness.

I hung up. Bad luck to my coworkers meant dropping a carton of eggs in Star Market. Low water pressure. Not getting the summer house they wanted on the Cape. My bad luck was of a whole different caliber.

Bobby leaned against the wall a few yards away.

"One more call, Bobby?"

"How'd you know my name?" His round cheeks were flushed and his gray eyes narrowed with suspicion. In my sophomore year, I had taken the subway to Dorchester and had a drink at the O'Halloran Pub, a grim bar full of Irish guys who yelled at the television all night. The older men looked like Tip O'Neill, the younger ones looked like Bobby. I never went back.

"Just one more call," he said, deciding that it was safe to let me use the phone again. "But hurry up."

I dialed Tucker's number, and his secretary connected me after a long pause.

"Larkin. How are you? Haven't heard from you in a while," he said in his soft Virginia drawl.

"Fair to poor. Actually, things are pretty screwed up."

"What's wrong?"

"I'm in jail."

Another pause. I suppose everyone found this news surprising. I didn't seem like the type to be calling from jail.

"What for?"

"Aggravated assault."

"Hmm. What'd you do?"

"Something stupid."

"Wouldn't be the first time. How stupid?"

"I beat up some kid who attacked me on the way to the bus. Now they've got me locked in a closet here at the Watertown police station. Any chance of you coming by here today?"

"Did they tell you when your arraignment was?"

"Tomorrow."

"Until then, you're kind of stuck. But I can come down and bail you out in the morning. In the meantime, you all right?"

"Things have been better."

"If you want, I'll drop by after work and talk to the police, but I don't think I can do much at this point."

"That's okay. I've slept in worse dumps," I said. Bobby glared at me from where he waited, pretending not to listen.

"I'll get you out as soon as possible. If I could cook, I'd bake you a cake with a saw in it."

"I'll wait."

"Have you told Laura yet?"

"No."

"Want me to call her?"

"No. Besides the assault charges, I need you to handle my divorce," I said. "She served papers today."

Tucker absorbed this new information and filed it away as he would with any other client. He gave a low whistle. "You sure got yourself in deep," he said. "You always had a way of stepping in it."

"It's not as bad as it sounds. I'm fine. I just want to straighten out all this stuff and get on with things." Optimism sounded ridiculous from a jail pay phone, so I dropped it. "You'll be here tomorrow morning, won't you?"

"You bet," he said, and I knew that he would help me in any way he could. In the future, I told myself, I would try to be more like him, regaining all the good qualities I had shed somewhere along the way. Tucker was honest, trustworthy, much too polite to ever beat up anyone.

"Thanks," I said.

"Don't mention it. You know, I haven't been in a jail since I got thrown in the Roanoke drunk tank when I was seventeen. My father sent the lieutenant governor to bail me out. It was quite an ordeal."

"I can imagine."

"So don't get all worried about anything. Be glad you're not in the hospital. I'll see you tomorrow at eight and I'll have you out by noon."

"That would be great. Thanks for everything."

I hung up and watched Bobby's head nodding slightly as he leaned against the wall, asleep from the fallout of a morning of doughnuts and coffee. He snored, each breath a struggle against the extra pounds of fat that encased him like aspic.

I could have walked slowly down the stairs, out the front door of the station, and home, but I decided I was in enough trouble already.

"Hey. Bobby. Bobby boy. Wake up!" He opened his eyes, confused for a minute, then angry as a bear whose hibernation has been interrupted.

"I wasn't sleeping." He reached out to pinch my shirt again, but I brushed past him and walked down the hallway. Bobby lagged behind a little, still fuzzy from his nap. I opened the door to JAIL and walked inside.

I waved. "Bye. Thanks for letting me use the phone."

Bobby locked me in, then stood for a moment at the door trying to figure out if anything was wrong. After he left, I sat on my bunk, a stack of yellowed copies of the *Watertown Press* in front of me. I read about city council meetings, and a column about Armenian-Americans called "Gold in the Melting Pot." All the time we had been in Watertown, I was aware that we lived in a separate world from the one the Armenians knew. I caught glimpses of it at Barca's Spa, the liquor store, the shops in Little Armenia, the Armenian Benevolent Society. Officer Gosgarian was right, Watertown wasn't my home. I was as much of a stranger here as he would be back in Pine Bluff.

Late in the afternoon, the police station quieted down and the shadows outside grew long, then disappeared, replaced by blue streetlights and the headlights of cars going home. I stood at the window and looked through the chicken-wire glass at a liquor store parking lot two stories below, its dumpster overflowing with cardboard boxes. The restaurants on Mount Auburn Street had opened and the air was thick with roasting lamb.

An honorable man faces defeat with his head held high.

I heard Catlett Stride loud and clear, his voice filling the cell. Strides always got through the rough parts; otherwise my great-aunt's history of the family would have chapters titled "The Road to Failure" or "Stride Family Losers." Catlett Stride was on the wrong side in a war, went crazy, and burned down his house. But he was still remembered as a hero of sorts. It was up to me to turn things around, and as I sat looking out the window of my jail cell I knew that I could.

"I'm not defeated," I said, then louder: "I may not be exactly honorable right now either, but I won't give up."

Two men moved quickly across the parking lot from the liquor store, looking like twins in their blue banker suits. Safely locked away, I watched them the way a cat might watch bugs—because they moved. They climbed into a black BMW; then each opened a beer and raised it to his lips like a trumpet, toasting another day finished, a piece of real estate developed. They smiled at each other just as in a beer commercial, and then the BMW moved silently across the parking lot and turned toward Cambridge.

I heard the key in the lock.

"You okay?" Bobby said. He walked in slowly and put a paper bag splotched with greasy stains on the small table next to the bunk.

"Yeah. Why?" I said, looking back out the window. I wished I were home now.

"I heard you say something."

"I was talking to my great-great-grandfather, hero of the battle of Chancellorsville."

"Oh." Bobby looked at me suspiciously. I could have been joking or not; he wasn't sure. "Here's your dinner."

"Thanks." I reached for my wallet before I realized it was still gone.

"You don't have to pay for it." Bobby walked toward the door. "It's free. I mean, no one pays for food here." He paused for a moment and turned. "Don't yell anymore, all right?"

"I won't," I said. Bobby locked the door and his heavy steps faded into the distance.

I walked over to my bunk and picked a newspaper from the stack. I read about rug auctions and holiday bazaars at St. James's Armenian Church. I wondered what would happen now that I had beaten up an Armenian kid. It was a small town, as Officer Gosgarian had said, and news would travel fast. Maybe tomorrow there would be a short item in the *Watertown Press* about a hometown boy getting beaten up in a cemetery.

I picked up the bag Bobby had left and looked inside. A gyro sandwich, fries, and a Greek salad in a small foil pan from Temo's, a restaurant around the corner. We used to get dinner there sometimes, before Laura discovered cholesterol. It had been a long day and I should have been hungry, but my appetite was gone along with my watch, my reputation, and Laura.

19

A NEW LEAF

TUCKER SPOKE quietly with the judge at the front of the courtroom. From my wooden bench I could hear only a few words—"mental stress . . . no prior record . . . gainfully employed." When I closed my eyes I found myself sitting on a pew in the Pine Bluff Methodist Church with my father and mother. The church was filled with families, old ladies in flower-print dresses, farmers tanned the color of clay. The rustle of church programs fanning the hot, still air. The smell of dusty hymnals and candles burning. Colored light from the stained-glass windows covered the floor with jewels. It was so good to be home that I had to fight back tears, but when I opened my eyes the church was gone, leaving only rays that streamed from a skylight at the center of the crowded courtroom. Pale as moonbeams, the light fell on burglars, barroom fighters, disrupters of the peace, redeeming everyone it touched. No religious conversion brought on this vision, just a sleepless night in jail. But I knew it was time for a change.

Someone tapped my shoulder and I turned around. "Come on, jailbird. Let's go." Tucker handed me a plastic bag containing my wallet, keys, change, and a buckeye I carried for good luck. We had been waiting in the crowded courtroom for what seemed like hours, but Tucker had managed to fix things in just a few minutes. I looked at him and wondered how long I had been gone.

"You're released on your own recognizance." Tucker leaned down and looked me right in the eyes as he spoke, as if I were mentally impaired, which in a way I was. "The judge set a court date in June. You can't leave the state before then."

"I'm not going anywhere." We walked down the aisle and through the swinging metal doors that led to the courthouse lobby, past families huddled on benches, blue clusters of cops. "What'd you say to the judge?"

"I told him you were attacked by a band of delinquents and you acted in self-defense. That's what happened, right?"

"Not exactly."

"From now on it is, unless you want to get in more trouble," Tucker said. "We'll have to do some careful planning for the hearing. Until then, I want you to be a fine, upstanding citizen."

"I will be. Sure." We walked down the concrete steps in front of the courthouse to Tucker's car, a mint-green Mercedes 300D. I hoped none of my dirt would rub off on the leather.

I sat with my head in my hands for a minute, pressing my fingers hard into my scalp. Despite my worrying last night, there hadn't been any finger-pointing Armenian parents or lectures from the judge. I wasn't going to complain. I was free from Officer Gosgarian, Bobby, and the smell of burnt coffee.

I sat up. "You probably don't have to spring people from jail very often."

"Everyone gets in scrapes now and then."

"You don't even know the half of it," I said. "I need to tell you some things. You're my lawyer, I guess I have to. Got a minute?"

"All day if you need it."

The sun beamed down on the parking lot and I squinted at Tucker. Where to start? "Before Laura left, I was seeing another woman. Her name was Mariah. I met her at a bus stop. Anyway, we were together a lot."

"Did you tell Laura about her?"

"No. I think she knows, but I'm not sure she'd tell me if she did. Mariah did something I have to ask you about. I don't think it's legal. She tricked me into getting her pregnant."

"You may have to explain that a little." Tucker handed me a fresh pack of Marlboros from his shirt pocket. "Brought these for you."

"Thanks." I lit one, inhaled deeply, then exhaled, the smoke coming out followed by words. "She wanted a baby and I happened to have good genes. Now that she's pregnant she doesn't want to have anything to do with me."

"Sounds like you're better off without a woman like that."

"You don't understand. She's going to have my child. Think about your kids for a minute. How would you feel if someone was holding them hostage?"

"That's not quite the same thing, but I get what you're saying. I don't know if legally there's anything you can do about it. Just hope she doesn't sue you for child support."

"I don't care about the money," I said. "That's not the point. I just don't think it's right for a woman to bear a child against a man's will, do you?"

"The Constitution just covers bearing arms, not children. But first things first. I'm going to call Laura's lawyer on Monday, and I don't think it would be a good idea for him to know you were fooling around."

"I don't care about the divorce either." I spoke a little too loudly; then more words tumbled out. "It doesn't matter. I mean, Laura can have everything. Anyway, her friends already came and took her things. I just want all this to be over." Tears ran down my face. Tucker sat stunned into silence, then reached over and gave me a tissue from the glove compartment. He put his hand on my shoulder in a serious way that only fathers and lawyers can pull off, and Tucker was both.

"You've been through a traumatic experience," he said. "You're tired and you're under a lot of stress. It isn't a good time to be making decisions. Especially financial ones. Giving away all your money doesn't mean your problems will go away. Just your money."

"Maybe that would help."

"I think there're millions of poor folks who would tell you different. Get a grip on things. You still have a good job. You're smart. You have friends. You got the whole rest of your life."

"I know. I know," I said, fumbling for the elusive grip. What could be more pathetic than weeping in Tucker's Mercedes?

"We'll get together in a couple of weeks and plan for the divorce. Until then, take better care of yourself. You look like a wreck. You don't need to do anything except change the locks so Laura's friends can't come back for seconds. I'll check the custody laws and we can talk about that too."

As much as I appreciated his help, Tucker still didn't get the point. He had come up with legal solutions, ways to save money. What I really needed couldn't be measured in dollars and cents. But I didn't tell this to Tucker, who clicked the ignition slightly, waited a moment, then pushed the starter knob on the dash-board. Starting a diesel engine seemed a manly, superfluous ritual, an *Esquire* kind of skill—like fly-fishing, mixing compli-cated rum drinks.

We drove through dumpy Watertown Square, really more like a gigantic intersection than a square, then headed up Mount Auburn Street. The morning sun warmed my hands. Maybe winter was finally over, I thought, imagining that this turn in the weather had something to do with my decision to become a better person.

Tucker pulled into my driveway and parked. "I'll call you next week about setting up a meeting. Maybe we could get back on schedule for our monthly drink."

I smiled. "I'd like that." As long as we didn't have to go to the Quiet Bar.

239

"I mean, it's kind of silly that we don't see each other more often. We live so close."

Tucker lived in a huge house with his wife and kids in the best part of Cambridge. I lived alone in a half-empty Watertown condo surrounded by Armenians. Somehow, this didn't seem so close to me.

I got out, looked back at Tucker's shining car. "Listen. Thanks again. I mean it."

"Get some rest. And keep your wheels between the ditches, you hear?"

"Yeah. I will."

Tucker drove away and left me standing in a cloud of diesel fumes worthy of a Greyhound depot.

I didn't want to face my ravaged apartment yet, so I walked back to the tiny backyard. Bordered by a chain-link fence, it was about the size of my cell at the Watertown jail. The house blocked out most of the light, so the yard was usually shady and cool, covered with a kind of mossy grass that was always wet. But today the sun trickled down through branches tipped with rust-colored buds.

I wandered around the melting yard, the ground spongy beneath my feet, and looked at everything with new eyes. Grassy shoots of crocus poked out of the ground, their purple flowers fluted like tiny champagne glasses. Laura and I had planted them when we first moved in, hoping to make our condo seem more like a home than one floor of a residential property. These first flowers of spring seemed to point toward a bigger change on the way. Then again, everything felt heavy with significance.

I lay on the ground and breathed deeply. I would rest here for a few minutes. The ground was still cold and water soaked through my jacket, turning my skin clammy. It didn't matter. Like a napkin after a long meal, the suit bore grisly reminders of my recent history. I shut my eyes and sprawled spread-eagle as if I had just fallen from the roof.

240

* * *

A shadow covered me as I slowly sank and became one with the earth's crust. I opened my eyes with a shiver only to find that it wasn't a cloud; it was Mrs. Gregorian. For a hundred dollars a month, she and her son, Ishtar, did all the yard work and maintenance we claimed to be too busy to do. Short and dark, she wore a heavy black coat and black boots that laced all the way up her ankles. Her thin black hair was pulled back in a painful bun. In one hand she held a rake; in the other, my answering machine, cracked in two and sprouting wires and tape.

"Is this yours, Mr. Larkin? I found it in the bushes." She seemed unfazed by my condition. You'd think that Mrs. Gregorian regularly found her employers taking midmorning mud wallows in their backyards.

"No," I said, lying.

"I'm sure it's yours." She leaned down and placed the answering machine gingerly next to me, an offering.

"You have no right to go into my apartment without my permission." Mrs. Gregorian had keys, and I had always suspected that she came into our apartment while we were at work, and nosed around, criticizing the way we kept house.

She turned her head slightly to the side and narrowed her eyes at me. "I didn't, Mr. Larkin, really." Like many of our neighbors, Mrs. Gregorian seemed capable of casting the evil eye, and I didn't like the idea of her prowling around our apartment.

"So how do you know it's mine?" It was hard to look intimidating when I was lying on my back in the mud.

"It has your wife's name on it." She leaned down and pointed to where Laura had written her name and Social Security number on the back in indelible marker.

"I guess you're right," I said. "I wonder how that got out here. Thanks."

Mrs. Gregorian began to rake furiously next to the fence. She dug into the bed of leaves and dead grass, shredding the new green sprouts. I closed my eyes again, but the sound of the rake

241

didn't go away. I lifted myself out of the mud with the sucking *thunk* of a tarred shingle being pulled from a roof, then walked around to the front of the house to escape the little black cloud, Mrs. Gregorian. Officer Gosgarian was right; it was a small town. Soon all the Armenians would hear that I had beat up a neighborhood boy. Mrs. Gregorian could tell about the other strange things she had seen and heard around our house—the sacrificial answering machine, the filthy apartment, screams out the bedroom window late at night. Now she could add a new story about finding me lying in the backyard, blood-splattered and crazy as a loon.

Rake in hand, Mrs. Gregorian shuffled down the sidewalk after me. "Mr. Larkin!"

I stopped at the front door and watched her approach, a shrunken version of a life-sized person, her black eyes shiny as a crow's.

"Yes?"

"Another thing. You have not paid me since January." Mrs. Gregorian didn't need to be raking lawns; she owned a couple of properties on the street that were worth at least several hundred thousand dollars each. Gentrification had been kind to her, but she still acted as though every penny were her last. I had seen her out next to the street at night picking bottles and cans out of my trash.

"Sorry, I've been traveling," I said. Mrs. Gregorian's eyes flashed; she knew I hadn't been anywhere.

"If you do not pay me, we will not get the oil tank filled. We will not sweep your stairs. We will not . . ."

"Okay. Okay." I took a check from my wallet and wrote it out for five hundred dollars, enough to cover the months I owed and then some.

"Here you go," I said, trying to sound friendly. "Thanks a lot." She grabbed the check and charged back down the sidewalk. Mrs. Gregorian became remarkably spry when she had been paid, living proof of the curative powers of greenbacks. I opened the door and walked up to the apartment.

* * *

I looked in the bathroom mirror and discovered a hybrid creature—half businessman, half demon—staring back at me. I undressed quickly and wadded all my clothes in a dank ball which I tossed in the trash. Then I ran hot water in Laura's beloved bathtub. As it filled, I scraped off beard and dirt with a disposable razor.

I lay in the tub and scrubbed until the water turned gray. When I was finally clean, I put on my favorite jeans, a white shirt, and boots, then opened all the shades to get a better look at the bedroom, a mine field of memories.

I brought in some huge trash bags from the kitchen, the kind for fall leaves, then went to the closet and started tossing clothes that reminded me of Laura into the bag. In went jackets she had bought me, suits she helped pick out at Louis. I closed the bag, then opened another and stuffed it full of Perry Ellis shirts, silk ties from Solo. With the closet nearly empty, I moved on to the rest of the bedroom, tossing in the Braun clock radio, a stack of photos from a vacation in St. Croix, and a Totes umbrella she made me buy against my better judgment. I had always considered folding umbrellas the mark of the truly emasculated.

In the kitchen, I threw away most of the Calphalon pots and pans, wedding presents. I shoved the Cuisinart and all its accessories into the garbage, since it reminded me of all of Laura's gourmet experiments. Armed with a copy of *Food & Wine*, she would spend Sundays buying ingredients, mixing, sifting, using every utensil in the kitchen. The final result would always be awful and fruity—shrimp with a strawberry-pepper glaze, pork stuffed with ginger and blueberries.

I opened the refrigerator and scooped out the deliquescent contents of the crisper, then slam-dunked the wheat germ into the trash. When I finished, nothing remained except the lonely box of baking soda. Like a reverse Santa taking away all the toys, I hauled the heavy bags downstairs and lined them up on the sidewalk for the garbagemen.

In the living room, the VCR was the first to go. It reminded me of the Saturday nights spent watching movies, watching television, watching anything except each other. I stuck it under my arm, its cord dangling behind like a tail. Then I piled up the CD player, the coffee-table art books we never read, the framed Monet posters Laura had bought at the Museum of Fine Arts. It took almost a dozen trips down to the trash, but now the living room could just be a room again. The walls were marked with shadows where pictures once hung, the floors were scraped by ghost furniture, but nothing remained to drag me back into the past.

In the hallway, I left only the pile of bills next to the front door. I figured I'd sit down and pay them all later, over the weekend. On second thought, I shoved them deep into the trash bag. If any of these companies really wanted to get paid, they would write again. In my new life I would keep an orderly desk. I would keep my checkbook balanced. I would volunteer to take meals to old people, to teach kids how to play baseball. The refrigerator would be filled with healthy food—fruits and vegetables, tofu, mineral water, all the stuff I used to make fun of. I would even go jogging in the evenings. Maybe.

I carried down a few more loads from the hall closet—tennis and squash rackets, the unused rowing machine, ski parkas fluttering with lift tickets—leaving behind only the shoe box that held Catlett Stride's skull. Then I took a broom and started sweeping. An itchy haze of dust filled the apartment as I rounded up the herd of elusive dust bunnies, chased down every lint tumbleweed. After about half an hour I had collected a dirt pile the size of a small dog, which I nudged down the stairs with the broom so it landed on the Thompsons' doorstep.

I swept, scrubbed, and mopped late into the afternoon. The day had grown warmer and warmer but the cold crept back into the neighborhood at sunset. I slid the storm window up and smelled the wormy, melting lawns. The last of the gray snow next to the street was gone now, leaving behind lost change and sodden mittens. If it had warmed up a day earlier there wouldn't have been any snow left for Nicky Badrosian to throw at me. I wouldn't have beaten anyone or gone to jail. Fate or bad luck, I could call it either.

My garbage bags sat next to the road, a row of fat green men hunkered down on the curb. In the distance, the radio towers throbbed red on the horizon. A dark line of clouds gathered in the west. It would rain tonight, a cold rain to wash away the winter. I leaned outside and watched the blinking lights for a minute, then closed the window and did the dishes.

Late at night the clatterings and voices echoed from down on the street, loud enough to wake me up. Naked, I walked to the kitchen and looked outside. About a dozen people gathered around the bags I had left next to the street, scavenging through thousands of dollars of my possessions, my going-out-of-Laura sale. They ripped open each bag with a vengeance, angry that someone would throw away things this good. A shriveled old man held up an Armani suit, then tossed it aside. Too big. A kid in a leather jacket went through a stack of CDs, spinning the ones he didn't like across the yard like Frisbees. A small woman hauled away a stack of pots and pans. Looking more carefully I could see it was Mrs. Gregorian, followed by Ishtar, who carried my tape deck. Chairs, appliances, and clothes all drifted down the street like crumbs on top of ants.

When someone died in Boston's North End, the Italians put his clothes out on the sidewalk so anyone who wanted could take away this dead person's things. I had always thought this was kind of strange, but now it made perfect sense. I was glad to be rid of these possessions and I hoped they brought their new owners better luck.

I watched the looting for a while from the window. Glass broke. People shouted. Car doors slammed. My new leaf was the neighborhood's gain, but no one would ever thank me for it.

245

20

THE CAREER PATH

I STOPPED TO LOOK next to the road for a good rock to skip across the river but found only broken glass and flattened cans. Walking to work was part of my new discipline, and also a necessity since I hadn't gotten the Volvo fixed. I watched the last thin ice travel in rafts down the river, creaking like floor-boards. In the distance I could see the low Weeks Bridge and the spires and cupolas of the college. The dome of Dunster House was blood red; the Business School's glimmered gold.

I walked down the jogging path through a morning thick with clichés. A new day dawned. I saw the big picture. Today was the first day of the rest of my life. Or at least my first day back at work.

Ahead, cars lined up on Memorial Drive, each waiting to dash across the intersection like a squirrel. My shoulders hunched a little and my hands hid in my overcoat pockets as I walked past the budding sycamores and bleary drivers. I thought of how healthy walking was, compared with sitting in the Volvo. I breathed in, breathed out, the cool air a heady mixture of spring and exhaust fumes. I was always more comfortable in cars, and I had owned a string of them—the muscle-bound Chevelle, a sleek Charger, a boxy Dart, the unfaithful Volvo. When things got bad, I always had a car in front of my apartment building. I could just drive somewhere else, find a new job, another apartment. But I was determined to stay here and get things straightened out, to keep my head held high. For now, this meant walking.

As I got closer to Harvard Square, the river widened and the path along the banks grew crowded with trench coats. Each walker carried something—backpack, gym bag, umbrella, briefcase, newspaper—clutched the way a child holds a stuffed animal. It made me glad my briefcase had disappeared somewhere between the bus stop and the cemetery.

Unencumbered, I walked toward Harvard Square fueled by a new energy that sent my mind reeling. I would learn how to row and would spend serene spring mornings gliding down the Charles from Watertown. I would buy a mountain bike and race along the banks in skintight shorts. But as I passed the same familiar sights, the Crockett Company building looming closer and closer, I realized that I was still on my dogpath, despite my attempts to turn over a new leaf. As I rode the elevator to our floor, I stared at my reflection in the brass doors and tried to hold on to the notion that this day would be different.

Everyone stopped talking in the bullpen and stared at me as if I had just trotted in buck naked. I couldn't believe that Ellen would break her promise, but judging from the chilly silence, I could tell everyone knew I had been in jail. Lillivale and Gillman stood in the middle of the room, bloodless as statues. I nodded at them as I walked toward my office, all eyes on me.

"How you doing?" My voice broadcast through the office.

They said nothing, and then suddenly everyone started talking again, unfrozen. Lillivale and Gillman were probably pleased to see me screw up. Once Davy's favorite, I now would be forced to climb my way back up the invisible ladder. I knew I'd have to work hard and keep on Davy's good side for a few months. But I could do it. I was a Stride, descended from Cherokees and pioneers. Lillivale and Gillman were lightweights; one setback and they would crumble, run to another company.

In my office I found post-ums stuck to my computer, papers stacked on my desk, a pile of mail on my chair. I would have to stay late to make a dent in it all, but the hard work would make up for the three-hour "lunches" I used to take with Mariah, the afternoons spent daydreaming at my desk.

I heard a soft knock at my door, and Ellen slipped in.

"I'm glad you're back," she whispered. She closed the door quietly behind her.

"Glad to be back," I said. "Why're you whispering?"

"I wanted to catch you before Davy did. There's something that you should know, and it's not good." She paused. "They're really pissed."

"Who?"

"Davy. McCormick. Lillivale. Gillman. Even me a little," she said.

"So they found out. Of course everyone's pissed. It doesn't look good to have a senior consultant thrown in jail. You didn't tell them, did you?"

"No, of course not."

"Anyway, there's nothing to worry about. I never mentioned the company and I don't think it'll make the papers. I've got my lawyer working on it." Maybe someone from the police station had called to confirm that I worked for the Crockett Company.

"Honestly, Larkin. They don't know about it," Ellen said.

"Then why's everybody acting so strange?"

Ellen looked me right in the eye. "It's low, Larkin. Really low. I helped you out when you needed it, remember? And now you've taken advantage of me." Ellen shook her head. I had never seen her angry before, her green eyes dead as emeralds, her mouth a tight, unwavering line. "Maybe you were my friend just because you knew I could help you."

"That's not true," I said. "What're you talking about?" Ellen had something besides my life of crime on her mind, and I wished she would get to it.

Davy walked in without knocking.

"I was just welcoming Larkin back," Ellen sputtered. She backed away, caught someplace she shouldn't be.

Davy jerked his head toward the open door. "I need a few minutes alone with your friend." He held the door open and Ellen walked out, ducking under Davy's outstretched arm in an awkward limbo dance.

"Get your coat. Let's grab a couple coffees and get some air." I had heard Davy use this line before. It was an invitation to go down to the Career Path.

"I don't think so." In my years at the Crockett Company I had managed to avoid visiting this heartless patch of concrete, and I didn't want to go there now. All the people in the office would watch from their windows as Davy yelled soundlessly below. He might as well have set up a wooden stockade for shackling bad employees.

"What do you mean? I said let's take a walk."

"I'm not going down on the Career Path, okay? If you've got something to say, you can tell me here. I've worked here too long for that," I said.

"Fair enough." He closed the door. "But when I'm done you'll wish you had decided to go downstairs where no one can hear us, because I plan to chew your ass into bite-sized chunks."

"If it's about the jail thing, I don't blame you for getting mad. But I promise it won't get the company into trouble. No clients will ever hear about it."

"I don't know what you're talking about. I don't care about your personal life. You can stick Coke bottles up the pope's butt all weekend, for all I care. It's *this* that really pisses me off." Davy took a large folder from under his arm and waved it at me. He slapped it down on my desk and some pages from *Strategies for Success* fell out.

249

"I took the liberty of having Lillivale look through the manuscript, and he found some monster typos," Davy said.

"I was under a lot of stress when I wrote that." A queasy wave washed over me as it did every time I got caught lying. I breathed deeply and summoned up my best defense, more lies. "It's not my finest work, but I had a tight deadline. You know that." I could tell he wasn't really listening. A conversation with an angry Davy was never give-and-take. It was a lecture, a dressing-down.

"That's no excuse. It's like that guy who said he killed his wife because he ate a bunch of junk food. That shit just doesn't fly with me. Lillivale found whole paragraphs lifted from other books. He found bogus quotes. Explain that."

"If you want me to take a second pass at the draft, I'll be glad to work in Lillivale's comments," I said.

"Take a look at this thing before you promise me you can kiss it and make it all better." Davy spread out the manuscript, spider webs of red ink covering every page. Whole sections were crossed out while others had huge question marks in the margin. At the end were about a dozen pages of notes on the people I had quoted. Lillivale had divided them into "Never Contacted," "Misquoted," and "Deceased."

It made me angry to think of Lillivale searching through my book for ways to trip me up. I had never expected anyone to dig through the manuscript so carefully. What did it matter if I lifted a few quotes here and there, when middle managers were just going to buy the book and put it on their shelves? They got their ideas from sports figures, who in turn stole them from the military, who stole them from the Greeks and Romans. There had probably been an original thought a few millennia ago, but businessmen didn't want originality. They wanted hot buttons, bulleted checklists, action steps, pathways to progress.

"So I made up some stuff. You can't tell me you never stretched the facts a little. Think about back when you used to sell cars."

"I never had an unsatisfied customer. Never."

"But you can't say you always told the truth, can you?"

"Most of the time I did."

"Exactly. Let reporters worry themselves to death about the truth. The truth is *boring*. What sells is something that sounds good, that tells people what they want to hear. That's what I was trying to do."

"Maybe so, but the truth can also keep the Crockett Company out of court. If we publish this we'll be up to our peckers in lawsuits. People don't take kindly to seeing their names in print with some quotes attached. I can't believe you'd do this to me and the company after all we've done for you." Davy stalked away from my desk and shook his head.

"I'm sorry," I said, not meaning it. This was the part where I was supposed to feel guilty, but I didn't at all, just a little surprised.

"I don't care." Davy looked at me with a stare that told me he meant it.

"I know the book has problems, but I think I can work them out. I can do some new research and patch it together in a month. I'll do it on my own time, and I won't . . ."

"No can do, Larkin. It's a dead end. Briefcase Press is breathing down our necks. We've broken our contract. What the fuck am I supposed to tell them? That the author, Larkin Stride, made up all the good stuff because the truth is boring? Oh yeah, Lillivale found something else."

"What's that?"

"You never got your MBA. Wharton's never heard of you. You barely scraped through Harvard. Am I right or am I right?"

"Depends on what you mean by 'scraping.' "

"God damn it!" Davy slapped his hand against the side of my bookshelf and knocked a withered spider plant to the floor. "I will not be lied to anymore. Just answer my question."

"I didn't go to business school. I made it up because I didn't think you'd hire me."

Davy's face turned splotchy. This part was no act. When he walked toward me I backed away, expecting him to throw a punch. Instead, he picked up the draft of my book and dumped it in the trash. "I hired you because you didn't seem like all the other assholes coming out of business school every year. And now I know why. You didn't even go there. I hired a liar." He said the last line slowly as a poem.

"I worked hard for you."

"Everyone does."

"Then I'll work harder, if you let me."

"I can't." Davy turned and looked me right in the eyes the way a salesman would when he was about to give a price that was too high. It was an old trick. If you looked people in the eyes, they wouldn't be so shocked by what they heard.

"You're fired," he said. "I don't have any choice. I hear what you're saying, and even though I don't agree with some of it, if it were totally up to me I'd probably give you a second chance." Blaming things on some invisible third party was another salesman's trick. *Listen, miss, if it were up to me I'd sell you this car for a dollar, but my sales manager, he's got my tit in a wringer, and if I don't make my quota . . .* I had to hand it to Davy, he was consistent. Once a salesman, always a salesman.

"Look. This is your company," I said. "If you want to fire me, then just fire me. Don't blame it on someone else."

"Okay, then. I want to fire you too. But not as much as Lillivale and Gillman. If I don't, they say they'll jump ship, start their own company, and take some clients with them. They've got me backed in a corner. McCormick says to do this quick and dirty, so I'm not going to argue with you. You're out of here. Don't even bother packing. I'll have Ellen put your stuff in a box and send it to you."

I said nothing. Outside I could hear the phones ringing as the office slowly started its daily parabolic climb in motion and volume. Davy waited for me to say something. I felt the velvet coffin's cool crush on the back of my neck, breathed its dead, thick air. I would have to beg to keep my job, but it seemed too late, as if all this had happened a long time before and I was far away, remembering the conversation.

"I did it on purpose." The words shot out like cherry tomato seeds.

"What?"

"I knew the book would get me fired. I wanted to get fired." I looked past Davy at the bullpen, dissected into stripes by the venetian blinds. "I don't care about business. I don't like taking people out to lunch. Making deals. Writing proposals. I don't even like my office much." I had to keep the velvet coffin at bay. I could feel it sneaking up on me again, tempting me to plead for my job. I picked up my stapler and threw it across the room. It hit the wall with a tiny crack that made me laugh.

"I never liked that stapler," I said. I picked up my desk calculator in one hand. There were lots of good things to throw in my office. The phone console would be next, then the computer.

"That's office property. You break it and I'll call the police." Davy pointed at me. Bad dog. I put the calculator down. "Stop acting like the governor just granted you a reprieve. I don't get it. I think maybe you have a screw loose someplace."

I sat down at my desk and swiveled toward Davy, who gathered up the stapler debris and dropped it in the trash. "If I begged for my job back, would you give it to me?"

"No. Probably not."

"Then why bother?"

"Because this is important. Wake up and smell the fucking coffee, Larkin! You're getting fired. This means no more cushy job. No more big office. No more expense account. It means you're through in the consulting business."

"Fine. There are other things to do," I said, not sure what they were.

Davy quit being an angry boss for a minute and sat down on the edge of my desk, hands in his lap. Even though weekly visits to Tan-o-rama gave Davy a thin veneer of health, I saw the loose, pale skin above his collar twitch.

"You know, some mornings I want to get back out there and sell, get the blood flowing again," he said, shaking his head. "Roll up my sleeves and do some real work instead of standing in front of clients like a bozo." By not caring, I had set off a sympathetic vibration in Davy, and now he was being honest with me, probably for the first time. Davy saved the truth for last, like dessert.

"I know it's a crock of shit here," he said. "The Crock-of-Shit Company. Isn't that what they call it behind my back? But it's my crock of shit. And it's easier than hauling demo cases through airports, making cold calls and getting the door slammed in my face by secretaries."

"Lillivale and Gillman put you up to this, didn't they?"

"Not really. It was a group decision." I thought of everyone sitting around the conference table, deciding my fate. "They're dicks," Davy said. "The worst kind, smart and greedy. They asked me to make you return the advance you got for the book. They think the money should be split between them for uncovering this snafu, if you know what I mean."

"A little payoff so they don't tell anyone about the book?"

"Right. But I'm going to do you one more favor. Consider the twenty grand my parting gift, like the stuff they give people on game shows when they lose. I'll pay them the money out of the marketing budget and no one will ever know."

"Thanks," I said. Davy was being fair. He had always been fair to me. The velvet coffin tugged at my sleeve one last time before it drifted out of range.

"Don't mention it. Just send me your firstborn." Davy stuck out his hand, and for the first time I could remember, his palm felt sweaty.

"I'd be glad to. Believe me."

I checked the clock as I put on my overcoat. It was only nine-thirty. Half an hour ago, I had been an overpaid consultant;

now the Crockett Company already withered and sputtered in my mind like an apple tossed in a fire.

"Thanks again," I said, trying to get this part right, my exit line. "For everything, I mean, and don't think that I don't . . ."

"Good luck." Davy shook my hand one more time. I looked behind him through the office window, where white dots of cloud drifted through a turquoise sky.

I found Lillivale and Gillman lurking outside my office like schoolboys, hoping to overhear a few bits of choice screaming and begging. They didn't say a word when I passed, just surveyed my face for evidence that I was crushed, miserable. I suppose I should have said something, but I didn't want to give them the satisfaction. Instead, I just gave them a big hillbilly grin.

I walked through the front office, invisible. Junior consultants shuffled papers and moved in jerky caffeine rhythms, rushing to answer phones as if they might explode after the first ring. The Crockett Company suddenly seemed like a huge ant farm with all its scurrying and its cubicles. Maybe it had been like that all along and I just hadn't noticed, having been one of the ants.

Ellen stood at the head of the table in the conference room making a presentation to a group of clients, pointing to a bulleted list on a flip chart. When I walked by she looked up and watched me through the glass. She waved slowly, her fingers curling and uncurling like a child's, her mouth crinkling. Then she turned back to her clients.

I took the elevator downstairs and walked out of the building, and crossed the Career Path without looking back. It was a beautiful day. The sun warmed the warped sidewalk and steamed out the winter from the bricks. I tossed my cashmere overcoat into an alley where bums would find it. I had always hated that coat. Three trips to the tailor and it still didn't fit right.

The bar was just a few blocks away, but as I climbed the narrow staircase at the entrance, I traveled back to when Tucker, Ash, and I had holed up there. I stopped at the door and looked inside. My exponential memory had raised the Elysium to a higher power not matched by the bar I saw before me. In my mind, the Elysium was a holy shrine, small and dark, lit only by a television, a couple of bulbs with paper plates taped on them for shades. Mystical red lights illuminated the shelves of liquor from below. The bar I entered was as brightly lit as a bank, the silver wall fixtures beaming off Formica tabletops. The floor was covered with black and white tiles, the booths had been replaced with black tables, and ferns hung where the tilted trellis once held its dusty crop of plastic grapes.

A few couples sat at tables, drinking coffee and reading the *Globe*. This bar could have been at an airport or a mall. The Elysium was gone.

"Can I help you?" A young bartender pulled me from my stupor. I stared at his white shirt and black pants, his round tortoiseshell glasses and neatly trimmed beard. He smiled.

"Is this the Elysium?"

"They used to call it that. Now it's called Timmy's Black and White Pub."

"Oh." Now I knew why the bar looked so familiar. Timmy's was a chain. I had been in lots of them on business trips. They were bars without histories, without drunks, without color even, since the black-and-white theme carried over to the bar stools, the menus. Even the television.

"Can I get you something, sir?"

"A beer."

"We have Miller and Miller Lite on tap. Heineken and Amstel Light in bottles."

"Any other imported beers?" I remembered the Elysium's beers from around the world—skunky spring lager from Czechoslovakia, motor-oil ales from Scotland.

"No, that's it. And we have wine coolers."

"I'll have a Miller." I sat at the bar and watched Jackie Gleason and Art Carney running around on the television. *The Honeymooners*. Timmy's played old black-and-white shows on videotape, and the flickering, fuzzy picture reminded me of when I used to stay up late and watch TV until my eyes hurt.

"Here you go." The bartender placed my beer on a black-and-white coaster. I took a twenty from my wallet.

"Run a tab, will you?"

"I'm sorry, but I have to ring up each beverage item separately." The bartender took the bill and walked over to an ancient brass cash register. Looking closer, I could see that it housed a computer with a glowing green digital display.

"Why?"

"It's the way they have the computer set up."

"Oh." I had hoped that time would have left the Elysium alone, that it would be preserved like the frozen squadrons of World War II planes that kept popping up in the Alaskan tundra. But progress was the great leveler of memories and Harvard Square had changed a lot in a dozen years. Gone was Buddy's Sirloin Pit, with meat as tender as a rawhide chew toy. Fire had claimed La Piñata, a dumpy Mexican place where I had often heaved sangría into the toilet. The list went on—Bailey's, Casablanca, the Half Penny. I suppose it was too much to expect that the Elysium would be immune to destruction, but I raised my glass to the old place, to Tucker, to Ash, and to me.

Several separate beverage items later, I turned to the bartender and signaled him toward me with a wiggle of my fingers, pale as fungi beneath the unsavory lights of Timmy's. Lunch was over and he gathered glistening salad plates from the tables.

"Yes?" He wiped his hands on his apron and walked around the bar, smiling. The Stepford Bartender.

"So. I've been meaning to ask you. It's something that I've been wondering for a long time, and I think you may have the answer."

"Sure. Ask away."

"Who's Timmy?"

"Timmy?"

"You know. The name. Timmy's Black and White Pub?"

"I don't think there is a Timmy."

I shook my head and watched the bubbles rise slowly through my beer. "What? No Timmy?"

"We're a division of BevCo. And I think some Japanese investors just bought the German parent company, InterBev."

"Oh." I was drinking beer at a multinational conglomerate.

"So you used to come to the old place, the Elysium?" The bartender leaned forward on his elbow, careful to roll up his sleeves first although the bar was spotless. He looked expectantly at me, as though I were about to tell a mighty tale. *Gee, Uncle Bud, tell me about the time you caught the ten-pound trout with a Bic pen and a shoelace.*

"It was a dump. We used to come here after the library closed. Or before. I used to come here with two other guys. One's my lawyer. The other's dead."

"Sorry to hear that."

The bartender's black-and-white badge said "Jim." I decided to give Jim a much-needed dose of reality. "He was in the wrong bar at the wrong time. Some rednecks beat him to death in a parking lot. He was from Alabama. His name was Ash."

"Unusual name." Jim latched onto the details, missing the point.

"Not really, Jim."

"This is someone else's name tag. Jim's not my real name."

"That's all right. This isn't a real bar, either."

"We grossed five thousand dollars last Friday night." Jim gave me a new smile, this one a little too smug for my liking.

"Not bad. Another Miller, please." I pushed some limp dollars toward him.

Late in the afternoon, I retreated to the only dark spot in Timmy's, a little alcove with a pay phone and a video game called Yen. The object of the game was to move a lever so your little round man gobbled up lots of little gold pellets. Different objects showed up in the round man's way—a TV, a bomb, a pile of money—and you had to make quick choices about whether the things were good or bad before you gobbled them. I did pretty well at first, racking up a couple of extra games. But I got tired of the greedy round man, and I made him swallow the bombs until he kept exploding and the game ended.

Back at the bar, the ever-friendly but unnamed bartender put a new beer on a coaster and emptied my ashtray.

"So you went to Harvard, huh?" This same line had been a prelude to insults from strangers and fond memories from wistful alumni.

"Yeah."

"I'm taking courses at the extension school." The insatiable thirst for continuous schooling in Cambridge meant everyone was taking courses somewhere, although they didn't necessarily learn anything. I didn't tell that to my smiling bartender, who seemed uninterested by the world's downside.

"What're you taking?"

"European economic history and a poetry workshop."

"Heard of Baudelaire?"

"French, right?"

"Uh-huh."

The bartender nodded at me and gave me one last professional smile as I stood up to leave at about five. I think I had set some kind of record at Timmy's for beverage items. Outside, people rushed past me like flashing schools of fish. Fish darted to the bus. Fish swam toward the Cambridge Savings Bank. Fish gathered around the newsstand.

The air grew cooler as the sky faded, and I wondered if it had been such a good idea to throw away my overcoat. Free from the Crockett Company, I was in no particular hurry. I might rise slowly into the slate-blue sky like a beer bubble. Today had been different after all. As I started to walk along the river toward Watertown, I laughed loud and long enough that the fish swimming around me left plenty of room.

21

A LIFE OF SUNDAYS

*At Chancellorsville, Catlett Stride crossed the Rappahannock,
hiked twelve miles across scrub brush hills called the Wilderness,
then fought for ten hours without rest in a battle where more
than 13,000 valiant southern men would fall. His efforts that
fateful May afternoon did not go unrecognized by his commander,
General Stonewall Jackson, who is said to have commented that
if Arkansas had sent more like Catlett Stride, the Confederate
Army would soon be standing on the steps of the U.S. Capitol.*

—OPAL STRIDE BUEL, *A History of the Strides*

SWOLLEN BY RAIN, the red buds on the trees in my
backyard unfurled fragile leaves the color of luna moths. In May,
the world was covered with fuzz, tendrils, blooms. Every day
found me sitting in my backyard, enthroned in an overstuffed
chair, its springs spongy as the backseat of an old car. I had
bought it at a flea market and kept it in the basement to await
the reupholstering that I never got around to learning how to
do. When I cleaned out the storage area, I couldn't bring myself
to throw it away, since it reminded me of home, where we used

to keep old furniture outside for when friends dropped by, the couches rotting gradually into clots of stuffing and rusted springs.

Next to my chair was a small table stacked with paperbacks from the drugstore and my great-aunt Opal's family history. With time to kill, I read more than I had since college, sometimes deep into the night by the light of my lamp, connected to a long orange extension cord that ran up the side of the house and into the bedroom.

I assumed that the less I did, the less chance there was that more things could go wrong. On particularly ambitious days I walked to Little Armenia to buy food. Boys about Nicky Badrosian's age watched me as they unloaded crates of fruit. The shopkeepers narrowed their eyes and slapped my change down on the counter. I couldn't tell if my reputation as an Armenian-basher preceded me, but even if they did know, they would forget in time, the way any small town forgets, their anger fading slowly as they realized that these things happened. Fires burned. Cars smashed together. My arraignment approached but I wasn't worried about it. One incident in a cemetery on a March morning was too small for any town to hang on to for long.

I retreated to the backyard, where no one sought me out except the meter reader and the mailman. A couple of reminders came from the efficient people at American Express, who knew that my nonpayment was certainly an oversight because I was leading such an active life. I mailed my credit cards back with final checks. I had the phone shut off. I canceled the magazine subscriptions, the newspapers, and everything else. I wrote Mrs. Gregorian and told her not to come around the backyard anymore, that I would take care of it myself. When I had settled my accounts with the world, my checking account dwindled to a pre–Crockett Company balance, just enough to cover the mortgage for a couple of months.

I couldn't really say where all the money had gone, the big paychecks and bonuses. I had pissed it away at restaurants and liquor stores, doled it out to car repairs, insurance, the Gold

Card. All I had left was my share of the condo and the Volvo that sat out front, abandoned, a pile of parking tickets thick as a paperback beneath its windshield wiper. Maybe I would push the car behind the house and put it up on blocks to complete my hillbilly still life.

I took my cigarettes from the table, then lit a match, the flame pale in the sunlight.

Stand and fight.

Catlett Stride's voice came from a sunny corner that I couldn't look at without having my eyes water and swim with tiny flakes. Upstairs, his skull waited in its shoe box to remind me I was no hero, as if I needed another reminder.

"There's no one to fight." And anyway, what was I supposed to do, charge into the Crockett Company on a horse and reclaim my office? Hide behind a tree with a rifle and pick off Laura's lawyer?

The honeysuckle vines on the fence shuddered a little in the breeze.

"I found you, you know. I can put you back too. Maybe I ought to take your skull back to that bookstore. What do you say to that?"

"Hello?" A woman's voice came from behind me and I turned around to look over the tall back of the chair. I squinted into the sun and tried to see who it was, then watched a graceful silhouette move slowly down the sidewalk, past the Thompsons' barbecue grill and into the backyard.

"Hi," Mariah said.

I stood up and noticed the smallish curve beneath Mariah's pale blue sundress. The hollows of her cheeks had filled in a little, taking the edge from her cheekbones.

"Here, sit down." I pointed toward the green chair. "It's my favorite chair."

"Looks like you're having a yard sale back here." She sat down slowly. "Are you all right, Larkin?"

"Couldn't be better." I sounded loud and awkward, a community-theater version of my voice that came from spending too much time alone.

"I've been trying to call you for about a month. Your phone's disconnected."

"It's broken. I've been meaning to fix it but I've been really busy."

"And I called you at the office but they said you didn't work there anymore."

"I got tired of all the bullshit. It was good money and all, but . . . " I had pushed Mariah as far as I could from my thoughts, and now that she had appeared in the backyard I couldn't help acting as if she were some kind of ghost, a glimmering memory in a sundress.

Mariah caught me looking at my watch. "I only came by for a minute," she said.

"No, I'm glad to see you. You look great." I wanted to rub my hand along her taut belly and feel our child inside her, to lift the dress over her head and lie with her beneath the forsythia.

"I just wanted to tell you that you were right. I haven't been able to work at all. The doctor told me darkroom chemicals were bad for the baby. I'm moving back to Charleston. I figured I could save some money living down there."

"You're leaving?" Why would Mariah come by just to tell me she was leaving?

"My family has been really great about it. My mother's even knitting little sweaters. Can you believe it?"

"I don't think that's such a good idea," I said. "I mean, the hospitals are better here, and you've got your business and your friends and everything else. . . . " I realized that in the cluttered back of my mind I still held out hope that Mariah and I would get back together after I got things straightened out. I hadn't told her about this plan since I hardly knew about it myself.

"I don't care about any of that," she said, not hearing me. "Right now I have to do what's right for the baby. I haven't smoked or had a drink in months. I throw up every morning. I feel him kick sometimes when he's mad at me."

"I don't think he's mad at you."

"Are *you*? The least you could have done was call or something. I haven't heard from you in months. I couldn't leave without at least saying good-bye."

"I haven't been . . . You see. It hasn't really been a very good . . . " I dropped the stage voice and found my own, quieter words. "Look. Some things have happened, Mariah."

"What things?"

"Laura's asking for a lot of money in the divorce settlement."

"You should be able to cover it."

"Not anymore." I sat down at Mariah's feet and plucked at pieces of grass, speaking calmly, as if I were telling someone else's story. It all seemed far in the past, dry as history. "I got fired a couple months ago. There was something wrong with my book."

"Like what?"

"I made up some . . . a lot of the research. And they caught me."

"You were always complaining about that place anyway."

"I know, but it paid the bills."

"I'm sure you can find another job." Mariah tried to sound optimistic, but as she looked at me, she saw a different man, a stranger.

"Not right now. I've got to go to court for an aggravated-assault charge next week."

Mariah looked down at me from the chair. "Jesus, Larkin. What happened?"

"It's a long story. I beat up some kid on my way to work."

"Did you have a good reason?"

"He beaned me with a snowball."

"That's unbelievable," Mariah said. "You've got to be making that up."

"No. I got thrown in jail for a night."

"You're kidding."

"I wish I was. It wasn't so bad, really."

"Anything else?"

"Well, my car's broken and I don't have enough money to fix it."

"Sounds like you've had a streak of bad luck," Mariah said.

"Streak? More like a whole season of it." I used to find money on the street. I never broke any bones. I won contests. "Oh yeah, and one other thing. You know that bar I used to talk about? The Elysium? The one I told you about from college?"

"I think so."

"They turned it into a fern bar."

Mariah reached down and put her hand on my wrist. "So what are you going to do now?"

I quit pulling grass stems apart. "About the ferns?"

"No. About your life."

"Oh. Nothing."

"Nothing?"

"I think things have got to start getting better soon."

"I hope they do, Larkin. I really hope they do." Mariah moved her hands to her knees, which she rubbed gently as she spoke. She had come to say good-bye, to take one last look at me, not hear about my problems.

I was seized with a new idea. "Why don't you stay here with me? I think I'd have better luck if you were around," I said. "Aren't pregnant women supposed to be lucky? Don't people rub their stomachs or something? Anyway, I've got enough room upstairs for you and the baby, believe me." It was a good idea. Mariah would give me the courage I needed.

"Come on, Larkin." She looked exasperated. "I'm sorry you're having such a tough time. But you can't just tell me to stay because you need good luck. I've got my own life and I've decided I don't want to live it here."

"I know, I know," I said. "So why don't you take me with you to Charleston? I'm good with parents. They always used to like me. I got their daughters back home on time." This idea sounded equally good. I had always wanted to go to South Carolina.

"No. You can't just make things up as you go along." She shook her head. "I thought long and hard about what to do, and I've made my decision."

"I'm tired of having to figure things out." I suddenly hated Mariah's careful consideration of the future, her decisions. "You don't know what the hell you're doing either. You're going home to live with your parents. You call that a life of your own?"

"You've got some nerve telling me what to do."

Mariah's comments irritated me, made me impatient to have her gone. "I think you'd better leave now," I said quickly. "I've got a lot to do. I'm sure you do too, packing and all that. I don't really have anything else to tell you except I'm sorry this didn't work out some other way."

"Come on," she said softly, smoothing a wrinkle in her dress with a gentle pass of her hand. "It worked out this way because we let it." She looked right at me, eyes unwavering, then stood and walked slowly out of the backyard.

"Mariah!" I called, but she didn't turn around. I rose to follow but stopped when I realized I had nothing to say, that I didn't mind her leaving. I wanted the afternoon to be quiet again.

The backyard that had felt so peaceful closed in, a cage. I reached over to the table and picked up Aunt Opal's book. I arched back and heaved it as hard as I could toward the fence, where it hit the honeysuckle vines and fell into the muddy bed of hyacinths. I took a few steps toward the flower bed to retrieve the book. But as I watched the pages flutter like the wings of a fallen bird, I realized that I didn't want it anymore.

I stayed up late the night before my court date drinking beer in the kitchen. Outside, the traffic had died down except for cars pulling into the crowded parking lot of the Armenian Benevolent Society. They were probably planning their next parade or organizing a church bazaar, something civic-minded and well intentioned, the kind of thing I never did. Voices and applause drifted down the street. Otherwise, the neighborhood was quiet, the windows open wide, thin drapes hanging still in the dense spring air, alive with a spermy perfume of sap, lilacs, and apple blossoms.

The cold March morning in the cemetery played over and over in my mind like a tired rerun. In full-color cinematic memory, I pulled Nicky Badrosian's head back like a puppy's, by the nape of his neck, then shoved him down on the frozen ground, his nose breaking with the sound of a pencil snapping. But that wasn't the way Tucker wanted me to tell it. We had invented a story somewhere between the truth and a lie, a fiction that made me look less guilty; I had been minding my own business when attacked by a gang of kids on drugs.

Tucker had assured me that I would probably get off with a fine, maybe a few hours a week doing community service, but it wasn't the punishment that concerned me. It was the crime. Even if everyone else forgot about that morning, I wouldn't.

During his visit, Tucker had cast a clinical eye around my new backyard home as if he were a psychiatrist instead of a lawyer. I told him that I planned to plead guilty to the assault charge, that Laura could have whatever she wanted. Tucker wanted me to say I was innocent even though I wasn't, and to offer Laura nothing and make her fight. But my interest in fighting was at an all-time low. Tucker squatted down next to my chair, getting his wing tips dirty. "You've got to be willing to do things you don't want to sometimes, to bend a little," he said. "After all, life's a compromise."

His words stuck in my head as I opened another beer. No one had ever told me life was a compromise when I was a kid, and I wasn't ready to start believing it now. I tried to forget about the court date but the phrase stuck like a burr—aggravated assault. I suppose this would have been the right time for several stiff, worry-dissolving drinks, but I would need all my wits the next morning when Tucker picked me up to go to the courthouse. In any case, like most of the apartment, the liquor cabinet was empty.

Outside, the streetlights filtered through a green canopy of leaves. A few walkers drifted toward the Armenian Benevolent Society.

"I'm turning in," I said to no one, then walked down the hall to the bedroom, took off my clothes, and lay down. Sleep would take a long time to come this night, and I couldn't think of any way to speed it up. Laura always had her Valium, a chemical mosquito netting that kept away all pests, present company included. I figured sleep was earned, like money, and if I didn't have it I would have to work for it. I picked up the thick book Tucker had lent me on criminal law. It was boring enough to put me to sleep but might remind me of the next day and get me all stirred up again. I set it back on the nightstand.

Voices murmured from somewhere outside and I hoped they would lull me to sleep. But they grew louder. I crept to the window, cautious as a deer, and looked down. Dozens of people milled in the dim, moonless backyard. I couldn't imagine what they were doing. Maybe they were lost. I thought about leaning out the window and talking to them but something held me back. The crowd grew as I watched from behind the gauzy curtains.

I recognized the old men who hung around Barca's Spa, the butcher from the Meat Spot, a few clerks from Little Armenia. I saw Mrs. Gregorian and Ishtar, who stood next to Mrs. Pakarian, the garbage can thief. The old neighbors I had watched playing cards at night stood near my chair. From mothers carrying babies to skinny men in T-shirts, all were Armenian. I left the window and ran down the hall. One accidental beating didn't merit a lynch mob. But from the front window I could see more people walking silently toward the house from the Armenian Benevolent Society.

They've got you surrounded.

I locked the front door and pushed a small table in front of it, as if this would stop any intruder. I moved quietly through the apartment with the lights off, hoping the mob would think I wasn't home.

In the backyard, a guy in tan Sansabelt pants and a white shirt with a wide collar stood on my chair in his muddy shoes and signaled for silence. Looking closer, I made out Officer Gosgarian from the police station. It didn't seem right to have a policeman trespassing in my backyard, especially one out of uniform. Officer Gosgarian spoke so quietly I could barely hear him. For a few minutes all I could pick out were a few isolated words. *Violence.* Something about strangers in their own backyard. *Justice.* The police couldn't always take care of these problems. *Action.* It was time to take a stand here in Watertown.

Officer Gosgarian's brief speech ended in applause loud as hoofbeats. Now my neighbors would drag me from the house, cover me with tar and feathers, or maybe ladle scalding hummus over my head. Anything seemed possible. I decided to open the window a little more so I could hear better. I grabbed the top of the window frame and pulled up, but spring rains had swollen the window in place. I pulled harder. As the applause died out, the window moved up slowly and emitted an ear-splitting squeal. I froze. The crowd turned as one and looked up at the bedroom window, where I stood in my underwear.

I ran from the bedroom, my bare feet slapping on the floor, then retreated to the kitchen and waited for the angry crowd to thunder up the stairs, for the pounding on the front door to begin. I sat down on the floor, a hot wind blowing from beneath the refrigerator, and waited for what would happen next. Sweat trickled down beneath my arms.

Go out in flames.

I closed my eyes. Catlett Stride whispered the same tempting offer he had given in to himself. There was lighter fluid beneath the sink, enough to start a good fire in the hallway, one that could save me from what waited outside. I thought of flames that spread through the house with the sound of hands clapping.

The fire would scorch the white walls and char the carefully sanded floors. I saw flames gushing from every window until the top of the house exploded out into the neighborhood. I waited for a sign to tell me if I should take out my lighter and get to work.

But no one broke down the door. No windows shattered. A few minutes later the voices grew fainter and I got up from the floor. From the kitchen window, I could see people leaving the Armenian Benevolent Society. After good-byes and handshakes, they got into their large American cars and drove slowly away. I walked to the bedroom window and saw that the backyard was empty. The soft grass bore no footprints, my chair still presided over flower beds untrampled by any mob.

It was after midnight now, and all I could do was sleep, a confused slumber that came on quickly, filled with dreams. When I heard the buzzer ring it was easy to convince myself that it was only a dream. But the buzzer rang again and again, pulling me awake to stumble down the hall to the kitchen, where the digital clock on the stove read three o'clock.

Out the window, I saw a police cruiser and a red station wagon from the fire department. Someone's car had burned. I opened the window to get a better look, letting in an acid breeze. Firemen in yellow coats pointed belching fire extinguishers through the car windows to put out the last of the flames. The metal skeleton sat in the middle of a dark pool of ashes, water, and glass, the windows shattered from the heat.

In the burnt frame, I could still make out the familiar boxy shape of my Volvo. I cringed as one of the firemen opened the driver's door gingerly with a gloved hand and hacked at the smoldering front seat with an axe. Then he stood back as a second fireman sprayed the inside with white foam.

Policemen leaned against the patrol car and smoked cigarettes, waiting. Two figures in bathrobes stood at a safe distance in the yard. The Thompsons. The firemen stood back and watched the car for a minute, then put their fire extinguishers in the back of the station wagon. They said a few words to the cops and drove off, lights flashing. In a few minutes the policemen got in their patrol car and left the ruins of the Volvo scattered on the road like fallen space junk.

As the police car drove away, the Thompsons walked back inside to sleep with visions of shrinking property values dancing in their heads. In the morning they would probably leave a note asking me to please remove the unsightly wreckage.

I got dressed, then took a battered suitcase with tarnished brass clasps from the hall closet. At one time, it had ridden next to me in the passenger seat of the Chevelle, carrying everything I owned—my shirts thin as dishrags, jeans slick with restaurant grease. I had kept the suitcase after I no longer needed it, after I had settled down, after Laura's parents had given us a set of luggage from Brooks Brothers.

In the bedroom, I threw in a couple of my favorite shirts, a few pairs of underwear, socks, jeans, and the last of the cash I had hidden in the box on the dresser. In the kitchen, I grabbed things that at that moment seemed right—a ballpoint pen, a pack of cigarettes, a transistor radio, a hunting knife, an apple, a can of Pepsi, a couple of beers, a deck of cards. I ran back to the bedroom and threw these things in on top of my clothes, then wrapped a belt around the suitcase and cinched it closed. I reached into the dark closet and pulled out the leather jacket I had worn all during my travels. When I put it on I was safe, protected by a second skin.

I picked up the suitcase and walked toward the front door, stepping lightly across the floorboards. It was time to go, but as I paused at the door I remembered something important that sent me running back to the closet to feel around blindly in the dark, since I didn't dare turn on the light. Whoever had set fire to my car might still be watching. I found the shoe box and reached inside, the cranium cool beneath my fingers, then put the box in with the other things. Leaving the keys in the door, I walked down the stairs, suitcase in my hand.

The street was deserted and quiet except for the water dripping from the burnt car. I moved quickly down the front path, then stopped at the remains of the Volvo and put my hand on the metal, heat bleeding from the sooty hood. I tossed my wallet into the pool of gray water where the driver's seat used to be.

I walked down Mount Auburn Street past the Armenian Benevolent Society, gray and unfocused in the dim half-light. In an hour, a new sun would stain the horizon blue and another warm spring day would begin. I stood on the curb and watched a few cars drive by, then a *Boston Globe* truck and a delivery van for the Watertown Bakery. After a few minutes I flagged down a taxi.

"Where to?" the driver said. I tossed in my suitcase and jumped in the backseat, slamming the door behind me.

"South Station. Fast."

I kept my eyes straight ahead as the taxi glided through the empty, grainy town until we had passed Little Armenia and turned downtown along the Charles, its banks lush with alders and wisteria. The river curled like a dark snake, and I raised a hand slowly as if to wave, the sweet smell of smoke on my fingertips.

ALONE IN THE CITY
OF DREAMS

I DRANK a lukewarm Coors from the club car and watched the no-man's-land of Rhode Island speed by. The gray grass whipped next to the tracks as we passed a factory, some trucks parked next to a diner. The sleeping passengers breathed in rhythm, pulling in one slow inhale and then exhaling with a sigh. In a few minutes, I would join this army of breathers, heads bobbing in time with every lurch of the Southern Crescent. I thought it was a good name when I bought my ticket, and pretended that I actually knew my destination. The Crescent just happened to be the next train out of Boston when I got to the station.

In hazy semiconsciousness, I tried to remember Laura—the thin line of freckles beneath her eyes, the curve of her full breasts, the way she moved her lips in her sleep. But I had recorded the details and lost the bigger picture. I couldn't remember if I had thought we would be together forever or if I knew that one of us would leave. From the beginning, the conclusion of our life together had always been lurking somewhere on the edge of every day.

The train stopped in New Haven with a jolt, and talking and

coughing broke the silence in our car. When the conductor announced that we would be delayed for a few minutes while the train switched engines, I hurried outside for a cup of coffee and some candy. Men in raincoats stood on the platform waiting for the train to New York. In Boston, businessmen always looked a little ill at ease in suits, as if they'd much rather be wearing corduroys and boat mocs. The commuters here seemed crisper, more irritated. I stepped carefully between them.

A bank of phones next to the newspaper racks gleamed irresistibly in the morning sun. I put in some change and dialed my number back in Watertown. I expected to find Tucker or maybe the police, since by now I had missed my court appearance. Even Laura, at home waiting for me. Instead, a recording reminded me that my number had been disconnected.

I hung up and called the Crockett Company's toll-free number. When the receptionist answered, I asked to speak to myself; she told me that Mr. Stride no longer worked there. I wondered who had gotten my office.

I put in the rest of my change and punched the familiar buttons of Mariah's number, my heart pounding.

"Hello." It was early and Mariah had been asleep. Mornings were probably hard for her now. I thought of hanging up but didn't.

"It's me. Larkin."

"Hi. What's up?"

"I called to say good-bye."

"I don't leave for another couple of weeks. My parents are afraid if I go up in a plane my stomach will pop or something, so we're going to drive all the way to South Carolina."

"Should be a nice drive."

"Hey. You had me worried the last time I saw you."

"I was tired."

"Seemed more crazy than tired. I hope you're not calling to see if I'll take you with me to South Carolina."

I cringed when I remembered my pathetic performance in the backyard. "That's not why I called."

274

"Well, it's a little early to say good-bye."

"Not for me. I left."

"What?"

"I decided I had to get away for a while, so I left town."

"Where are you?"

I paused, waiting for a lie to pop into my head.

"You can tell me."

"Vermont," I said. "I'm in Vermont."

"It must be nice there now."

"It is. There're cows. Pigs. Maple syrup. Cheese. The whole nine yards."

"How long are you going to be there?"

"I don't know. For a while. Maybe I'll build a little shack and live in it. I always wanted my own place in the woods."

"You still sound kind of strange."

"I'm fine. Really. How're you doing?"

"Larger every day. None of my dresses fit anymore."

"When will you . . . I mean, how much longer."

"Until the baby's born? Sometime in August, when it's nice and hot. In one of my books it says something about Norwegian women giving birth in saunas. I expect it'll be about the same in Charleston."

I glanced over at the train platform. Passengers began to get back on board. "I won't be back before you leave. So I've got to ask you something now. It's important."

"Ask away."

"If it's a boy, will you name it Catlett?"

"What?"

"Will you name our child Catlett? I know it's a strange name, but it'll fit right in down south."

"I don't know, I hadn't really thought about names yet."

"I'll never ask for anything else from you." Suddenly the name seemed very important to me.

"Big deal. I'm the one who isn't asking for anything."

"Just say you'll think about it."

"I'll think about it."

"Good."

"What if it's a girl? Do you have any name in mind for a girl?"

"Call her Mariah. It's a beautiful name. I always liked it."

The intercom on the platform began to screech, and a voice said, "All aboard." The train hissed, then shivered like a dog shaking off water.

"I've got to get going now. . . ."

"You're not really in Vermont, are you?" Mariah asked.

"No."

"You never were much of a liar."

"I'm telling the truth from now on," I said. The train doors slammed closed.

"Well, if you work real hard at it, maybe you'll get it right someday."

The train moved backward a little, then began to inch forward. "I've got to go. Take care, Mariah. Maybe I'll see you again on a bus sometime."

"I doubt it."

"Don't be too sure. Stranger things have happened," I said. "Good-bye."

The phone twirled at the end of its cable as I ran toward the train moving down the platform. I ran as fast as I could, after years behind a desk, cases of red wine, and enough butter to clog a garden hose.

As the train was about to clear the end of the station, I grabbed a handrail and swung onto a small platform at the back of the last car. My heart beat in a frantic rhythm that made me dizzy. Inside was a small, noisy compartment where a man in an Amtrak uniform sat on a little metal bench folded down from the wall like an ironing board. I collapsed on a second bench and let my head hang between my knees until I got my breath back. Sweat dripped down my nose and rained on the dirty metal floor. To think that I, once a stalwart two-miler for the Pine Bluff High track team, was now unable to do a simple sprint without risking cardiac arrest.

I looked up and watched as New Haven receded into the distance, no bigger than a toy town with plastic skyscrapers and a little balsa-wood train station.

I recognized the man as the ticket-checker; he was a young black guy who wore his blue and gold conductor's hat backward like a catcher. He leaned toward me and shouted over the sound of the tracks.

"Who you think you are, anyway? O. J. Simpson?" He smiled, and gold teeth sparkled in the sunlight. A small constellation of ingrown hairs clustered on one cheek.

"No. I just had to get on the train," I shouted.

"I hear you. Now you'd best be getting back *in* the train before you fall off. No passengers allowed out here with me. I'm busy driving. Don't bother the driver." He laughed and nodded toward the metal door.

I rose slowly and walked to the door, which bobbed in front of me like a rowboat.

A guy in a gray suit sat in what had been my seat, pounding furiously on a laptop computer. I pulled my suitcase down from the rack, walked farther back in the car to an empty seat, where I fell asleep within minutes. The tracks were bad in this stretch of Connecticut, and I woke several times convinced that I was lost at sea, tossed around by heavy waves. Each time I opened my eyes I saw the heads of other passengers nodding along too, and it made me glad not to be alone.

At the next stop, I stared out the window at another bank of telephones, but the urge to use them was gone now. After a few minutes, more commuters got on and packed the aisle with a forest of raincoats. A puffy guy entered the car. Like McCormick back at the Crockett Company, he had the inflated-with-a-bicycle-pump look usually found in marine life. I found myself watching him, amazed that someone about my own age could look so bad. Two tufts of wiry hair stuck to the sides of his head like old cotton candy. His eyes were small, pig eyes shining from

277

a face moist as a stamp pad. He carried a folded newspaper in one hand and a tan briefcase in the other. I guessed he was a stockbroker, or maybe a lawyer, although no lawyer I knew would be wearing a three-piece brown wool suit in late spring.

The overstuffed businessman plowed down the aisle, his width forcing people to squat on strangers' laps until he had passed, muttering, " 'Scuse me, 'scuse me." He folded his jacket with incredible care and put it in the overhead rack, then dropped down into a seat about ten rows in front of me with an audible sigh.

I closed my eyes and dozed off for what seemed like seconds. But when I opened my eyes the train had stopped again. The ticket-checker I had talked to earlier stood in the aisle next to me, his hat on the right way now. At the far end of the train I could see a couple of policemen talking to the conductor. They were here to arrest me for leaving Massachusetts. My cab driver must have tipped them off. The policemen started walking toward me and I reached out and grabbed the ticket-checker's sleeve. "Hey. What's going on?"

He glanced at an older conductor, his boss. "A passenger, sir. He had a heart attack in the club car. They're removing him now for medical assistance." He punched a ticket efficiently with a shiny tool, then leaned over after the policemen and the conductor had passed. "The fat motherfucker choked on a potato chip. Vinegar and salt," he whispered. "Happens about once a month on this run. People get so excited about being on my train they just *die*."

He punched the next ticket. "Don't be eating no in-between-the-meal snacks, you hear?" He gave me a gold-toothed grin, then moved down the aisle.

Through my window, I saw two paramedics struggling on the platform with a stretcher that bore a large mound covered with a sheet. As they walked by, the sheet blew back to reveal the guy in the ugly brown suit. His face was reddish blue, as if it were cold outside, which it wasn't. A third paramedic ran along next to the stretcher and tried to shove a thick plastic tube into the man's mouth. They moved by quickly, but I saw the fat man's mouth open and his tongue loll out, gray and slick as old liver. His hair was damp and matted, and his eyes were glazed as if he had been clubbed.

I looked over at where he had been sitting and saw his suit coat in the overhead rack, still neatly folded. Above me, my suitcase jostled in the rack as the train started to move again. Inside it, Catlett Stride's skull lay nestled in its cardboard box. Although I knew I couldn't just abandon it back in the hall closet, bringing the skull with me seemed all wrong now. It was a piece of baggage that would weigh me down, and the time had come to shed this last vestige of my previous life—an idea so final it scared me. I closed my eyes and said a quick, useless prayer for the puffy guy, and a longer one for me too.

On my first morning in New Orleans I slept late, then lay in bed and watched smoky light drift through the grimy little window of my hotel room. The window faced the back lot of a radiator repair shop, the ground stacked with twisted pieces of rusting metal. If I leaned out and craned my neck to the right, I could catch a glimpse of St. Charles Street at the end of a narrow alley. Hearing it was easier. The bars were open and a saxophone warbled on the jukebox at a corner tavern. A door slammed somewhere down the street, and a car drove off, tires crunching on broken glass. The trolley clanged by.

A cheap hotel room can be a palace or a prison, depending on its occupant's point of view; right now this room was exactly what I needed. The sheets smelled of cigarettes, and the neighbors had screamed at each other in the middle of the night. Red paint on the brick wall crumbled when I reached over and touched it, sending a trickle of dust onto the sheet. Next to the bed, round stains from dozens of sweating beer bottles marked the nightstand's veneer, its edge charred from forgotten cigarettes. But I was happy here, and happiness cost twelve dollars a night at the Magnolia Hotel & Grille, certainly less than I had paid for it in a long time.

Outside, the late-morning sun hovered like a blister in the chalky sky, sending down an unrelenting heat that almost made me retreat to my room. I carried the familiar battered shoe box under my arm, along with my New Orleans guidebook with its foldout map. I had studied the route and knew where I was going—not far, just a few blocks down St. Charles. The bars were already filling up. As I passed Clem's Place, a cool, beery breeze wafted from the door and I heard an old Professor Longhair tune with a drunken rhythm.

A tattered Confederate flag hung over the red-brick building near Lee Circle, the red and blue Stars and Bars faded to two versions of gray. From all appearances, the flag might have survived the Civil War. To me, much of New Orleans seemed like that flag—rotting and worn. I read the inscription over the entrance: MUSEUM OF THE CONFEDERACY. THEY SHALL NOT BE FORGOTTEN.

It was slightly cooler inside but every surface felt as if it had been sprayed with sugar water. I looked around at a large room lined with tall display cabinets full of uniforms, rifles, and photographs. High on the walls hung portraits of Confederate generals—Stonewall Jackson, Jeb Stuart, Jubal Early—serious men in gray staring down at all visitors. Valiant. Defeated.

A small man read a book at a desk lit by a circle of green light. Gray-flecked hair topped his pasty face, and behind silver-rimmed glasses his eyes were the color of soapsuds. The cream-colored suit he wore was rumpled but accented by a small yellow bow tie, precisely aligned across a white collar. He looked up when he realized I was staring.

"You can look around as much as you like up front, but if you want to go into the main part of the museum, admission's two dollars." He nodded at the rest of the room.

"Actually, I have a question," I said. Closer now, I could see that he had a small curled moustache, a gold watch chain, and enough other affectations from the last century to make me wonder whether he was the curator or the curated.

"Yes?"

I sat down opposite him and put my hands on the sticky desk. "Do you take donations?"

"Well, the two dollars is a donation if that's what you want to call it. It goes toward new displays, rent, scholarly research on the struggle . . ."

"Not cash donations. I mean do you take Civil War memorabilia, things like that."

"Many of our finest pieces came from private collections. In fact, see that settee over there?" He pointed across the room and I turned to see a plush red couch as big as a station wagon. In the middle were several dark stains. "Those bullet holes were fired by General Sherman's troops during his march to the sea. A Daughter of the Confederacy in Atlanta had that shipped here several years ago at considerable personal expense. We must have a dozen couches like it downstairs. Seems like during the war almost as much furniture got shot up as soldiers." Judging by his eagerness to talk, I could tell the clerk had spent too much time alone in the museum. But this was good: I had a strange request and he seemed odd enough to receive it.

"So you do take donations, then?" In a dim corner of the museum, I saw a darker shadow walking among the displays.

"Yes."

"Then I'd like to make one." I put the box on the desk and pushed it toward him.

"Did you write to us about this?"

"No, I just happened to be in town for a few days on business and I figured I'd drop it off." Although I wanted to appear nonchalant, my hand shook on the top of the cardboard box.

"Then we'll need to fill out this donation form." He pulled a piece of paper from the top drawer of his desk, then carefully licked the tip of his pen before looking up at me.

"Your name?"

This wasn't part of my plan. So far, I had remained anonymous. Now I ran through the possibilities in my mind and blurted out the first name that seemed right.

"Lillivale," I said. "Tom Lillivale." So much for trying to tell the truth all the time.

"Address?"

"I'm staying at the Maison de Ville in the Quarter."

"Your home address?"

"I don't have a permanent address right now. I'm in the process of moving. The company's relocating me." The clerk's eyebrows rose slightly as he moved on to the next question.

"And let's see what you're donating." He opened the box.

"Yahhhh!" The scream was unusually powerful for such a small man, and it echoed through the empty museum. He pushed his chair away from the desk and tugged at his moustache.

"My God! Why didn't you tell me it was a skull? You almost gave me a heart attack."

"Sorry. I figured you got things like this all the time."

"Look around. See any other bones? No. Know why? Because they're *scary*. We can't scare our visitors. This is a family museum." Still flustered, he sat down and pulled a half-pint of rum from a bottom drawer. He took a quick sip and then tossed the bottle back in the drawer with a familiar motion.

"I didn't mean to scare you," I said.

"I know. It's just that the thought of death simply paralyzes me." He wiped a thin mist of sweat dramatically from his face with a white handkerchief. My father would have called this man a sissy. I'm sure Catlett Stride thought even less of him, but he wasn't talking.

The clerk placed his pen down carefully, calmer now. "Mr. Lillivale. Your donation is very unusual. We get photographs, diaries, uniforms, rifles, and things of that sort. Skulls usually stay buried with the rest of the soldier. Might I inquire as to how you gained possession of such an item?"

"I bought it at an auction. It was in with some other antiques."

I smiled and looked the clerk right in the eyes to build confidence. But I could feel my mouth getting dry. A drop of sweat rolled slowly down to my chin and fell quietly to the floor.

"I'm a collector."

"Oh?" the clerk said.

"I collect books. Old books. First editions. Prints. Leather bindings. You know."

"And this skull was just stuck in with a pile of books?"

"Yes. That's exactly where it was," I said. "From the papers in the same lot, I found out the skull belonged to a Confederate hero. He fought at Chancellorsville."

"That's very interesting," the clerk said. "But I'm not sure we can accept human remains. I'll need to check with the museum director."

"Is he in now?"

"No. He's on vacation with his family. Goes to Gettysburg every year at this time."

"I like a man who gets into his work," I said, "but I'm afraid I'm only in town for another day. You're the assistant director, aren't you?"

"Actually, I'm just . . . why, yes. I'm the assistant director." A good salesman could play this guy like a violin. But I wasn't trying to sell him anything, just give something away.

"Listen, maybe I'm wrong, but it doesn't seem like people are exactly beating down your doors here," I said. "I've got an idea. What you said about skulls being scary? Well, you're right. I'll tell you something, though. People like to be scared. Take this skull, hunt up some other bones, and put together a complete Confederate skeleton. You know, like the Hall of Dinosaurs."

The clerk leaned toward me. "Are you joking, sir?"

"No. As a matter of fact, I'm not. I'm in advertising in New York and I get paid to come up with ideas like this every day. But you can have this one for nothing. Run it up the flagpole with the director and see if he salutes. If he doesn't, put the skull away in your archives. Either way, you get a chance to score a few points with the chief."

"Well, I'm not really sure about people wanting to see bones," he said.

I stood up and pulled the shoe box across the desk. "Listen. If you're not interested, I'm sure there're other museums in town that would . . . " I turned to leave and felt a hand on my shoulder, smelling of Old Spice.

"As a matter of fact, I think we already have a couple of leg bones from the Battle of Chickamauga."

I sat back down.

"Just one last question," he said. "Do you have the papers with you? The ones that you bought with the skull? They could be helpful placing the deceased in the Confederacy. Many people claimed to have fought, but a lot of them joined on after the war was over, if you know what I mean. Out of romantic notions."

"I don't have the papers. But I know his name. It's Catlett Franklin Stride. He was at Chancellorsville with the Arkansas cavalry."

"Arkansas didn't have a cavalry," the clerk said softly. He turned toward a bookshelf and ran his finger across the spines until it came to the book he was looking for. "This usually sets it straight." He pulled the book out and I could see the title, *A Complete Accounting of Those Who Served During the Late War*, written in spidery gold letters the color of a tarnished penny.

He opened the book and read out loud: " 'Stride, Abraham. Stride, Brother Elisha. Stride, Catlett Franklin.' Here he is," the clerk said. "Served in the Army of Northern Virginia as a sharpshooter. Fought in some skirmishes in the early part of the war. And yes, here it is, in Chancellorsville, where he was . . . Oh, my stars!"

The clerk closed the book but left his finger between the pages.

"The papers said something about him being a hero."

"Well, that depends on whose side you're on," he said. "He played a decisive role in the war, but see for yourself."

He opened the book and put it on the desk, pointing to the words as he read. " 'Catlett Stride was dishonorably discharged after he and other pickets from the Stonewall Brigade mistakenly fired on another group of Confederates the night after the battle, wounding three, including General Stonewall Jackson, who later died of his wounds.' " He nodded toward Jackson's portrait.

"Many historians consider this the turning of the tide for the Yankees," he said.

"There must be some mistake."

"Jackson's last words were, 'Let us cross over the river, and rest under the shade trees.' "

"But that can't be right. Catlett Stride was a hero. I'm sure he was."

"Time has a way of changing everyone's role a little bit," he said. "Soldiers turn into officers. Incompetent commanders become geniuses. Everyone fought bravely and no one turned and ran."

My eyes began to water and I knew I had to say something to keep the tears away. "So I guess this Catlett Stride was kind of an unlucky footnote to history."

"Yes, you could say that." The clerk closed the book and put it back on the shelf.

I tried hard to swallow and keep my balance. Beneath my feet, the floor of the museum shifted sideways and down. "It's hot in here, isn't it? I think the heat's making me funny. Does that happen?" I said.

"Yes, it can do strange things." The clerk opened the desk drawer and offered me the half-pint of rum. "Here."

I took a drink and handed the bottle back. "Make sure you keep that skull in a safe place, will you? I got kind of attached to it."

"We will." He pushed the donation form across the desk. "Please sign at the bottom." I drew an unrecognizable scrawl and pushed it back toward him, then put the cover on the shoe box.

In a dark corner of the museum stood a small hunched man with a gray beard that hung to his chest. His clothes were tattered, his ruined boots were clotted with mud, and his beard was snagged with twigs and leaves. One eye was pinched shut; the other stared at me with the carnelian glow of a fading ember. But his voice was strong and I heard it clearly across the cavernous museum.

Good-bye.

"Good-bye, friend," I said to him. "Maybe I'll see you again?"

Not for a long time.

"I do hope so, Mr. Lillivale." The clerk shook my hand. "It's been most enlightening. Come by the next time you're back in town. I think you'll find our new display very interesting."

I took one last look back as I left the museum but I could see only the Confederate generals staring down from the walls. Catlett Stride had a little explaining to do, but then again so did I.

The street radiated a powerful new heat, as if someone had been turning up a gas flame beneath the pavement all morning. I made no attempt to dodge the sun, just walked as fast as I could, sweat pouring down my face. I didn't slow down until I reached my own seedy stretch of St. Charles Street, lined with blood banks and bars. Inside the Magnolia Hotel, the air was heavy with grease from the all-night café off to one side of the lobby. The smell of bacon reminded me of home as I climbed the stairs.

In a frenzy, I searched every inch of my tiny room. I threw out an empty vodka bottle from under the bed, a necklace of blue glass Mardi Gras beads, a tiny pair of panties, and a Spanish–English pocket dictionary covered with oily smudges. Having freed myself from the last relic of my past, I didn't want to share my quarters with any artifacts from former tenants.

Safe and alone, I fell asleep in my sweat-soaked clothes.

I walked downstairs for breakfast, past the sullen woman at the front desk. A handwritten sign above her head reminded renters that rooms couldn't be paid for with bottles or cans. In the café, unsteady bums, rotund cops, and joke-cracking cab drivers jockeyed for tables with clumps of Japanese tourists and German kids with backpacks. I sat at the counter.

The counterman flashed a smile missing several teeth. "Mornin'," he said. A skinny guy with greasy shoulder-length hair, he wore jeans, a wide belt, and a football jersey printed in large letters with the name "Eugene."

"What's your pleasure?" Gene asked in a thick drawl.

"Two fried eggs, grits, bacon, white toast, coffee with milk, large orange juice."

"Coming right up."

I watched as he broke the eggs over the grill with one hand while flipping a mound of home fries with the other. I had always thought fry cooks had the hardest jobs in a restaurant. They needed patience, an unshakable calm, and perfect timing. Gene worked the grill with two deft spatulas, keeping up with all the orders from the crowded restaurant.

A waitress leaned against the silver milk dispenser, watching Gene work. She had ginger-colored hair and broad shoulders beneath a tight black T-shirt. Although her face was lined, her pale blue eyes seemed to belong to another, younger woman.

An older man hunched over a sink in the back washing dishes in slow motion, same as he had yesterday and the day before. Bent forward at the middle like a stiff doll, he sloshed a plate in the gray wash water, then dunked it in the rinse sink and put it on a plastic rack. When the rack was full, he carried it to the counter and slowly placed each dish on the lower shelves, kneeling directly in Gene's way.

I watched for several minutes as the dishwasher scrubbed a chipped coffee mug. Then he dipped a plate into the wash water without scraping it, so pieces of toast bobbed on the surface. The rinse water probably wasn't hot enough, and it wouldn't be long until someone left the Magnolia Grille with food poisoning. The dishwasher seemed preoccupied, probably with his meager pay and the whiskey it would buy. He didn't see the graceful way Gene's hands moved as he cooked, didn't notice the waitress's blue eyes as she passed by.

Gene walked toward me carrying my breakfast in one hand and a mug of coffee in the other, almost dropping everything as he squeezed past the dishwasher. He set the plate down on the counter and slid salt, pepper, and catsup in front of me.

We had talked on other mornings, and he knew I was a regular guy from Arkansas, a traveler, new to town. Behind him, eggs sputtered on the grill and hash browns steamed. The waitress stood with her arms folded and waited for her orders to come up. The dishwasher dropped a glass on the floor with a shatter that quieted the room for a moment. I bent a finger and drew Gene closer. I had an important question for him, and as the cops, cab drivers, and drunks all turned back to their plates, I asked it.